TAKEN BY STORM
M.J.Schiller

Copyright © 2013 M.J. Schiller

All rights reserved

1

CHAPTER ONE

Bashea had gone to the well in the dark. She knew it was unwise, but it seemed so safe, just outside of the light from the fire where her family and other tribesmen sat telling age-old stories. If they had heard her scream, her brothers would have been at her side in an instant. The only problem was, her captors didn't give her time to scream. They were waiting, watching before she even lifted the handle on the gourd and stepped forward.

It all seemed so innocent. Her family was laughing, re-telling stories, ones oft repeated when they got together, like the one about her brother, Bagrat, and the camel. Bagrat meant "made by the gods," and, in Bashea's opinion, her brother believed he was. That was why the story about the camel spitting on him, just as he was about to ask for the hand of the woman who was now his wife, was so funny. Bagrat would always laugh good-naturedly and counter with a story about one of Bashea's other brothers, or something she had done; there were plenty of those stories. They all would join in on the fun, talking over each other and repeating old dialogue word-for-word. Bashea possessed a wickedly fast tongue, and had so often stuck her foot in her mouth, it was permanently shaped to accept it. So, time and again, she was the one being teased when they gathered. Not that she minded; it was all part of being a big family.

It was this she was thinking of as she made her way to the well, feeling warmed by the comfort of kinship. It was cool outside the cozy ring of the fire, and Bashea was pulling her scarf tighter when they jumped her. Before she could even draw a breath, they took her own scarf and forced it into her mouth. She struggled against her attackers, but there were so many hands on her, she could not inflict the damage she wished to.

As they dragged her backwards, she could see her father's face, lit by the fire, as he stood, the crowd laughing loudly at something he said. No one could hear her grunts or groans, or see how she dug heels into the sand to try to slow the abductors. A short, squat man stepped into her line of vision, smiling evilly as he used a huge palm branch to wipe away the drag marks they were creating. The only signs left behind to point to her presence at all were a cracked gourd and a puddle of water.

The men brought Bashea to a camp, and then they really had their fun, each taking a turn with her until she finally passed out. Even then, they did not stop. When she would awaken, someone new would be over her, and she would thrash about, fighting against the others pinioning her arms and legs. She used teeth to try to stop what they were doing to her, even head-butting someone, which had him drawing a knife to cut her arm in retaliation.

Bashea was sure they would kill her, or she would be abandoned in the middle of the desert, left to die. But in the end they rolled her up in a carpet, where she fought against the panic of suffocation, head giddy, lungs aching for air. Tossing her onto a camel, or some other beast of burden, it was hard to say which, they brought her to dump their load on the floor of a beautiful bedroom. With a brutal yank on the carpet, they sent her rolling out across the floor to the hearth, almost into the mouth of the fire that chased the chill from the room. Then they just left. She attempted to get her bindings off by various means, but finally fell asleep. On top of her exhaustion, the warmth of the fire lulled her. Besides, she needed to conserve her energy to fight off the next attack.

It was all so surreal. She wondered what her family must be thinking. They would have searched for her, if they had any idea where to start. But even she had no idea where she was. She knew her father would be very upset, and that pained her. She tried not to think about what the soldiers had done; it made her sick.

THE KING OF AVISTAD was dying, and there were those who wanted to hasten his death all the more. Young Prince Tahj knew this. He knew it as he was walking down to the throne room, his footsteps ringing in the empty hallway, his heart beating a mile a minute. The twenty-three-year-old prince had found that very thought weighing on his mind day and night since his older brother, Kadeesh, was killed in a war with the neighboring kingdom of Subda.

Tahj remembered the day he learned of Kadeesh's death. He was knocking around a cloth ball with his friend, Radeem, juggling it on his ankles and knees, when the messenger arrived. His mother's wail pierced through him, ripping a hole in his life that left Kadeesh on the other side of a great chasm. Kadeesh had been the brightest jewel in his father's turban, tall, with a bronzed, even complexion, radiant teeth, and a heart bigger than the very breadth of the good king's lands. He was a kind brother to Tahj, though six years his senior, and had always managed to spend time with the younger boy when he was home.

Since the fateful day Kadeesh was killed, the king had trained Tahj to take his brother's place as heir to the throne. Tahj accepted the mantle unwillingly; he did not believe himself to be the born leader his brother was. Maybe it was because Kadeesh was always there to lead the way; Tahj had become comfortable in his role as the understudy. And now, thrust into the limelight, he felt like a fool, strutting around and putting on airs he did not deserve. The place belonged to another. But, no matter what his feelings on the subject were, he knew it was his obligation to step up and bear the responsibility as best he could, for his mother, for his father, and for all of Avistad.

Tahj felt the little stab that had become so familiar whenever he thought of his brother and accepted the pain as he traversed the long hall, glancing up at the dozens of colorful, triangular banners rolling in the breeze off of the adjoining courtyard like waves in the sea. Light still streamed in, ducking between the pillars separating the courtyard at his left from the hallway. Though it was late afternoon, its rays still felt warm on his shoulder as he strode purposefully forward. It always amazed him that outside the thick walls of the palace, the sun could roast you alive, but within its shadowed walls, there was a chill that could never be permanently shaken.

As background music to his thoughts birdsong rang, sounding almost mournful as it ricocheted off the palace walls, coupled with the sound of a fountain somewhere nearby. The closer Tahj got to the throne room, the tighter his chest became, knowing any misstep on his part would be met by the derision of his father's counselors, especially the grand vizier, Lord Boltar. The man was a pompous ass, as far as Tahj was concerned, but he still wielded a lot of power, and so Tahj kept a close eye on him.

When Tahj entered the throne room and strode forward, he could already feel the others sniveling behind his back.

"Look, the boy prince has come."

"The fool!"

"He is not worthy to wear the royal turban."

Still, Tahj squared his shoulders and approached the throne, passing through the others as if swimming upstream.

The throne room was unnecessarily large, the back three-fourths of the room unused and in shadow. The only time these corners were lit was during a ball, when the whole room seemed to come alive as if it were put under an enchanted spell, broken only by the sound of music and laughter, and the tantalizing smells issuing from the kitchen just beyond. Now the room managed to smell both musty and, at the same time, like an odd combination of pine and jasmine. Columns sprang up in regular rows like soldiers, marching up to the bottom of a short but wide staircase that led up to his father's throne.

At the foot of the stairs, Tahj got down on his knees and bowed from the waist, his hands stretched out in front of him on the floor, as was proper, holding the position for several seconds before slowly rising.

"My son." The king reached out to clasp Tahj's hand warmly in his long, slender one. He was taller, thinner than Tahj, with steel-gray hair and a long, drooping moustache.

"Father," Tahj returned with feeling, stepping up and bending to kiss the ring on the king's hand.

His father was not looking well these days, he noted. His skin had taken on a gray pallor, and his hands shook uncontrollably. His golden robes hung from him, limp, as if suspended by the pair of hooks that were his shoulders. The older man coughed, the air rasping through his lungs like the clash of metal.

As the king fought to get his fit under control, Tahj slid his gaze to the group of advisors to his right, searching for the face of the grand vizier. He located the man with ease, his prominent red robes setting him off from the rest, his thin face looking strangely stretched, cheek bones and chin pointy under the dark, thin skin and smooth goatee. Was it his imagination, or did the minister's coal-black eyes seem to sparkle with menace, his thin lips lifting almost imperceptibly at the corners as he gazed upon the weakened king?

"You look well, Tahj," the king said, regaining his voice at last. "I take it things went well in Moleeda? You had no problem collecting the tribute there?"

Tahj turned from his scrutiny of Boltar and grinned easily at his father. "Things went well. The sultan sends his regards—"

"Aaaactually, Sire," Boltar interrupted, drawing out the word with feigned politeness, "I'm sorry to interrupt, Your Highness—" His voice was oily as he gave a slight bow in Tahj's direction. "—but the prince did not collect the entire tribute." He stood back, his arms crossed, a slippery smile splitting his face, above which his thin mustache twitched in anticipation of a conflict.

Tahj waited a beat before responding, his eyes like cold steel as he glared at Boltar. He returned his attention to the king. "This is true, Father, the sultan was a little short on his gold. He is in the middle of building a mausoleum to his late wife, and is drawing heavily from the treasury right now." Tahj glanced again at the grand vizier. "I believe, since he is grieving, we can give him a bit more time," he added pointedly.

"Sire." Boltar pounced. "This is exactly what I was speaking of. Everybody has a sad story they could share. If we allow people to go without paying tribute every time someone is ill or—"

The King waved a hand dismissively in Boltar's direction without even looking at him. "If Caspar says he will pay, he will pay. We've never had a problem with him. Was your travel pleasant, son?"

Tahj beamed, happy to have scored a point against his nemesis. "Very pleasant, Father." He chanced a glance in Boltar's direction. The grand vizier scowled, a vein pulsing in his elongated neck. "Very pleasant."

"Good, good. You must tell your mother and me about it at dinner, then."

Sensing he was being dismissed, Tahj clicked his heels together sharply and bowed. "As you wish, sir."

He left the throne room quickly, and was surprised to hear a second pair of boots accompanying him. A hand dropped over his shoulder. "It is good to see you, Prince Tahj. Welcome home. Your trip was good, then?"

Tahj tried to ignore the chill running down his spine. "Yes, as you just heard, Lord Boltar, it was good."

"Ahh...fine, fine. Well, we have a gift for you, the men and I." His tone was amused. "Something we brought back from a small village in the desert, just under the foothills of the mountains. Something to make you a man."

Tahj knew he meant a bottle of some strong drink. Unlike his men, Tahj rarely imbibed alcohol, and it had become a point of ridicule among the troops. "Thank you, Grand Vizier. I'm sure it was very thoughtful of you. Now, if you don't mind, I'm going into my private quarters now to open your gift." Tahj took the other man's arm from his shoulder as if it were contaminated and dropped it, turning to enter his room. The last image he had, as the door closed, was of Boltar rubbing his hands together with a sneer of sick satisfaction.

With a sigh, Tahj leaned against the door. "Like I would really drink anything *he* would send me," he said to the thin air. He straightened up and removed his short, robin's egg-blue, silk, beaded jacket, crossing through his sitting room to dump it on the curtained bed in his inner chambers. He removed his turban, too, throwing it unceremoniously across the bed. He hated the thing as it was both hot and uncomfortable. He only wore it for formal occasions or when conducting business, to lend himself an air of dignity his youth and inexperience robbed him of. He ran his hands roughly through his thick, black hair and then, with a loud, exaggerated exhale of breath, he flopped down on his mattress. Tahj worked to undo his loose blouse at the wrists where it was tied, at the same time tugging it out of the waistband of his tight, white, dress pants, also saved for formal occasions.

"Where is this dubious bottle of mead?" He glanced around the room at all the flat surfaces and saw no glittering bottle. Having freed his wrists, he dropped them to his lap as he continued to scan the room, realizing it felt good to be home in his own familiar surroundings. The brightly colored bedspread, the red drapes, the ornately carved bedside table, along with the spicy aroma of incense, all spoke of home. Light flooded the relatively small apartment from a wide bank of windows on the far side of the room, which still smelled of the fresh air he'd let in when he first arrived home. A crow cawed loudly in the courtyard off his bedroom, overriding the trilling of a warbler in a nearby acacia tree. A knock on the door interrupted his thoughts. He rose to open it.

He cried out with joy. "Oh, ho, ho! Radeem, my friend." He was swallowed up by a large man with a wide, open face and hair as black as his own, who began to thump him vigorously on the back. "How good it is to see you. How long has it been?"

"Too long, Tahj...or should I call you Your Highness?"

Tahj laughed. "Oh, and am I, then, to call you Captain?" He snorted. Tahj had given his cohort the title of captain in his army a few years back. "Just Tahj will do. You are too much of a brother to me for it to be otherwise." He flung an arm around the taller man's shoulders. "Why are you back here?" he teased. "Missed all of the Avistad beauties, did you?"

"Well, assuredly yes. But that is not why I am here." His open face clouded. "Actually, Tahj, the reason I have come is rather serious."

Tahj couldn't have been more surprised. Something serious, from Radeem? Responsibility seemed to have matured him. "You seem troubled. Come in. Sit down." The two men grabbed the only chairs in the small parlor. Of the same dark, ornately carved wood as the bedside table, the chairs were high-backed and hard, with red, satiny, cushioned seats. A small round table separated the chairs, but the men were still almost knee-to-knee as each leaned forward to speak to the other.

Radeem glanced around. "You are certain no one is listening?" Tahj nodded solemnly. "It is bad, Tahj."

Tahj put a hand on Radeem's shoulder. "Tell me."

"It is about Kadeesh," his friend added hesitantly.

Tahj felt a lump rise in his throat, but nodded again in silence.

"I think he may have been murdered."

"What?"

Now he had begun, it seemed Radeem could not wait to tell his childhood friend all he knew. "He was not killed on the battlefield, like Lord Boltar said. Kadeesh was found in his bed in the morning, his throat slit

Tahj knew he should be shocked, but he didn't feel all that surprised. He had known Kadeesh was too good of a swordsman to be killed by an untrained peasant, as reported. "How do you know this?"

"There is talk among the troops." Seeming to anticipate Tahj's objection to talk not being proof, he held up a hand, continuing, "But there is more. I'm afraid not only did Lord Boltar assassinate your brother, but he may also be preparing to overthrow your father. A friend of mine, a soldier, reported to me he was approached by two men and asked about his loyalties to the crown, and, although he swore his allegiance, he got the feeling it wasn't really the answer they were looking for. He told me they seemed disappointed rather than reassured. I asked him to describe the two men for me, and I am certain they were Boltar's men." Radeem stopped to study Tahj. "But you don't seem all that surprised by what I have to say."

Tahj rose so suddenly Radeem almost tipped back in his chair, but Tahj barely noticed. Standing behind his own chair, Tahj gripped the back as he spoke. "I've had my suspicions." He raised his hand to stop Radeem's interruption. "Nothing solid, mind you, it's just... I was afraid my own dislike for the man was coloring my thinking, but maybe I was right after all." He gazed off for a moment but then returned to his explanation. "He seems to undermine me at every turn. Every order, he questions; every mistake, he scrutinizes." Tahj threw up his hands, gesturing with each statement as he began to pace behind his chair. "And lately he almost seems vulture-like, as if he were waiting to swoop down and peck the eyes out of my father's corpse."

Radeem stood, too, his brow uncharacteristically furrowed. "I'm afraid we may have underestimated Boltar. His following may already be too strong. You know..." He hesitated. "...the rationing your father ordered was not a very popular move."

"Yes, but a necessary one all the same," Tahj argued. "Those people in the North were starving." The decision had cost his father many of his wealthy friends, friends who saw the rationing as simply money out of their pockets. And it was a decision that had made Tahj proud. "The floods washed away most of their wheat and barley crops along with many vineyards—"

Radeem put a hand on his friend's shoulder. "You don't have to convince me. I've always known your father to be a fair and intelligent man. But there are those who like to complain, and the rationing certainly gave them fodder to do so." The captain lifted his hands innocently. "That's all I am saying." Tahj nodded his understanding. Radeem paused, calculating. "I'm going to hang around here for a few months, keep my eye on things. I don't trust Boltar, and I want to be here if anything goes awry. Besides," he added, perhaps trying to lighten the moment, "there are those Avistad beauties you spoke of..." He let his voice trail off with a wide grin.

Tahj smiled and punched his friend lightly in the stomach. "You're all talk. I know you're quite pleased with that beautiful new wife of yours."

Radeem paused, as if considering. "You're right, I suppose," he returned with a sigh. "But I'd at least like to know I could find myself another wife, if I so desired. I haven't had a girl cast her eye in my direction in many a moon, my friend." He tapped his somewhat rotund stomach petulantly.

"Ohh, what a shame," Tahj commented, his voice dripping sarcasm. His smile spread. "Seriously, it is good to have you back, Radeem." Tahj took his friend's hand and placed his other hand on the captain's broad shoulder.

"It is good to be back," Radeem consented. "Now, I'm going to go spruce up for dinner. Maybe I can seduce some willing servant girl." He winked and headed for the door.

Tahj halted at the doorway. "You haven't changed a bit. Remember the time we snuck into that sultan's tent and you bedded about half his harem before he caught on?"

Radeem's eyes sparked, his laughter loud and robust. "Now *those* were the days." He sighed. "Still, I wouldn't change a thing. I do love my Aara." He shook his head. "I've turned into an old married sap. I never thought it would happen."

"Me, either," Tahj retorted mildly.

Radeem smiled. "I'll see you at dinner."

"Shortly, my friend."

Tahj closed the door on Radeem and turned to stroll back to his bed, absorbed in thought.

LORD BOLTAR WATCHED Prince Tahj enter his quarters and rubbed his hands together wickedly. He loathed the prince. He'd seen the boy as a toddler running naked through the castle. How could anybody be expected to take orders from someone after seeing that? And, damn it all, if Prince Tahj hadn't turned out to be a fairly competent commander on top of it. That fact alone had him grinding his teeth at night.

And before Prince Tahj it was Kadeesh. Kadeesh, well-proportioned, good-looking, and with an air of authority, even as a young lad; unlike Tahj, who spent most of his childhood playing games in his nursemaid's shadow. Kadeesh was a natural-born leader, and the

King sensed it from the start. But royal blood ran through your fingers just as easily as peasant's blood, Boltar thought with a laugh. Kadeesh was no longer a problem. What people failed to remember was that Boltar, too, was once a prominent man around the palace. Before the king met and married his wife, it was Boltar he turned to for advice, Boltar whom he left in charge during his sometimes lengthy absences.

But, as soon as Kadeesh could walk, it seemed, Boltar's position in the palace diminished. It was infuriating. Boltar's father had been the grand vizier before him, and his father's father before that. In fact, somewhere in the past one of his family members had been second in line for the throne, and no one in the family had ever forgotten it. No, never forgotten. Boltar could still remember his father's deep bass voice reminding people time and again, "We're from royal blood, you know." Even as a young lad, Boltar was told someday the throne would belong to his family again.

But as it was, here he sat, keeping books while Prince Tahj went out to collect the tributes, which had been the Grand Vizier's duty in years past. Now, not only was he stuck behind in the palace, but he was also expected to manipulate numbers instead of people. It really wasn't his strongest skill, and it certainly didn't give him the rush of power he got when he was out dealing with the troops.

Boltar turned with disgust and headed away from Tahj's doors, still stewing. He hadn't gone far when his sharp eyes caught sight of a figure through the arched openings to his right, striding down the hall on the other side of the courtyard, facing the opposite direction. Radeem, he thought, sucking in a hissing breath. What would he be doing here? Boltar snuck behind a column and watched as the younger man met an intersecting crosswalk and changed direction. Radeem ambled through the courtyard which was sparsely covered with grass, the expanse broken up with tall, willowy trees and ornamental fountains, and approached the prince's rooms. One of the

Grand Vizier's spies had warned him the captain had been asking a lot of questions lately. Was Radeem here to warn the prince?

Perhaps it was time to act. He'd planned on just a few more weeks to let the poison he gave the king do its work, but perhaps it was time, after all. It was just as well the current reign end in blood, rather than a quiet death. Besides being personally satisfying, it would also serve to establish Boltar as someone to be reckoned with. As Boltar thought about it, his pulse began to quicken. Nothing got his blood pounding faster than the rush of power he felt when torturing or killing someone. He turned, and as his heels clicked down the tile hallway, he ticked the next steps off in his mind.

CHAPTER TWO

Tahj wondered if he had time for a nap before dinner. His head was swimming from all Radeem had told him. Could Lord Boltar really be planning something so evil? He unstrapped the scimitar from his side and set it across the bedside table, then ran a hand fondly along its length. It had been his father's weapon. The king gave it to Tahj on his eighteenth birthday, telling his son he no longer felt the need to wear a sword as he was always in the castle, surrounded by friends, advisors, and guards. He entrusted it to Tahj and told him never to use it in anger.

Tahj drew his sword from its scabbard with a sad smile, laying it across his knees to examine it. The sword was beautifully and intricately engraved with the family crest and intertwining vines which ran the length of the blade; he never tired of looking at it. He wondered now if he could live up to the trust his father put in him when he gave Tahj the weapon. Lately he could feel a darkness gathering around him, and he knew eventually he'd be called to act on it. He didn't relish the thought. Wearily, he bent to remove his boots, but as he did, he caught sight of what appeared to be a pair of slippered feet poking out from around the corner of the bed.

Blinking in surprise, Tahj rose slowly and stepped around the corner of his bed, curiosity piqued. He found a girl spilled out on the mostly white, llama-skin rug in front of the fireplace. He gaped, frozen in shock. A low fire burned to fight off the chill from the drafty palace, and, in its flickering light, the girl lay on her side, absolutely still except for the rhythmic rise and fall of her chest. Her hands were clasped over her head in what appeared to be an awkward position, and her glossy black hair was splashed across her face, hiding it from view. The hair was mussed, with bouncy, loose curls so lush it brought to his mind a prize-winning horse's mane.

Tahj was stunned to find someone in his private quarters. His gaze darted around, checking if anything else was amiss, but, besides the girl lying at his feet, the room seemed to be untouched. She wore an airy, one-piece jumpsuit which was a swirl of color. At her shoulder was a sweep of vivid pink, edged in lighter pink, which faded into purple, and then, in turn, bled into a thousand shades of blue which seemed to capture the myriad of colors of the sky at dusk. Tahj squatted down beside her in a relaxed stance, resting his forearms on his knees and clasping his hands between his legs. He paused, listening for a second to the soothing sound of her breathing. He let his gaze flow over the outline of the girl, from her impossibly tiny waist, over the subtle yet sumptuous curve of her hips, and finally to those wonderful, slippered feet that had first drawn him to her. She was tiny, this one, he mused, although she appeared long, stretched out as she was in front of his fireplace like a lazy cat.

He reached out to touch her shoulder gently, but she didn't stir. He was filled with a strange desire to see more of her and carefully moved to brush the hair back from her face, surprised by the warmth of the smooth skin there. To his utter amazement, he saw the girl was gagged, with a bright new bruise purpling her cheek where a diagonal cut along her cheekbone oozed.

She woke with a start, screaming in terror, though the cries were muffled by the scarf tied in her mouth. She shrunk away from him, curling up defensively, her dark, almond-shaped eyes wide with fear. She brought her arms down, and now he could see they were tied at the wrist, the bindings hidden by the long, flowing sleeves of her outfit.

His own heart racing, Tahj tried to calm her. "Shh-shh-shh-shh," he murmured sympathetically. "I won't hurt you."

So this was what Boltar had meant as a gift—a servant girl they had captured on some unauthorized raid into the desert and brought back against her will. Of course the grand vizier would find it humorous, as all the men teased Tahj about his lack of female company. Though surrounded by men who would bed any number of women on a given night, Tahj was still a virgin.

The girl shook the hair out of her face angrily, still screaming, near hysterics as he tried to comfort her, tears flicking out of her eyes in all directions. She was stunningly beautiful, with even, caramel-colored skin, high cheekbones, and a voluptuous mouth. Realizing he was gaping at her, he dropped his gaze, but not before noticing the light smudges of dirt on her right cheekbone and the beginnings of bruising on her right temple.

"It's okay," he continued desperately. "I won't hurt you. No one is going to hurt you anymore."

Tahj was overwhelmed with pity for the girl. She pushed away from him and managed to somehow get into an upright position. Her feet bound, she was still able to scoot away until her back thumped into a heavy wooden trunk at the foot of the bed, knees bent in front of her. She glared at him, eyes wild, seeming shaken equally by fear and anger. Again Tahj made a move toward her, and she jerked away.

"I only wish to untie you." He spoke with kindness, gazing steadily into her eyes, even though doing so had a strange effect on him, making *him* feel like the frightened hare. Each time she cowered, he felt a jab of guilt. Slowly he reached out again, and this time the girl stilled, watching him warily. He moved his hands inch by inch until they were poised on either side of her face, ready to remove the gag. She flinched and looked away as he drew near, her body tense. He froze for a moment, again chastised by her actions, closing his eyes to wipe away the image of her pain. With a heartfelt sigh he opened them again, gazing into her eyes and whispering as softly and reassuringly as he could, as if to gentle an unbroken stallion, "You'll be fine, I promise. I won't hurt you."

She observed him out of the corners of her eyes, which were wet with tears and darker than any eyes he'd seen before. Still, there was a light in them, a fire of passion that could not be denied, as if the vibrant life within was barely contained. Ignoring the slight thrill that ran through him when he brushed her velvety skin, as well as the way her silky hair made his gut clutch as it slid over his knuckles when he reached behind her neck, he tried to loosen the knot on the gag. It was tied so tightly he was shocked she wasn't choking on it.

"I can't get it. It's too tight," he said after a while. "Can you turn your head a little?" As Tahj got closer to examine the knot, he was captured by her perfume, which reminded him of the exotic fruits travelers would sometimes bring to the castle from faraway places. Since she was turned the other way, he closed his eyes for just a second to enjoy the fragrance of it as he inhaled. He shook his head, laughing at himself, and concentrated on untying her, but, the more furiously he worked at the knot, the angrier he became. How could someone do this to another person? Not to mention a smaller, more vulnerable one?

After several minutes, when the knot gave way to his prying fingers, he snapped the scarf back in anger. He instantly felt bad for doing so, as the girl jumped and her gaze flew to him in fear. He remained still, purposefully relaxing his features. Seeming to determine he was not an immediate threat, the girl began to work her mouth, which was no doubt sore from being stretched, though still watching him. "What's your name?" Tahj asked kindly.

She eyed him but remained silent. Of course she wouldn't speak to him; she wouldn't trust him any more than she trusted the men who did this to her. Tahj moved to release her hands from their ties, but she again pulled away, shrinking back against the bed. "I only want to help you," Tahj murmured with a sigh. He touched her wrists. "I'm just going to untie you."

At that moment, someone began to pound on the outer door. "Tahj! Tahj!" Without waiting for an answer, Radeem barge into the front room.

Recognizing his friend's voice and the breathless urgency in it, Tahj jumped to his feet. With one last glance down at the girl, he turned and met Radeem in the doorway to his bedroom.

"Oh, thank the heavens!" Radeem cried in relief. Tahj was alarmed to see his friend's sword was drawn. "Something's wrong. I heard screams and shouts, and it seems like all hell is breaking loose."

Without waiting for further explanation, Tahj grabbed his sword and bolted through the door with Radeem. He was nearly out of his apartment when he remembered the girl. "Wait." He returned to his bedroom while Radeem stood with his mouth hanging open.

Finding the girl in the same position, Tahj bent to talk to her. "I'll be back to free you later. Stay here. You'll be safest here." On impulse he touched the side of her face and then drew away before she could form a reply.

He grabbed Radeem's arm as he passed through the doorway, and they took off at a dead run in the direction of the throne room. As they passed through its arched entryway and weaved through pillars they saw a horrific sight. Strewn on the few stairs to the throne lay several of his father's closest ministers, like kindling dropped in flight. Many lay face down. But one in particular lay face up, haphazardly draped across the steps, his head near the bottom, eyes wide open but not seeing, blood dripping eerily down the steps from his body and pooling below. The room was filled with a foreboding silence and permeated with the faintly metallic odor of blood.

"My father!" Tahj cried in a panic.

He took off again, this time angling past the corpses to a doorway hidden off to one side behind a curtain. He drew the golden, velvet drape back and took the few short steps down in one leap. Radeem followed, his face ashen, his breathing coming hard now. The hallway before them was totally enclosed, with no outside windows. It was brightly lit as wall sconces lined either side, set about a foot-and-a-half apart all the way down the forty-foot length. The walls were of the same chalky white as the rest of the palace, and the tiles were the color of sand. At the end it took an abrupt ninety-degree, right-hand turn.

Tahj sped toward the section of the palace containing his parents' bedroom, willing his feet to take him faster. As he slid around the corner, he caught sight of a trail of bloody footprints leading away from him. Tahj's stomach dropped, a coldness sweeping along his spine and up his neck, where the hair stood on end. He could hear Radeem's voice behind him asking him to wait, but he ignored it. Lifting his head, Tahj could see the door to the inner chamber splintered and cracked open a few inches. He stumbled forward several paces just as he heard Radeem rounding the corner behind him. Radeem's footsteps stopped, but the sound of his panting filled the hallway.

"No," Tahj breathed, freezing in place. A short set of stairs led to the door, similar to the ones in the throne room, and tall pillars flanked it, spreading out wider as they descended the stairs. Tahj saw, as he lurched forward, that one of the pillars was smeared with blood and could just make out behind it the body of a guard who had given his life to defend those within. The other guard's pointy helmet lay at the bottom of the stairs, but he wouldn't need it anymore. His decapitated head could be seen a few feet beyond.

"Wait!" Radeem called, staggering forward, still breathless. He put a hand on Tahj's shoulder to detain him, but Tahj shrugged him off, reeling toward the end of the hall.

Stepping over the guards' bodies, he climbed the stairs and slammed through the door, causing a section of it to fall to the ground. Tahj's heart stopped when he saw his father's legs hanging off of the right side of the enormous bed, which was sheathed in a white, filmy fabric. Heavier curtains, which were drawn back and tied to the footboard, blocked the rest of his view. Tahj moved slowly now, as if wading through honey, afraid to see what he knew to be the king's lifeless body. He made a wide circle around the end of the bed and brought a hand to his stomach to fight back the wave of nausea that overtook him.

Radeem rushed in the door, but then held back. If the blood splattered everywhere hadn't alerted him, the complete silence would have. When he caught Tahj's eye, and no doubt saw the horror on his face, Radeem seemed to understand they were too late, lowering his weapon and dropping his head. But a second later his head jerked up, as did his sword, and he advanced toward a green-and-gold pleated curtain along the wall to the left of the bed. "Tahj!"

The sound of his name awakened Tahj from his stupor and he came around the foot of the bed. Holding his sword aloft in his right hand, Radeem used his left to yank open the curtain. For a split second, Radeem seemed to be at a loss, but then his gaze was drawn down. Hearing his friend's soft curse, Tahj stepped around Radeem to find his mother at his feet. She must have crawled across the floor toward them from where the soldiers had found her in the inner chamber. The rustling of the curtain was caused by her shaking hand as she used the curtain to pull her more upright.

With a cry, Tahj fell to his knees. All along he had been concerned for his father's safety, knowing he would be the prime target, but he had never dreamt anything could happen to his mother. As close as he and his father were, Tahj and his mother were much closer. They had consoled each other after Kadeesh's death while the king remained in denial. And even before, when Tahj was only a small child, when his father spent all of his time and energy on training Kadeesh, he and his mother had been nearly constant companions.

Tahj gently turned his mother over and gave another strangled cry as he saw her clasping a wound above her abdomen, trying desperately to staunch the flow of blood. In despair, he sat down, pulling her partially onto his lap.

"Mother, oh, Mother!"

Radeem looked away.

The queen sputtered softly, "Shh, shh, shh. It's fine, Tahj." She closed her eyes, her skin uncharacteristically pale. Blood saturated her jade green gown, but, even with her elaborate headdress askew, she was the picture of elegance.

"It's not fine. How can you say that?" Tahj replied, sounding like a little boy, the tears running down his face now.

Ignoring his remark, the queen appeared to gather her strength to speak again. She seemed to have something important to tell him before the darkness swept her away forever. "You have to get out of here."

As if coming to a sudden decision, Tahj argued as he shifted to pick her up. "Not without you, I'm not."

"No, son. Son." She moaned, and, frightened he had hurt her, Tahj set her gently down again. "My time is over, but you must flee."

Tahj shook his head vehemently, sniffling. "No!" and then again, with calm resolution, "No."

"You have to go." With surprising swiftness, she reached up to clutch his tunic, opening her eyes and saying earnestly, "But promise me you'll come back someday and set things right, for your father." Her gaze trailed to the bed. With what little strength she had left she shook him and demanded, "Promise me."

Tahj lowered his head, fighting to suppress his sobs. "Yes," he managed after a few seconds, lifting his head to gaze into her eyes one last time. "I will, Mother." He brushed her hair back, accidentally wiping some of the blood on his hands onto her forehead.

She didn't move her eyes from his face, but they became unfocussed. She lifted her trembling hand, blindly reaching for him. "Go now," she said, her voice a choked whisper, and then her head tipped back a fraction, lips still parted, but the life fading from her open eyes.

Tahj wept bitterly, saying over and over again, "No. No."

Radeem squatted down beside Tahj. He opened his mouth as if to say something, perhaps wanting to offer some words of comfort. Seeming to find none to suffice, he remained silent. As Tahj looked on, Radeem's gaze shifted to the dead queen's features. His tears fell on her motionless face, and Tahj recalled she had been much like a mother to his friend when they were young. Radeem reached up slowly to close her eyes.

In a flash, Tahj grabbed his hand. Saying nothing, his face still contorted in pain and damp with tears, Tahj looked at his friend beseechingly, and then once more at his mother. Tahj placed a quivering hand over her eyes and closed the lids with care. He sniffed, becoming slightly more composed, but continuing to stare at her.

"Tahj."

He looked up.

"Your mother's right, we have to go. They'll be looking for you."

Tahj nodded stiffly. She was gone. Carefully, oh, so carefully, he shifted so his legs were out from under her body. He cradled her back and neck in his hands and slowly lowered his mother to the floor. He stood, still staring at her.

They could hear shouts in the distance. Radeem lifted his head, a sense of urgency returning to his demeanor. Grasping Tahj's elbow, he nudged him toward the door, repeating, "We must leave here. I'm sorry, Tahj, but we have to escape before they come."

Tahj shook himself, as if waking from a dream. He glanced at the bed, but he didn't really need a reminder of what he saw there; it was burned into his psyche forever. Blindly, he turned and followed Radeem out the door. They jogged along, Radeem talking about his strategy. "We'll take the side door to the stables. If I can get you on Balamore before they see us, he'll outrun any mount."

Tahj nodded, but his mind was rewinding through the discovery of his father's body and his final moments with his mother. He heard Radeem's words remotely, but they didn't register in his besieged mind. They reached the little-used door leading out to a courtyard, across from which was the royal livery. Radeem cracked the door and peered out. Sunshine pushed inside, and Tahj wondered that it could be daytime when such dark and horrendous deeds had been done within the walls of the palace.

"It's clear," Radeem said excitedly, but Tahj was rehearing his early statement. *They'll be looking for you. They'll be looking for you.*

The girl! Tahj thought in alarm. He spun and started running in the opposite direction. Radeem turned, and then in shock began to call after Tahj, but ended up biting back his words, perhaps thinking it unwise to alert anyone to their presence. He shook his head and started after Tahj, muttering, "Where in the name of Airyaman are we going?"

CHAPTER THREE

Bashea sat dumbfounded as the dark-haired stranger took off, leaving her alone. He seemed different from the others, his warm, brown eyes so sincere. And when he touched her face so gently, she almost melted. After the blows the others gave her, to have someone touch her in such a way made her want to cry. He told her he would be back to free her, that she was safest where she was, but Bashea wasn't taking any chances. He seemed nice, but she wasn't about to wait around to find out for sure.

Feverishly she worked on her bonds, using teeth, now the gag was out, to loosen the knots. Even so, the cords were tied so tightly they were digging into her wrists, which were chafed and bleeding in some places. She cried as the efforts caused her further pain and tears fell on the ties, wetting them, though she only became more determined. After several minutes she felt the fabric slip and give, and within seconds more, her hands were free. She sighed with relief and indulged herself for a moment by gingerly rubbing the cuts and raw skin along her wrists before moving on to her legs. In only a few short minutes, after removing her shoes, Bashea had that scarf loose enough to slide her feet out of the loop. Without hesitating, she got to her feet, throwing the hated scarves across the room and stretching her sore muscles experimentally.

Bashea was in such a hurry to leave, she barreled right into the six-foot-eight behemoth waiting for her on the other side of the door. He held her scarves to his nose, inhaling, having picked them up from where she had thrown them, just outside the door. With a shaved head, the man was easy to recognize, and her stomach dropped. He was one of Boltar's men. With an evil chuckle, he threw the scarves behind him and picked her up by the arms.

"I hoped you'd still be here, and I was right." A wide grin played on his face as he pulled Bashea in to smell her hair. "By the gods, you are beautiful." His voice was deep and gruff. With very little effort he tossed her the few feet onto the bed.

Bashea bounced off, right into his massive arms. She frantically attempted to squirm out of his grip, but, try as she might, Bashea had little effect on his bulk. She couldn't get away from him, and her blows hurt her hands more than his body. "Release me!"

"You can scream all you want, Beautiful One, but anyone who would have helped you is dead by now. We will have some fun now, *Ziba*." He laughed heartily, kissing her neck.

Bashea recoiled, panic seizing her. *This won't happen again.* Reacting instinctively, she turned her head and struck with the weapon she'd used to untie her scarves.

"Argh!" Throwing Bashea on the bed again, he brought his meaty hand up to his neck. "You bit me!" He cursed her as he rubbed the tender spot.

Bashea tried to scramble across the bed, but she felt hands seize her ankles, dragging her back. She clutched at the covers, but they only came with her.

Her attacker flipped Bashea onto her back like he was flipping the pillow to the cool side. "You'll pay for that," he snarled ominously. He raised his hand and, before she could react, cracked her sharply in the face with his open palm, making her cry out in surprise and pain. Swiftly he moved forward, trapping Bashea's legs with his lower body and growling down at her. "Why don't you just relax? I know you enjoyed it when I had my turn last night because you calmed down."

Tears stung her eyes but they blazed with hatred. "Don't mistake my being exhausted, or passing out, for being aroused. I hated every minute your cur-like hands were on me!" she spat.

"Really?" he replied as if disbelieving her. "Well, we'll just see about that, won't we?" He whipped off his jacket, and Bashea sat up and began flailing at him with all she had left in her, though she knew from experience it was useless. She refused to be complacent. If it was the only thing she could do, she would let him know with every last fiber of her being she detested him.

TAHJ RACED THROUGH the hallways, Radeem skidding around corners in his wake, huffing and puffing. Though he was a full head taller and barrel-chested, Radeem still had a tough time keeping up with his less bulky friend.

When he reached his door, Tahj found it was open a few inches. He burst through the doorway, and the first thing he noticed was the scarves the girl had worn lying on the floor of his parlor in a heap. He heard a man's voice within, and then the girl's, rising in pitch.

"Don't mistake my being exhausted, or passing out, for being aroused. I hated every minute your cur-like hands were on me!"

Tahj felt himself seized with a white-hot fury.

"Really? Well, we'll just see about that, won't we?"

Tahj drew his sword, but just as he did, he heard an outer door open and a familiar voice say dryly, "Down, Mahtab." Radeem entered behind Tahj, drawing his sword, and they crept forward, Radeem moving to the side of the doorway opposite Tahj. "Release her!" the voice barked, angered at not being listened to the first time. Radeem's eyes opened wide. It would seem that he, too, recognized the voice of Lord Boltar. The pair listened intently, trying to still their breathing, both to hear better and to keep from being heard.

Tahj stepped up and peered through the doorway, keeping well back from view. Boltar walked into Tahj's line of sight, his red robes swishing. A hulk of a man stood pinning the girl's arms behind her, unnecessarily, as she stood perfectly still, eyes wide, watching Boltar but giving no heed to the other men who had come in the door from the outer courtyard with their leader.

"She was, oohmm, a pleasant distraction," the grand vizier said smoothly, running a finger up the girl's arm and sucking in his breath. He paused a beat, staring into her eyes wordlessly before adding, "Wasn't she, men?"

There were low murmurs of agreement and sniggers. The girl's face was red, though still determined. She shivered.

Boltar chuckled mirthlessly. "Unfortunately, we don't have time for that...*now*." The emphasis on the last word was a clear threat. The girl bristled at his touch, her whole body visibly tense, strung tighter than any of the sitars that ever played at the king's court. Abruptly Boltar's attitude changed. "Where is the prince?" he asked, his voice snapping like a whip.

Radeem and Tahj exchanged worried glances. Tahj peered in again, counting. Just the two of them against...six of the others, if you only counted the brute holding the girl as one.

"Who?" the girl asked, her voice trembling despite the firm set of her chin.

Without warning, Boltar backhanded the girl so viciously she almost flew out of her capture's grip. In the stunned silence which followed, the grand vizier rubbed his long, thin hands, studying them and seeming to admire the large ring he wore. "The prince," he said casually, as if exchanging every day pleasantries, "where *is he*?"

The girl turned her face back, a new cut opened beneath the previous one, no doubt left by the ring, her skin fire-red. "I-I-I don't know what you're talking about." Her eyes were wild now. With a swiftness unexpected from a man of his age, Boltar punched the girl in the stomach, knocking the wind out of her.

Tahj jumped forward, but Radeem rushed across the threshold to push him back behind the wall again. They both froze for a minute, but apparently everyone was too busy watching the action within to notice Radeem when he crossed in front of the doorway. "We can't help her. There's too many of them," he hissed, his arm across Tahj's chest, pinning him in place.

"Let go of me," Tahj whispered loudly, his voice covered by the groan the girl made as she sagged to the ground and was again yanked to her feet. "I'm not going to just let them beat her."

Boltar took a step forward, yanking the girl's head up by her hair. "Now, you tell me where the prince is—" He drew a dagger. "—or I'm going to carve your pretty face up."

The girl glared at him. She was breathing heavily. "I d-don't know where your...p-precious prince is. And even if I did—" she paused, straightening her spine a little. "—I wouldn't tell you if my life depended on it."

Boltar screamed in rage and lunged forward, bringing the tip of the knife to the girl's neck. She gave a little squeak, but then closed her eyes, her face tense, but with a sense of resignation. A thin line of blood trailed down her neck where the point nicked her.

Boltar hesitated, seeming surprised by the girl's bravery. "Very well, then." He switched his grip on the knife and drew it back to bury it in her heart, but as he did so he lifted his head a little, turning it a fraction in the direction of the doorway.

With a cry, Tahj and Radeem entered the room brandishing their swords.

In a heartbeat Boltar hauled the girl to him and spun so he was behind her, with the knife to her neck.

"Release her!" Tahj ordered. "It's me you want, Boltar. She has nothing to do with any of this."

Boltar eyed him with a sneer. "True. But she's such a pretty thing." He squeezed the girl tighter, pressing the edge of the blade into her skin.

"*Stop*! Stop!" Tahj gazed into the frightened girl's eyes for a beat, and then held his hands out wide, loosening his grip on his sword. "My life for hers, then," he said desperately. "That's a fair exchange."

Boltar studied Tahj, his eyes steely. "But why would I do that, when I could have you *both*!" Without warning, Boltar pushed the girl roughly away from him toward Tahj. She stumbled forward into Tahj's arms just as Boltar made his move.

But Tahj was expecting the grand vizier's thrust and quickly brought his sword up to meet it as he wrapped his other arm around Bashea's waist. Using a trick Kadeesh had taught him, Tahj jabbed. With a neat twist of his wrist, Tahj sent Boltar's dagger up and over his head, where it clattered to the floor behind the bed.

In the next seconds, several things happened at once. Boltar's men rushed forward, but, weaponless, he moved out of the fray. till holding Bashea around her waist with one arm, Tahj countered assaults with the other, his sword clashing noisily with two soldiers at once. Radeem quickly took one soldier out of play and had another one back on his heels.

Boltar watched from the back of the room expectantly, like a dog waiting for a bone, but he clearly wasn't happy with what he was seeing. One of his men slashed at Tahj, but the girl screamed a warning, and they both ducked just in time as the sword whizzed over their heads. Before the man could correct his balance, Tahj scored a deadly blow to his midsection. He released his hold on the girl to strike at his next attacker with a two-handed grip, and she backed away to the outskirts of the fighting, looking on just as Boltar was but undoubtedly hoping for a different outcome.

Tahj dodged a blow and jumped up on the bed to gain advantage. Boltar stealthily retrieved his dagger, hoping to bury it in Tahj's back while he was occupied. But just as Boltar was getting ready to position himself, the huge form of Mahtab blocked his path. Tahj was able to finish off his man, but wasn't ready when Mahtab grabbed him from behind by the seat of his pants and collar. He threw Tahj right into Radeem. The two fell like a pair of dominoes and then looked up from the floor at the hulking figure towering above them, casting a shadow on their alarmed faces.

"This isn't good," Radeem muttered.

The big man above them stepped forward and grabbed Tahj's sword out of his hand, tossing it aside like a piece of lint. Radeem struggled to get his sword out, as it was trapped between his body and Tahj's. Mahtab bent down and grabbed Tahj by his collar, but, unnoticed by anyone, the girl had climbed up on the bed and now catapulted herself onto the beast's back with a shout, wrapping her arms around his neck as tightly as she could.

But even this didn't stop the brute; he saw it as a mere annoyance. The girl cursed him, digging heels into his sides and jerking on her arm to pull it back across his thick throat, trying to put pressure on his windpipe. It did provide a distraction and, as he brought his hands up to try to pry the girl off, he dropped Tahj. He managed to pull her arm away and reach around with his other hand to grab the girl's waist and throw her off. She landed heavily by Radeem and Tahj's side.

With a roar, Mahtab dove for the girl, intending to teach her a lesson for the last time, but he never laid a hand on her. With a mighty swing, Radeem sliced right through the big man, and his body fell at the feet of the terrified girl whose screams now filled the room. She brought her hands, splattered with Mahtab's blood, up to try to cover her eyes and remove the horrifying image she just witnessed.

Boltar ran out of the door and into the courtyard, shouting for reinforcements. Hearing the sound of soldiers' feet pounding outside, Tahj knew they only had a few seconds.

"Come on." He grabbed the girl's arm and dragged her to her feet. She looked up at him in shock, and he tried to reassure her. "We've got to get out of here." He crossed to the door and drew the lock to the outside courtyard. "That may buy us a little time." He looked at Radeem, who nodded. Tahj turned to the girl, scrutinizing her to make sure none of the blood on her was her own. "Are you hurt?" She stared at him without speaking. "Have you been injured anywhere?" he repeated. She shook her head slightly. "Come." His voice was tender as he took her elbow, and they turned and followed Radeem out the front door.

CHAPTER FOUR

Radeem, Tahj, and the freed girl ran down the deserted hallways, the palace now eerily quiet. The screams and shouts had died away, and not a soul was in sight. No servant, no minister—everyone had taken cover or met their end. There was no conversation among the three fugitives. They retraced Radeem and Tahj's earlier steps, grateful with each twist and turn not to run into any of Boltar's men. Radeem led the way with Tahj following, the girl's hand clutched in his as she trailed behind.

When they got to the door Radeem had opened before, they only needed to glance out the small window in the top of it to see a handful of Boltar's men gathered outside. He mopped the sweat from his forehead with the back of his hand. "We have to get past them to the horses," he commented between pants, gesturing out the window. "It's the only way."

"I can distract them," the girl offered. Radeem and Tahj turned to stare at her. "I can distract them so you can get to the horses," she reiterated, trying to convince them. "Just be sure to return for me."

Radeem nodded, but Tahj wasn't convinced. He grabbed Radeem's sleeve. "It's too dangerous."

"She just rode that monster in your bedroom like he was an un-broken horse," Radeem protested. "She can do it."

"I can do it," the girl seconded. She glanced down at her outfit, splattered with blood, and it seemed to give her an idea. Before Tahj could argue further, she slipped out the door and into the sunshine.

Tahj clenched his jaw and sank down resignedly so he could watch safely from behind the door. The girl stumbled forward a few paces, moaning, and several of the soldiers looked up from their conversation, casting a glance in her direction. Tahj jumped up, concerned for her, but Radeem laid a hand on his shoulder.

"Wait."

"Are you crazy? Something's obviously wrong with her."

"No," Radeem said slowly. "I think she's faking to distract them."

Tahj took another look. Now, four of the soldiers had turned to watch the girl coming toward them with interest. She called out to them weakly and then swooned, falling hard to the dusty ground. The group of guards rushed to her side, dropping to their knees to form a circle around her, arguing with each other excitedly about what they should do.

"Come on." Radeem slid through the doorway. Tahj had no choice but to follow.

They stuck close to the wind-chafed walls, ducking into and out of the shadows as they nervously watched the group assembled around the girl. The girl had led the men off to the right a little, so Tahj and Radeem headed left along the building until they reached a gate. Seeing it as their best means of escape, they carefully lifted the latch, praying with each inch the rusty metal wouldn't squeak and give away their presence. Halfway up, the pin scraped loudly as it slid and the two men froze.

The argument over what to do about the girl at their feet became a heated one, providing a cover for the escapees' movements. Once the doors were unlocked, Radeem pushed them open several feet, and the two continued around to the intersecting courtyard wall, scooting alongside it until they reached the livery. They stole inside, unnoticed. Radeem quickly headed over to find horses but Tahj paused at the door, listening as the girl pretended to revive.

"Where am I?" she said faintly. There was a man on either side grasping her hand. They supported her back as she sat up shakily.

"Are you feeling well, *Doshizeh*?" Tahj heard a deep voice ask.

"Come on." Radeem stood behind him, leading two saddled horses by the reins with packs on their backs, which would hopefully contain something useful. Radeem stared at Tahj in wonderment. "If I didn't know you better, I would believe you weren't interested in getting away at all. You need to get away from that window before you're seen."

Seeing the horses, Tahj became more animated. One was a deep chestnut brown with a gleaming black mane, the other entirely black. Radeem handed Tahj the reins to the chestnut.

"But this is your horse."

Radeem patted the steed's neck lovingly. "But you're the prince. It's more important you get away. And Balamore is the fastest stallion east of the Mediterranean, so...you ride him."

Tahj knew what a sacrifice it was for Radeem, as he had saved his wages for a year to buy Balamore. He was certain Radeem and Balamore had bonded when taking part in various skirmishes along the borders of the kingdom. Tahj found himself at a loss for words. "Thank you," he managed, his voice rough.

Radeem gulped. "Yeah. So, get on." Tahj put his foot into the stirrup. "I'll get the girl," Radeem added off-handedly. Tahj's head snapped around. "For the same reason," Radeem explained. "Two riders will slow a horse down."

Tahj reached down to pat Radeem's stomach. "No offense, friend, but I think the girl and I will still be lighter than you." Noting Radeem was opening his mouth to protest he added, "Besides, I *am* the prince." He swung himself up into the saddle and gazed down on his friend with an amused smile. "*I'll* get the girl."

Radeem smiled in turn. "You are the prince," he said snidely, with a slight bow. He slapped Balamore's flank and then hopped up in his own saddle, steering his steed toward the barn doors, which were open on the opposite side. The pair spurred their horses forward and came around the side of the building at a full-out run, bearing down on the soldiers who had just recognized the sound of hoof beats and started to rise.

Even through the dust swirling around in the narrow courtyard, Tahj could see the girl's radiant smile as she caught sight of them. Unnoticed, she backed away from the group. Tahj and Radeem ran through the men, scattering them as they leapt to get out of way of the charging horses, the pounding of hoofs thundering in their ears. The riders flew past the girl, but then Tahj turned his horse's head back.

"It's the prince!" one of the men shouted with surprise, reaching for the sword at his belt.

The girl ran to Tahj's side, and he reached down to grasp her arm, hauling her on board behind him. She stuck her foot in the stirrup he had withdrawn his boot from and vaulted onto the horse. It was a difficult move, but she was light and lithe, and with Tahj's borrowed strength they made it look easy. Tahj turned his horse's head back to the east and they sprinted away, ducking through the low gate he and Radeem had opened, bolting off into the countryside.

Tahj bent over the horse's neck, and the girl followed suit, melding her body against his, hands strapped tightly around his chest. He glanced over and Radeem was doing the same thing, minimizing the wind resistance, he and his mount seeming like they were formed into one unit. They were in that state now where it seemed like the horses were almost flying over the ground, their hooves landing almost as one, necks stretching up and down, straining forward with every ounce of energy they possessed.

Tahj turned to look forward. They were about halfway to a forest at the foothills of the mountains, but when he chanced a glance behind, he saw they were being hotly pursued. They had to reach the trees to lose those who followed. He knew Radeem was thinking the same thing as he was: hit the trees then change course, perhaps doubling back in the direction of the palace just to throw the soldiers off all the more.

He tried not to think about how comforting the heat from the girl's body felt as they rode. Or about the way his heart had thrilled when her hands first slid up over his chest to get a firmer grip on his shoulders from beneath. Tahj banished the thought of the warmth that flooded him when she laid a cheek on his back so trustingly. He unconsciously drew himself closer to her, sealing all the gaps between them.

Their pursuers were also closing the gap. He could occasionally hear their horses' hoof beats landing in the quiet between their own, and catch a cry or two, or a horse's impatient snort. Tahj heard a *whoosh* of air close to his ear and saw a blur of motion out of the corner of his eye. Something buried itself in the sand a few feet ahead of them. He realized arrows were flying around them, a flurry at first, and then sporadically. He heard Radeem cry out and saw him fall forward, lying across his horse's neck and beginning to slip perilously to the side. Tahj called out his friend's name, the dust making his throat dry and muffling his shout. At the same time, the girl's arms squeezed him tightly and he heard her gasp once, loudly, and then she was again silent.

She saw the arrow pierce Radeem, and is frightened. Switching the reins to one hand, Tahj reached back to pat the girl's leg in an effort to reassure her, even though he was, himself, still concerned.

Tahj looked over for a second time and saw with relief that Radeem had righted himself in the saddle and was now using his arms to encourage even more speed out of his mount. The trees weren't far off, but it seemed like it was an eternity before they got to them, the branches seeming to reach out and pull the trio into the safety of their shade. Radeem and Tahj weaved through the trunks as only expert horsemen could, making a wide curve back toward the palace. Balamore seemed to be made for this sort of action. He instinctively avoided losing his riders to wayward limbs, leaning from side to side, almost performing a dance with the surrounding trees.

The group behind them immediately thinned out when they entered the tree line, some losing sight of their prey right away in the murky light. The sun had been dropping quickly as they shot over the wide plain, and its remaining, weak rays bounced off, unable to penetrate the foliage. As they traveled farther and farther in, the soldiers lost more men. Unseated by hostile branches, they found themselves lying dazed and bruised underneath the towering mulberry and witch hazel trees, which stood over them like old ladies, chastising them with hands on their hips.

Radeem and Tahj lost the rest, changing courses whenever they were out of their enemies' eyesight on the other side of a small hillock or outcropping of rock. They rode farther on, not wanting to chance running into anyone, until the moon became tangled in the branches above them and the horses became fatigued and slowed to a walk, snorting, and twitching the damp skin on their necks. The only sounds they heard now were the jingle of the reins and the plodding of the hooves beneath them.

"Let's stop," Radeem suggested wearily, bringing his horse alongside Tahj's. "I need to take care of this," he added, waving a hand, and even in the pale moonlight Tahj could see the arrow shaft projecting from the back of Radeem's thigh. Radeem swung his uninjured leg over the saddle and lay for a moment on his stomach, catching his breath, before carefully sliding to the ground. Even so, he cringed in pain and hobbled around for a minute, cursing loudly.

Behind Tahj, the sound seemed to awaken the girl, who stirred, though still leaning heavily on his back. She moaned softly and finally pushed off of him to sit up. Tahj dismounted and reached up to help her down. To his surprise, she practically fell into his arms, and as he supported her he realized her clothing was wet. He pulled his hand back and held it up in the silver moonlight, recognizing the crimson liquid running between his fingers.

"She's been shot!"

CHAPTER FIVE

"What?" Radeem asked, his voice high. He straightened up from where he leaned against a tree, observing his own wound.

Tahj swept the girl up into his arms and she mumbled something incoherently, perhaps in another language. He walked forward with his burden, kneeling down in the soft earth beneath the trees. Gingerly, he bent the girl's body so he could see her back, and there was the shaft of an arrow buried in her shoulder, broken off, no doubt from being bashed against low branches. Tahj couldn't imagine the pain that must have caused her. He cursed softly and laid the girl on the ground on her side. She lay limp, though again murmuring something he couldn't understand as he rose to return to Balamore. Maybe she was calling out for someone.

Radeem limped over to the girl, but couldn't manage to bend his leg so he, too, could examine her. Tahj came back, having ripped the pack from Balamore's back. "Where did they get her?"

"Shoulder," Tahj answered shortly, rummaging through the bag as he knelt beside the girl. He pulled out a lightweight shirt and tore it into strips. Radeem watched silently, now seeming oblivious to his own wound. Tahj carefully dabbed at the injury with one of his makeshift bandages, trying to steady his trembling hands. He looked up after a while. "What should I do?"

Radeem shrugged, apparently uncertain of the best course of action.

"Dammit, man! You're a soldier. Don't you know something I can do to help her?"

The captain thought about it. "You should probably pull it out, if you can."

Tahj peered down at his helpless patient. Her eyes were closed, face pale and still. With a sigh, he got a firm grasp on what was left of the arrow, which was about the width of his hand, and, whispering a short prayer, swiftly pulled it straight out. The girl cried out and, out of reflex, rolled over onto her back.

"No. No." He rolled her onto her side again, afraid the wound would get dirty.

"I'll get some water." Radeem began to hobble over to his horse, which was grazing a few feet away.

"But your wound—"

Radeem waved him off and retrieved a gourd, wrapped in goatskin, that hung from a string. Returning with it, he handed the gourd to Tahj, who unstopped the spout and poured the contents gently over the wound. Even so, the girl shook violently and opened her eyes. She seemed disoriented, confused, and frightened as she tried to jerk away from them.

"Ohh! What are you doing? Leave me alone!" Seeing the two men hovering over her seemed to frighten her. "Don't touch me!" she cried, scrambling onto her elbows and using her feet to back away from them.

Tahj bobbled the gourd as he tried to calm her, sloshing water everywhere. "Please, don't move. You've been shot."

The girl turned to peer at Tahj and seemed to recognize him then. Her head swiveled quickly to peer at Radeem in the darkness. "H-how d-did I get here?"

"We escaped on horseback." Tahj explained, moving tentatively closer.

She nodded, licking her lips and still looking from one to the other distrustfully. She shivered, her wet clothing no doubt making her cold.

"I'll start a fire," Radeem suggested.

"*I'll* start a fire," Tahj snapped, his nerves frazzled. "After I check your leg," he added more kindly.

Tahj rose and crossed to help his friend to the ground in order to examine his wound. "It doesn't appear to be too bad," he commented, grabbing the shaft to remove it with both hands.

"Wait!" Radeem was sweating, his face tense as he reached back to grab Tahj's arm. "That's going to hurt."

Tahj smiled, relaxing for the first time. "You are acting like a child."

"Well, why don't you let me pull a hunk of wood out of your leg, then," Radeem barked, glancing at the girl, seeming embarrassed by his weakness. She watched the two men, still reclining on her elbows but looking less frightened.

"On the count of three, then."

Radeem nodded uncertainly.

"One, two..."

Radeem screamed in agony. "By the light of Asman, man! Why didn't you do it carefully, like hers?" he grumbled.

Tahj ignored him, moving to retrieve the strips of cloth on the ground near the girl. Seeming to understand what he was doing, she handed one to him. He paused, gazing into those big, dark eyes of hers. "Thank you." She nodded again, and a glimmer of a smile touched her lips.

Tahj turned back to Radeem, shaking his head to clear it a little. She had such a strange effect on him. He wrapped a strip tightly around Radeem's thigh, and this time the captain only winced and sucked in his breath a little when Tahj tied it off, but then he scooted back, resting against a tree trunk with his injured leg bent at the knee, his other leg straightened in front of him. Tahj returned to the girl's side. "Can I bind your wound?" he asked, squatting and staring into her jewel-like eyes. She nodded, sitting all the way up.

Tahj tied the remaining strips together, making one long bandage. "I'm going to loop it over your right shoulder and then under your left arm." Again she nodded. He began to work the strip as he had described, chuckling nervously. "You're quiet."

The girl laughed, surprising him. "If only my brothers could hear you say that."

Tahj passed the end of the strip from hand to hand, careful to not touch her as he passed in front of her. "You have a big family then?"

She nodded. "Two sisters and five brothers."

His eyebrows rose. "Five?" He finished, tucking the end of the bandage into the folds he had created. He remained squatting in front of her, glancing down at the ground for a second, and then back up, squinting. "What's your name?" he asked her for the second time, wondering if she would again refuse to answer him.

"Bashea," she replied softly.

"Bashea," he repeated. "That's pretty." Her gaze shifted from one of his eyes to the other with an unreadable expression on her face. He watched Bashea, frozen by her beauty, until Radeem's loud snoring rudely broke the spell she'd cast. He laughed. "He's a jewel, that one." He gestured over his shoulder. Radeem's head had fallen back against the tree trunk, his mouth open wide as he slept. Tahj got up to retrieve a blanket and spread it over the sleeping man, still laughing quietly.

"He is your brother?" she questioned upon his return.

"What? Radeem? No. My friend." He busied himself by searching through the bag for a minute. "I'm Tahj, by the way." He held out his hand, and she slipped her slender one into it.

"Prince Tahj?"

He frowned, rifling through the bag again. "I suppose. But prince of what?" he muttered, unwanted images of his slain mother and father filling his mind. A breeze blew, and she trembled again, wrapping her arms around herself. "I'll get the fire started now."

She started to stand. "I'll help."

Tahj laid a hand on her uninjured shoulder. "You just relax. You've had enough action today."

Clearing a spot in between the trees, Tahj collected brush to start his fire. He pulled a flint box out of one of the packs and soon had small flames leaping to life. As he returned to Bashea, he found her face even more bewitching in the firelight.

"That feels good."

"Hmmm?" he responded absentmindedly.

"The fire. It feels good."

He stirred himself to respond to her. "Oh, yes. Well, I'm sure a bigger one would feel even better, but I don't want to take any chances on being discovered. We'll just have to stay close. To the fire, that is," he added lamely, but Bashea didn't seem to notice. She was staring into the fire, mesmerized by the dance of the flames.

"Mmm-hmm."

"I'll be right back. I want to find a boulder or something to rest our backs against."

Tahj's lopsided smile sent a strange shiver through Bashea. She looked down, afraid he would notice. After a second, she laughed at herself, shaking her head. Thick, wavy black hair, perfect, bronzed skin, a face that looked like it had been chiseled by a master, and that tantalizing flash of white teeth—what was not to like? But it was foolish to get all gaga over a man, and she was no fool.

Bashea watched him leave the already comforting ring of light from the fire, feeling a sort of pang as he slipped away into the dark. She glanced over at his friend, who was oblivious to it all, and wondered over how she had gotten where she was, in the middle of the woods with a handsome prince and a loveable buffoon.

Not for the first time, she thought about her family. Would they be sitting around a fire now, too, telling tales as they were the night she was abducted? Was Gaspard relating a story he read in some book he dug up, or was Bagrat horsing around with Jahmeel, coming dangerously close to the fire as they sparred with one another? Bashea hugged her knees closer, ignoring the pain it caused her shoulder, even as she was unable to ignore the pain in her heart. She rested her forehead on her knees and let hot tears roll down her cheeks where no one could see them, face buried in the little valley of her legs. Seconds later, hearing the crunch of a stick, her head sprang up and she hastened to wipe away the tears.

Tahj had searched through the brush and now came back, emerging from the dark with a five-foot section of log laid across his shoulders, arms looped over it like a yoke. He grinned at Bashea, obviously pleased with his find. Carrying the log left pieces of bark on his shirt, and long, smeared lines of gray to go with the red streaks of blood. Whether they were from their earlier fighting, or her own wound, she wasn't at all sure.

He would have looked almost comical if he weren't so darn good-looking, she thought. His right sleeve was ripped from shoulder to forearm, and, as he shifted his hands so they were underneath the wood, she could see the ripple of his biceps and felt an unwanted stirring in her blood. Tahj straightened his arms out over his head with very little effort, and the display of strength had her fighting back a sigh. He dropped the log to the ground with a dull *thump* and rolled it with his feet until he got it where he wanted it, near the fire. He planted a boot on it triumphantly.

"Our couch," he said, bending and waving his hand gallantly along its length.

He approached and reached down, sliding his large hand behind Bashea's good shoulder to help her up. She scrambled to her feet, shying away from his touch as much as she welcomed it. After she was comfortable by the log, he sat down next to her, crossing his legs in front of him. They sat quietly at first, surrounded by the night rhythms of the forest, the lazy sound of crickets chorusing with the popping of some of the greener kindling the fire consumed, and the deep bass of Radeem's snores. The pair soon was enjoying the soothing sensation of fire-roasted faces and clothes, even as the cool air chilled their backs to balance out the heat.

"How's your shoulder?" Tahj asked after a while.

"A little sore," she said hesitantly, "but, all in all, I think it could have been a lot worse."

He nodded in agreement. "Where are you from, Bashea?"

She liked the way he said her name, with care. She stared into the leaping, yellow-blue flames and sighed. "We call it Tamook. It's just a little village near the bottom of Mount Sabalan, to the north. My people are a nomadic tribe," she explained. "We herd sheep and move from place to place to find pasture." She felt embarrassed to be a mere sheepherder in the presence of a real prince, even though in her own tribe she was considered a princess, the daughter of the chief. But it was hardly the same, princess of a wandering land full of sheep dung, compared to prince of the glorious city of Avistad. She'd heard wondrous things about the city and all the goods that could be found there, all the things that could be done there, for the right price.

Tahj picked up a stick and idly played with the fire, trying to find a way to form his next question. "I'm sorry..." He stopped and started again, laying the stick aside and turning to her. "They took you away from your home, those men?"

Even in the firelight, he could see her cheeks flush. She quickly looked away from him, staring blindly again into the dance of flames. After several seconds had passed, she answered. "Yes."

"We will take you home, then, tomorrow."

She looked at him, her eyes wide. "You'd do that?"

"Of course." Reading the surprise on her face, an idea occurred to him and, his voice a bit panicky, he questioned, "You didn't think I ordered, or had anything to do with what those men—"

"No," she said quickly. "I didn't think that."

But he could tell it was a lie. He studied her profile in the flickering firelight. She still didn't trust him entirely. Her face still held the cuts and bruises from her tormentors, but it was no less beautiful, with a sense of pride and strength, framed with those tumbling black curls. She was unusual, this girl, and he found himself longing to unlock the secrets of her heart.

She drew her knees up and rubbed her arms. Tahj rose, and her eyes darted in his direction, still cagey and frightened. "I'm getting you a blanket." She nodded, but didn't speak again, going back to gazing into the depths of the fire. What was she thinking? Was she remembering the awful things that had happened to her the night before?

Tahj picked his way over the uneven ground to where the horses stood dozing. He pulled off the other blanket, which was rolled and tied to the back of the saddle. He stood for a moment, one hand on the horse, the blanket tucked under his other arm, and watched her. She was unaware of him, absorbed in her own thoughts. She was completely enchanting, magic in the firelight, intriguingly as fragile as she was strong. The holes he found in the cool distance she tried to maintain, the moments when she dropped her guard enough to let him in, fueled his desire to tear away all boundaries between them. He walked slowly back to her side, but she still jumped when he drew near.

Without speaking, Tahj knelt in the dirt, unrolling the blanket to lay it out by the fire. He lifted his eyes to hers. Bashea watched him guardedly, perhaps wondering if he expected her to join him in the bed he made. She glanced nervously in Radeem's direction, but he was still crashed out, snoring incessantly. It was as if she was measuring the odds, determining if she could fight Tahj on her own if she had to, or if Radeem would help him to subdue her, and do...whatever else to her.

Tahj rose and stalked to the edge of the clearing. He couldn't stand to see the pain in the girl's eyes, knowing, in a roundabout way, he had caused it. Sure, he didn't order the raid on her village, but it was undertaken to play a joke on him, so he felt some of the blame was his. As a leader, he hadn't won over his troops, and this was the result. She didn't trust him, and why should she? Her thinking poorly of him hurt. At the same time, it angered him that the men had acted out of hate and lust, and the pure evil dwelling within them.

These thoughts led him to others, thoughts of his father, whose body lay broken upon the bed, blood poured out upon the tiles Tahj had crawled over as a baby. And even as he saw this face, another one was superimposed over it—Kadeesh's, his dear brother. Boltar had taken Tahj's entire family away from him, and the need to avenge their deaths burned in his heart. But there was nothing to be done tonight, and he needed first to right things with the girl.

Tahj turned back to the camp. To his surprise, he found Bashea curled up where she had been, lying on her side against the tree he'd lugged out of the woods, the blanket abandoned. He headed silently toward Bashea, careful to avoid any branches that might snap and wake her. He retrieved the blanket, and, bending down next to her, noted how tightly she was curled up against the cold, how her hands lay clenched by her face. Tahj stretched out the blanket over her small body, being sure it covered the injured shoulder. He paused a second more, soaking in her face, and then unconsciously reached out to run the back of his hand down a soft cheek.

He felt a slight quiver under her skin. She had flinched at his touch. She was awake then, only pretending to sleep. He understood now—she was afraid to face him, afraid of what demands she imagined he would have. He drew back his hand and retreated to the other side of the fire. But, through the night, he continued to watch her as she slept. The moon traveled over the sky before he finally fell asleep, curled up on his side as she was, feeling suddenly very, very alone.

CHAPTER SIX

He was standing over the fire, mere feet away, with his back to her, gnawing on something, when the girl woke with a start. He heard the sharp intake of her breath and turned, holding a greasy finger to his lips. Radeem squatted down in front of her. "The prince is still asleep."

Straightening, he spun to sit next to her, too close, causing her to sit up and draw the blanket around her more tightly, though he pretended not to notice. He was staring at Tahj thoughtfully. Tahj lay on his side, head on his folded hands, with no pillow, no blanket, curled up against the cold. "He didn't sleep well," Radeem commented.

The girl followed his gaze. "He didn't?"

Radeem turned to stare at her. "Coming across your father with his throat slit, and then holding your dying mother in your arms will do that to you." He got up, disgruntled, angered at Boltar and his men and sore from sleeping on the ground. He was ravenous, having found only a small amount of dried meat in their packs, and all that made for a grumpy captain. Radeem rarely missed a meal.

He strode off to the horses to search the packs some more. He glanced up, catching the girl as she gazed at Tahj. There was something going on there, he was sure of it. The concern on Tahj's face when he found out she was hurt, the way she was looking at him now—there was definitely something going on. It amused him—he'd never seen Tahj with a woman—and irritated him. She was a beautiful girl, after all, and had no idea he was married, yet she chose Tahj over him. He fished an apple, which he had overlooked, out of a pack and then strode back over to her with purpose and sat down, chomping on his find it noisily.

"So," Radeem began uncertainly, "where is your home?" He turned toward her, resting a forearm on his knee, holding the apple loosely, in what he hoped was a casual position, not bothering to tie his shirt so she could see his massive chest. With his free hand he reached over to play with her hair.

She narrowed her eyes, but didn't pull away. "Tamook, at the foot of Mt. Sabalan."

He gestured to her bandaged shoulder. "Tahj do that?" he asked, with just a hint of accusation.

She nodded, but didn't elaborate.

"What's your name, *Ziba*?" he queried, using his best, honeyed tone, looking into those fathomless eyes and letting himself get lost for a moment with a stupid grin on his face.

"Bashea," she answered through clenched teeth.

"Bashea...pretty, like you." Radeem ran a finger down the girl's cheek, giving her his most charming smile, but in exchange he got a death stare meant to put him in his place.

Out of nowhere, a pack landed at Radeem's feet. He jumped in surprise. He had been so engrossed with Bashea, he hadn't noticed Tahj rising. "We need to leave," Tahj said coldly.

If Radeem had thought something was going on between them before, this only confirmed it. Oh, yes, he'd bet a silver coin on Tahj being jealous just now. Radeem smiled up at him. "You've got it, Your Highness." He rose and offered the girl his hand. She looked from him to Tahj, but the prince was walking away. She placed her hand in Radeem's, letting him help her to her feet. But when Radeem pulled Bashea in close she gave him the same icy stare. He backed up, holding his hands out as if offering her his surrender.

Tahj had stormed past them to the horses and now came back, squatting to roll up Bashea's blanket. She bent to help him, but he whipped the end out of her hand. "I've got it," he snapped, not looking up at her. He continued to roll the blanket up roughly and she backed away, rubbing a hand where the blanket must have burned as it was jerked from her grip.

Tahj would have felt bad about that if he wasn't too busy fuming over what he saw when he opened his eyes after a horrible night's sleep. Just as the bright sunlight chased away his nightmares, he heard their voices. He sat up just as Radeem was reaching out to touch her hair. She did not flinch at his touch. From Tahj's angle, he couldn't see Bashea's face, just Radeem's big, fat, foolish one, smiling at her like he was about to eat her up for dessert, and Tahj was angry.

It was perfectly reasonable to be angry with her. She sat there and flirted with Radeem, who was a complete stranger, and she shrunk away from Tahj's touch like he was diseased. Who wouldn't be angry? And then when Radeem touched her face, that was too much. Tahj thought about it as he threw the pack onto Balamore's back, nearly flinging it off the other side in his fury. He thought about it as he stamped out the fire, kicking the logs apart and spreading the remains high and wide.

"You all right there, Prince?" Radeem asked, peering at him curiously.

"Fine. Just ready to go," Tahj mumbled, not wanting to have to explain himself. Besides, at the moment he was pretty sure any extended conversation with Radeem would end up with the good captain being belted.

"Sure thing," Radeem responded in a chipper manner, which set Tahj's teeth on edge. Tahj reached up for the saddle horn, stepping into the stirrup. "Bashea," Radeem added, drawing out her name, "can ride with me today. Give Balamore a rest."

Tahj froze for a second, his muscles tense. "Fine." He finished pulling himself up and sat, staring straight ahead.

"My dear." Radeem offered Bashea a hand to help her onto the horse.

She took it, but muttered under her breath, "I'm only letting you help me because my shoulder is sore."

"Of course." Radeem winked and Bashea frowned at him. He climbed on in front of her. Tahj wondered about the exchange for a moment, but then decided he didn't care. Whatever was going on between the pair was none of his business. None of his damn business.

They took off, heading north through the trees, not running, but keeping a steady clip all the same. Tahj just wanted to be done with the whole thing, leave the girl with her family and... what? What was he to do now? His home was gone; his family was gone... But he'd escaped with his life; he would at least be grateful for that. He would start a new life somewhere else. Somewhere...far away from these two, he concluded. He tried not to look, but every once in a while, he couldn't help but glance over at her hands around Radeem's waist, as they had been around his the day before. Once, Bashea glanced back over at him, and he turned back around. He didn't want to look into those eyes of hers.

At midday they stopped in a meadow by a stream. Tahj chewed on some of the leather-like meat, which had been stored in salt in a pouch inside their packs. He lifted his eyes and saw Bashea. He froze, and his lips whispered her name involuntarily as he watched her dip to get water out of the stream. She brought it to her mouth and drank long, and then splashed some on her neck, stretching and closing her eyes. She was hot and weary, he knew, as he felt the same. A light breeze blew the hair back from her face, and he dropped his eyes, afraid she would see him watching her again, and, no doubt, think he was having perverse thoughts about her, which, he had to admit, he wasn't far from.

When Tahj glanced up again, Radeem had stepped up under the branches of the trees near the water, resting a hand against a limb as he talked to Bashea. She looked up at him and responded with something Tahj could not hear, but his stomach churned.

"Let's get moving," Tahj called out, packing things up again.

"What's your hurry, Tahj?" Radeem queried, returning from across the meadow.

"Nothing. No hurry. I just want to be done with it."

"Done with it?"

He shrugged. "Take the girl to her home. Done with it. Done with her." Tahj said it casually, but it was far from the truth. The last thing Tahj wanted was to be done with the girl.

"It is going to be an interesting trip from here on out," Radeem speculated. "The journey to the girl's home is only a day long, had we crossed the desert. But skirting it as we did, in the shadow of the trees, it will take a bit longer. I know this part of the kingdom, and we are going to run out of trees soon. We will need to cross out in the open eventually."

It was just this the two men were discussing when Bashea returned. "We'll need to get a hold of some tents," Radeem was saying. "We won't last a day without them in the desert." He looked up when she entered the shade where they reclined. "Our tree cover will be running out in a few hours. We are nearing the city of Shiraz." He turned back to Tahj. "We cannot enter as we are, dirty and bloodstained. It will arouse suspicion, and Boltar may already have sent some of his men there. They would have made it easily before us, crossing the desert."

"What are your suggestions?" Tahj listened to Radeem attentively. At least him could trust Radeem in this.

Radeem chewed on their dilemma for a minute before coming up with a solution. "I know. I know just what to do. I have a friend. He won't ask any questions, and he lives just outside the boundaries of the city. It's on the far side of Shiraz, so we will have to travel around it to get there, but we will go there, with your permission."

Tahj peered up at Bashea. He felt responsible for her safety, and exposing her to strangers, even if Radeem knew them, made him nervous.

She nodded her head. "If that is what we must do..."

Tahj stood. "Take us there."

CHAPTER SEVEN

Bashea sat uncomfortably behind Radeem. Not because of his earlier flirtation—she had put an end to that. It was simply because he was a large man, which left little room for her on the horse. No, Bashea could read Radeem easily. Probably married, with a couple of children, a flirt, but harmless. Though she had cringed earlier when Radeem called her *ziba,* "beautiful," she knew he had no idea those other men had used the same word, or that the sound of it now made her skin crawl. Radeem may be a letch, but he wasn't a threat; she was certain of that.

It was Tahj she couldn't figure out. Cool one minute, warm the next, like a desert gecko moving from sun to shade. He had barely spoken to her all morning, or Radeem, for that matter, yet he seemed so pleasant the night before. She mused over his covering her with the only remaining blanket and sleeping in the cold without one. She rubbed her hand down her cheek, remembering the way he touched her when he thought she was sleeping. She had been frightened it was just a precursor to more. That if she did not give him what he wanted, he would just take it, as the others had. But when she woke and saw him sleeping on his side in the cold without a blanket, he looked like a little boy. A cold, lonely little boy. She figured then that she had been wrong about him. Now, she was totally confused.

As she wondered about her traveling companions, the trees on her right began to thin out. Between the branches she caught sight of a solitary house ahead. Radeem led them until they were behind the small home, a hovel, really, with a thatch roof and a dirty wooden portico, though living this close to the desert, it was probably impossible to keep it clean. They broke from the trees for the first time to approach the house. The owner heard their horses and came out into the shade of an overhang that ran the length of the house, peering through the swirling dust quizzically. When he recognized Radeem, he bent and called joyfully into the house.

"Ah, Radeem, my friend," the old man said as the captain dismounted. He took Radeem by the shoulders and kissed him vigorously on both cheeks. "It has been too long. Welcome. Welcome." With the last he turned to Tahj and Bashea, who bowed slightly. "Friends of Radeem, you are welcome in my house."

Before the words were even out of his mouth, three girls swarmed out of the house squealing Radeem's name and gathering around to kiss him. Radeem blushed. "Girls! Girls! You must be calm. There's plenty of me for all of you." The trio's bright clothing stood out against the bland background of the desert like cactus flowers. Two of the girls took Radeem's elbows to lead him inside and the third followed behind, obviously fuming because she had been left out.

Tahj and Bashea looked at each other and smiled. One couldn't help being amused, it seemed. Appearing a little embarrassed by his girls' behavior, but equally proud of them, the father ushered his other two guests into the house behind them, their twittering almost making speech impossible.

Once inside the house's walls, however, the older man addressed them sternly, "Girls!" But then he chuckled. "I cannot even hear what my guests are saying."

He turned to Tahj and Bashea now. He was short and round, with a snowy-white beard and white clothing with a wide, gold sash, his eyes quick and merry. "I am Faraz, and these are my daughters. Etti—" One of the girls, dressed in the same sort of flowing jumpsuit Bashea wore, stepped forward and curtsied. She had on one of the traditional veils and shiny, metal medallions glinted from all over her vibrant orange clothing; her bright eyes swept over Tahj appraisingly before she stepped back. "This is my next eldest, Dariya." A second girl stepped forward wearing the same outfit in a pastel green, and the third, and youngest, daughter was introduced as Jessmyn. She was dressed in pink, and white sequins sparkled on her dress like grains of sand caught in the midday sun.

Each of the girls dropped their eyes when curtsying, as was respectful, but as they rose they held Tahj's gaze boldly. Bashea looked from them to the prince to gauge his reaction, but his face was unreadable. She felt the hair on the back of her neck begin to bristle and in turn became aggravated she was even aggravated at all. It was foolish. Of course the girls would admire Tahj, a young, handsome, eligible man. But did they have to be so obvious about it? They were practically throwing themselves at his feet.

"And you are...?" their host asked.

Tahj stepped forward. "I am Pr—"

"Pravin," Radeem corrected. "Pravin is my old friend." Radeem clapped Tahj on the back heartily, making him stumble forward.

Faraz's shrewd eyes seemed to catch the lie, but he graciously accepted it as the truth. "Welcome, Pravin."

"And this," Radeem added with a flourish, "is Bashea, Pravin's espoused." Both Bashea and Tahj cast him a look of surprise, but Radeem ignored them.

The older gentleman took Bashea's hand and kissed it while never taking his eyes from hers. "Bashea," he said with an odd tenderness, "welcome to our home." She curtsied.

From the moment they entered the house, the fabulous smell of some kind of savory repast had tempted them. Radeem, who seemed to almost drool as he spoke, addressed their host. "But it seems we have interrupted a meal. We should go and perhaps come back another time."

"Nonsense. Nonsense," Faraz answered. "There is plenty to share, isn't there, girls?" The three bubbled in response. "You must stay and eat with us. We insist."

Radeem bowed with his palms pressed together in front of his chest. "We would be forever grateful, my friend."

"Perhaps you would care to wash up after your travels," Faraz said tactfully, eying their soiled and bloodied clothing. "Pravin and your lovely Bashea, you shall have my room for the night."

"The night...?" Tahj began.

"And you, my dear friend, will have the girls' room."

There immediately seemed to be some infighting among the female trio, and from the snatches of whispers caught here and there, it was clearly evident they were fighting over who would share Radeem's bed for the evening. After a few seconds, the father made a sharp sound and the squabbling stopped, the middle girl smiling victoriously while the other two looked, at first disappointed, and then hopefully, in Tahj's direction. "Jessmyn, show Pravin and Bashea to their room."

"Our room?" Bashea questioned in a panic. Then, remembering they were supposed to be a couple, she added, "B-but we aren't yet married—"

Faraz winked. "We will keep your secret."

Bashea glanced at Tahj, who just shrugged, and she was forced to follow him across the room. As they walked past Radeem, the captain, seeming quite pleased with himself, slung his arms loosely around the pair's shoulders, leaning in to talk to them privately. "Since I went to the trouble of creating a lie to keep your identities a secret, the least you could do is act the part. Take your betrothed's arm, you idiot." Unseen by their host, he thwacked Tahj on the head. Tahj stuck his arm out begrudgingly and Bashea put her arm through it, equally unhappy. Radeem, for his part, seemed to be enjoying the fact that he was making them both uncomfortable.

Jessmyn sauntered in front of Tahj and Bashea, swishing her hips temptingly and glancing over her shoulder with a giggle now and then. Bashea looked at Tahj, but he wasn't watching the girl; he seemed to be stewing over something. "Here's your room." The obviously infatuated girl gave a wink, which was lost on Tahj.

When the door closed behind her, Tahj gave Bashea's arm an absentminded pat and withdrew his hand. It was suddenly very quiet. The room was tiny, with a double bed that took up most of one side, a small window at the head of the bed, and a fireplace on the adjacent wall. Tahj stepped up to put his hand on the mantle, staring into the barren depths of the fireplace beneath without speaking.

After standing just inside the doorway for several minutes feeling awkward, Bashea crossed to the window. Forgetting about her shoulder, she reached to move aside the curtain, sucking in her breath in pain. Tahj looked up, seeming immediately concerned.

"Let me look at that."

"No, I'm fine."

"Don't be foolish. I should check it. Come here." He sat on the bed and gestured for her to sit down next to him. When she hesitated he snapped at her, "Come here. I'm not going to do anything to you, for Arishtat's sake."

Bashea marched over, giving Tahj a cool stare, and sat down with her back to him. Slowly she moved her hair out of the way, looping it over her other shoulder.

The movement struck Tahj as very sensual, and the smell of her hair about drove him over the edge. Unsteadily he reached out and untucked the edge of the bandage and began to pull it off little by little. When it fell away, Tahj saw the blood had only gone through two layers, and he took that as a good sign. He pressed around the area gently.

"Does it hurt?"

"A little."

"I need to pull the fabric away to get a good look at it and make sure the edges are clean and sealed."

She nodded, but said nothing. Tahj put a hand on her shoulder, and his heart started to beat quicker. Chastising himself for being foolish, he carefully slid the fabric down off her shoulder, but the move was incredibly erotic, and when he saw the smooth skin of her neck and the top of her shoulder he fought an urge to sink his teeth into it, or, at the very least, brush his lips across the creamy expanse. He closed his eyes.

"So, how is it?"

"Oh!" he said, surprised by the sound of her voice. "Fine, fine. It looks fine."

His answer must not have been too convincing, as she jumped up to check herself in a large, rectangular mirror which had once been in a frame but now stood leaning against the wall. There was a long crack in it, and the glass was murky with age, but Bashea turned to look at her bare shoulder in its reflection speculatively. Since the wound was indeed clean, and looked like it was beginning to heal, she looked at Tahj quizzically.

The door opened a crack. "I've got...oh!" Seeing Bashea's top halfway off her shoulder and Tahj sitting on the bed behind her, Radeem commented suggestively, "Am I interrupting something?"

"No." Bashea bit off the word angrily, moving to the window and pulling her sleeve up.

Radeem winked at Tahj with a sly look, but, getting no smile in response, he continued. "I got you guys some clothes, if you want them," he added with a cheesy grin. He handed Tahj a stack of clothes, and Bashea turned and then rushed over to pull hers off the top. It was a beautiful piece, and she ran her hand over the fabric, her eyes wide.

Radeem turned to Tahj. "Uhh...I need forty Abbas to pay for them."

Tahj's head spun. "Forty Abbas!"

"I had to give my friend some compensation."

"But forty Abbas? That would pay for a whole new wardrobe and food and board for a week."

Radeem shrugged, still holding his hand out.

"Some friend," Tahj grumbled, pulling out a drawstring pouch and handing him the silver coins. "I've been gone a little over twenty-four hours, and I'm almost out of money."

Radeem accepted the money with a smile and turned to leave, counting the coins again into his palm, seeming unduly satisfied with their tinkling.

"Forty Abbas," Tahj muttered when the door closed. He laid the new clothes out on the bed and started to remove his shirt.

"You're not getting changed in here!" Bashea squeaked.

Startled, he asked, "I'm not?"

"Not in front of me."

"Oh, come on, *my sweet*." Tahj smirked. "We're engaged, remember?"

Seeming flustered, Bashea turned away when he proceeded to pull his shirt off. Tahj just laughed and shifted to dip his hands into a basin on a stand by the fireplace. He splashed the water on his face and chest, glancing over to where Bashea still stood by the window, her back turned, though peeking from time to time.

Bashea shut her eyes, trying not to think about the raw twist of muscle she had glimpsed as he had removed his shirt. "W-what about me?"

"You can get changed. I won't look."

"What?" She spun around, but finding his chest was still bare, dropped her eyes, nervously stammering, "I-I'm n-not g-going to change with you in here."

"Fine. Then you can change after I leave."

Despite his undressed state, Bashea looked up at him desperately. "But they believe we are to get married. If you go out there, and I stay in here to change, they'll suspect something."

"No, they won't. Women always take forever getting ready," he rejoined, slipping the fresh shirt over his head.

"Not me," she responded indignantly.

"Well, what's it going to be, Bashea?" he asked, sounding exasperated. "Do you want me to stay, or do you want me to go?"

"Ugh!" she cried in frustration, her face hot with suppressed rage. She took one of her shoes off jerkily, nearly falling off balance. "*Get...out of here!*" She winged one of her shoes at him, and Tahj dodged it. He just had time to duck out the door before the other shoe hit it.

EVERYONE AT THE SMALL kitchen table looked up at the loud bang of the door, followed by the sound of the second shoe battering it. Tahj lifted his shoulders apologetically. "Lovers' spat."

Faraz came over to put his arm around Tahj and usher him in. "My Talia and I had plenty of those. That's good," he whispered confidentially. "The feistier they are out of bed, the more fun they are in bed." He jabbed an elbow in Tahj's ribs.

Then she ought to be incredible, Tahj thought wryly. He grunted and then chuckled along with his host, feeling uncomfortable. His eyes searched the room for Radeem, but Jessmyn stepped forward, taking his hand and leading him to the table seductively. "You know, there are many men who choose to have a multitude of wives," she offered.

"Uhh..." Tahj didn't quite know what to say to that one. He had always thought it was strange when men took a number of wives. He hoped to find one very special woman to spend his life with, as his father had. Tahj sat down, and Faraz's two other daughters came to sit next to him, too, rubbing their hands over his arms.

"You're strong," Dariya said, and the others giggled. Tahj felt Etti's hand slipping lower on his thigh and shifted nervously. By the time Radeem came out, he felt like he had been fighting back three panthers. To his relief, Dariya and Etti rose to fawn over his captain, leaving him with only the one pair of wandering hands to deal with.

Tahj glanced up when he heard the bedroom door open and involuntarily rose out of his chair as Bashea entered. She was stunning in the white garb she wore, gold medallions hanging from the headpiece and the belt at her waist. The ties of the Choli top skimmed over her bare midriff, and she wore a traditional face veil, which only served to accent her mesmerizing eyes all the more, as they were the only part of her face which wasn't hidden. A triple strand of pearls hung below her chin, swaying as she walked forward, and Tahj felt as if the earth were swaying in time.

Radeem, who had stopped in mid-sentence when Bashea entered, gulped and bent down to whisper in Tahj's ear. "Bet you won't be complaining any more about the money I spent. Worth every damn Abba."

CHAPTER EIGHT

Faraz was the first to recover his voice; he went over to offer Bashea his arm. She placed hers gracefully on top of his, her palm flat against the back of his hand, as he led her to the table, but Bashea's eyes never left Tahj's. She was vaguely aware she should be listening to whatever it was her host was saying at her elbow, but she had become lost in Tahj's gaze, her blood humming through her veins.

Bashea felt a bubbling up inside, a strange warmth that seemed to come from her toes and spread upward and outward. For the first time in days she didn't feel scared, or angry, or confused. She suddenly understood the humor of the situation she found herself in, faking an engagement to a prince she barely knew, while his clown of a captain was strutting around like a peacock, three women throwing themselves at him in front of the proud eyes of their doting father. It was all so wonderfully odd and off-kilter, and somehow she found herself grateful to be sharing it with Tahj.

The others started their animated chatter again. "You look lovely," Tahj told her quietly.

"Thank you," she returned, her face growing suddenly hot underneath the veil.

Food was brought to them in mounds—exotic fruits, spicy meat, and heavy breads—and as they ate, Faraz entertained them with stories about his daughters. After the meal, they pushed the tables back and the three girls danced in front of the fire while their father played the nay. The music the small, wooden flute made was slow and sensual, and the dance was perfectly synchronized, as the trio had been dancing with each other their whole lives.

Tahj and Bashea and Radeem reclined on satin pillows, which were brought out and thrown on the floor for their comfort, and watched with rapt attention. When the dance was finished, the girls collapsed breathlessly on the floor in front of Radeem while they all applauded. Soon after, Faraz brought out a sitar and small cymbals, and Etti and Dariya accompanied their father in a more frolicsome tune. Jessmyn pulled a laughing Radeem to his feet and cavorted around the room with him.

Bashea laughed, too, a little lightheaded from the strong drink her host had served. Radeem, noticing how amused she was, grabbed Bashea's hands in turn, and forced her to dance along with him. Feeling carefree, Bashea spun with Radeem and then swirled around him, the alcohol loosening her hips as she shimmied closer and closer. On a whim, she took the scarf from her shoulders and wrapped him up in it, holding the two ends as if making him her prisoner.

Bashea was spinning and laughing with her head thrown back. Her eyes searched for Tahj, wanting to share her moment of joy with him and perhaps get him to dance, but he was no longer on the pillows. She completed her turn, still searching for him, when she spotted him on the makeshift dance floor, Jessmyn in his arms. As Bashea watched, the young dancer began to twirl around him, trailing her fingers along his chest as if in invitation. Radeem's head blocked her view, and she strained to see around him. Jessmyn took Tahj's hand and placed it on the small of her back and then bent away from him beguilingly so her hair nearly trailed the ground. Bashea's mouth fell open as Jessmyn sinuously straightened until she was hip-to-hip with Tahj, their faces inches from each other.

Bashea stopped dancing so abruptly she nearly stumbled, her momentum making her dizzy. The smile that had lit her face moments before fell away, and the warmth she'd felt welling inside her turned to an instant inferno. Her eyes snapped with fire. Blindly, she left the dance floor, intending to storm off to her room, if only Faraz hadn't stepped in her way.

The older man seemed to have noticed Bashea's reaction, the sudden heat in her eyes followed by the icy frost, and called for an end to the dancing. "Come, Bashea. Sit by me, please. I would like to talk with you."

Feeling it rude to do otherwise, Bashea sat rigidly on her cushion near her host as his daughter brought more drinks, constantly keeping Bashea's cup full of a sweet, heavy liquor that made her drowsy.

"You will forgive me, I hope, my dear," Faraz said, taking her hand gently. "But you remind me so much of my beloved, Talia." Bashea noticed how his face and voice softened when he said the name. "She died over five years ago, when Jessmyn was just eleven," he continued sadly. "I've tried to do my best by my girls, but I certainly lack a woman's grace and good sense."

Bashea was overwhelmed with compassion, the tears in her eyes a testimony to it. "That's not true. Your girls are lovely, and they seem happy and completely devoted to you. It can't be easy raising a family alone."

"It's not," he conceded.

Bashea studied her hands as they separated the strands of a tassel on the corner of one of the pillows she lay on. "My mother died when I was ten," she said softly. "It was me, my two sisters, and five brothers. My father raised us by himself. It was a struggle for all of us." She peered into Faraz's eyes with understanding.

Her host paused, something weighing on his mind. "Did he ever remarry?"

"No. She was his one true love, I believe."

"I've often thought, maybe I should have remarried, for the girls' sakes." He glanced over at where they were puddled in front of Radeem, feeding the captain grapes and talking to him blithely.

Bashea followed his gaze. "We all must choose our own paths," she said lightly. She reached out to squeeze his hand. "But you have raised three fine, strong young women with good hearts, my father. Who could ask for more?"

He regarded Bashea, his eyes soft, and touched her face. "Ahh" he sighed. "You remind me so much of Talia."

"How did you two meet?" Bashea asked hesitantly, not sure if it would please him to share or make him sad.

To her surprise, he laughed. "My cousin, Jobar, had eyes for my Talia. But once I saw her, I knew. I just knew." He paused for a minute, reflecting with a sad smile on his face. "So I challenged him to an arm wrestling match for the right to court Talia." He laughed jovially, his big stomach bouncing. "And I won."

"You arm-wrestled for your bride?" Bashea asked laughingly.

"Yes." He snickered. "It was the only time I beat the thug."

"You must have been inspired."

"I was. I wasn't about to lose that match to him, I'll tell you that."

"Umm." Bashea covered her mouth as she yawned. "I'm sorry, you've been a most gracious host, but whatever it is your daughters keep giving me," she noted, looking down into her now-empty cup, "is making me terribly tired, and I didn't sleep well last night."

Faraz rose and helped Bashea to her feet. "Then it is off to bed with you." He held her hands and kissed them in turn. "And the sweetest of slumbers."

"Thank you." She bent in to give him a kiss on the cheek, and was moved when she noticed the way this touched him.

Faraz squeezed her hands. "Thank you, for setting my heart at ease." She nodded. "Pravin, your bride is tired," he said with a wink. Tahj scrambled to his feet.

Radeem sighed, turning to the girls at his feet. "I think it is time for bed for me, too." He tapped Dariya and Etti on the cheeks. "The door," he whispered loudly, "will be unlocked."

WHEN THEY ENTERED THE bedroom, Bashea immediately took off her headband and set it on the mantle. Tahj leaned against the door, watching her and thinking of—and discarding—a thousand things to say to her.

"You will take the bed," he said abruptly.

She turned in surprise. "But you are the prince."

"I am the prince, and you will take the bed," he repeated sternly.

She leaned against the carved bedpost, her hands behind her back, studying him. A slow smile crossed her face. "You certainly use that prince thing when it suits you."

Tahj smiled back. "I do." He moved past her, pulling a straw-backed chair out from the wall and angling it toward the fire, which someone must have lit for them. He sat down, propping his feet up on a tiny woven ottoman, leaning back a little so he rested against the head of the bed. He folded his arms behind his head. "You enjoyed yourself?" he said with just the slightest edge to his voice.

Her smile dimmed. She turned away from him. "As did you, I suppose?"

He observed as her slender hands undid the belt of coins at her waist and laid it across the foot of the bed, his eyes traveling her slender form with a desire he longed not to possess. She bent to unstrap the sandals, which crisscrossed up her calves, and he pretended to not notice how deliciously curved those calves were.

Then, with a suddenness which made him chuckle, she flopped down on her back onto the bed, her head landing a foot from his elbow. He came to the conclusion then and there she was tipsy. One delicate arm hung off the bed, almost touching his knee, a wide, intricate bracelet wrapped snugly around her upper arm. He laughed to himself, but sat back and closed his eyes, his sleepless night combined with his own alcohol intake making his eyelids heavy.

In what seemed like only a few minutes, he became aware of her steady breathing beside him. He opened his eyes to look at her. Quietly he let the front legs of his chair come down again to the floor and stood to get a better view. The arm farthest from him lay flopped over her stomach, but her near arm was now carelessly tossed over her head. Her lips were parted, cheeks rosy, whether from the wine or the dancing, he didn't know. Her hair was splayed every which way, and she was the single most beautiful woman he had ever known.

It wasn't just the physical beauty, he knew now. She had a certain inner light, the strength he saw when they battled their way out of the castle, the compassion he saw in her eyes when she spoke to Faraz about his wife. "You are some woman, Bashea," he whispered, wanting again to just touch her face, if only briefly.

He flashed back to the moment she had entered the kitchen for dinner. He had admired the alluring way she set one foot purposefully in front of the other as she approached the table across from him, and he caught the moment her eyes changed from spellbindingly intense to tenderly warm. He knew she had begun to smile underneath her veil, though he could not see it, by the way her cheeks lifted and the light danced in her eyes, pleased and perhaps even amused by his reaction to her entrance.

When the dancing began later, Tahj watched the lively entertainment merrily, at first laughing as Bashea did. But when Radeem began to dance with her, his laughter faded and was replaced with a sort of sick feeling in his stomach. At the beginning, when she whirled about, a blur of white and gold, and tan skin, he was captivated, barely able to breathe. But when she wrapped her scarf around Radeem and seemed to be dancing only for him, he quickly sobered, remembering the intimate moment he'd witnessed between them that morning. He felt like he had been punched in the gut.

When she talked to Faraz, after dancing, Tahj watched her face in the firelight. Like a sunset, each instant it was more beautiful than the next.

In frustration, Tahj turned back to face the fire. None of it really mattered. Clearly she was attracted to Radeem and had no interest in him, so it was better if he just learned to deal with that right from the start and quit letting his heart have these little flights of fancy. He pushed thoughts of her from his mind and sat down again, but he couldn't sleep. He watched the fire burn down, the embers turning into that lava-like, red-gold glow, pieces breaking off and spilling onto the hearth. He got up again, restless, and kicked at the pieces of log which had fallen farthest from the fire, pushing them back into the stone fireplace.

"Tahj?" Bashea murmured.

Surprised, he spun to look at her. She had a dreamy sort of smile on her face but her eyes were still closed. Finding his voice, he answered her. "Yes?"

"Do you...find Faraz's daughters...pretty?"

Tahj believed she was asking out of jealousy for Radeem and so answered spitefully, "Yes. They are stunning, actually."

Without another word, she roughly twisted her body with a loud exhale of breath so her back was to him. She was mad then. Good. Just then, the low murmur of Radeem's voice came through the wall, coupled with at least two of the girls' giggles.

"Oh, heaven's mercy!" Bashea threw the pillow over her head. Tahj heard her muffled scream of rage and took a certain sick satisfaction in it. He returned to his chair, but what sleep did come was short and riddled with nightmares.

CHAPTER NINE

Somewhere in the middle of the night, Tahj woke with a start knowing something was wrong. He jumped to his feet and was alarmed to see the bed was empty. Cursing, he grabbed his sword from where he had hooked it over the back of his chair, jerking it from its scabbard, and marched out into the main room. It was dark except for the red glow of the dying fire.

"Bashea?" he whispered loudly. Getting no response, he peered into all the corners of the room to see if some shadow had swallowed her, but found he was alone.

He grabbed a candle from the mantle and bent to press its wick to the hottest part of the fire. After a few seconds he was rewarded when it burst into flame. He turned from the fire and clomped in the direction of the front bedroom, which was Radeem's. The door creaked as it opened, and the light fanned out to reveal the sleeping form of his captain with one girl slung over his chest, completely nude, from what Tahj could tell, the other two, in various stages of undress, within his outstretched arms on either side of him. Radeem had his hand on the naked hip of one—Tahj couldn't say for sure who it was in the dark—and the opposite arm curled around another's breasts as they were pressed against his far side.

Feeling like a voyeur, Tahj quickly closed the door. He felt a draft and turned to find the front door slightly ajar. "Oh, no, Bashea, you didn't." He stepped outside and immediately heard her piercing scream coming from somewhere in the forest behind the house. Tahj blew out the candle and dropped it at his feet; it was lighter outside with a three-quarter moon shining down. He tore off around the side of the house, calling out her name.

Again a shriek ripped through the air, followed by the all-too-familiar feline wail of a wild cat. Panicked now, Tahj ran forward, attempting to pinpoint the location the cries came from. Clumsily, he tried to draw his sword as its scabbard banged against his thigh, stumbling every now and then over tree roots and vines as he ran. After about twenty seconds he tripped into a clearing and saw Bashea several yards away, outlined by the moon as she swung a large branch threateningly in front of a pacing panther.

As Tahj watched, the panther sprang. With a mighty swing Bashea clubbed it, sending it flying back several feet. But the branch broke on impact, causing her to lose her balance and tumble to the ground not far from the injured cat. It was evident by the yowl which issued from the animal's throat she had inflicted some major damage, but, at the same time, it was clear the panther wasn't done with her yet.

Bashea searched frantically on the ground for another stick as the animal rose slowly to its feet. Tahj ran forward and Bashea, catching his motion, glanced in that direction just as the animal leapt. But before the cat could land on her, claws extended and teeth ready to rip her apart, Bashea's quick reflexes had her rolling out of the way. The cat took a swipe at her but missed and was about to advance when Tahj came running, yelling to distract it. The panther took one look at Tahj, flailing and screaming, and took off into the brush, leaving Bashea quaking on the forest floor.

Tahj fell to his knees beside her. "Are you all right? Are you all right?"

"Y-yes," she said, her voice trembling.

When he saw she had all her limbs attached, Tahj's adrenaline suddenly turned to rage. "What, in the name of all that is good, were you doing out here? Huh?"

"I don't know. I don't know." Her hands shook uncontrollably as she held them in front of her face.

Tahj stood and paced in front of her. "You could have been killed, Bashea! Has it really been that bad with Radeem and me you had to run away? We were going to take you home for goodness' sake."

"Home?" she suddenly screamed, her voice rising hysterically. She lifted her tearstained face to him. "Home? Do you really think I have a home, Tahj?"

"What?"

"They don't welcome women home who have been used by Avistad men, Prince Tahj," she said through gritted teeth.

Forgetting himself, Tahj responded, "What? I never touched you."

"Did you really think they brought you a virgin?" she exploded. "That they wouldn't have their way with me first?" Her voice caught as she stared into his shocked eyes. "Oh! I didn't just say that!" She collapsed in a heap, her earlier fright turning to horror and humiliation. "Oh, why did I say that?" she mourned.

"Bashea?" Tahj knelt again and put a hand on her back.

"*Don't*!" She threw back her head with a jerk. "Don't touch me!" Her words echoed in the night. Bashea focused on his eyes and rose, unsteadily, to her feet. "Don't pity me, Tahj! Don't you pity me!" She spun around and leaned with one hand against the tree, the other wrapped around her middle as she was again wracked with sobs.

Tahj stood dumbfounded, wondering what to do. He wanted to sweep Bashea up into his arms, but he was afraid to touch her again. He circled around her, trying desperately to come up with something to say to comfort her. He reached out to touch her again but she batted his hand away.

"Don't, please," she said more weakly.

He waited while her tears slowed. "Let's go back inside, Bashea."

"I don't know what to do. I don't even know who I am anymore."

Tahj could tell she was past reason; her brain had shut off and gone someplace else. "Come. Let's go inside." This time when he put his arm around her she didn't strike out. Tahj's heart broke when he felt her tremble under his touch.

"I don't know what to do," she repeated.

"Come on. We'll figure it out in the morning," he said kindly, leading her forward.

By the time they reached the house, Bashea had melted into his side and was no longer repeating, "What am I going to do?" over and over again. Tahj got her into bed, and she almost immediately fell asleep. He untied her sandals and let them drop to the floor. He sighed, weary to the bone, and fell into his chair, closing his eyes. That was when he heard things starting up again in Radeem's room.

"Ugh!"

WHEN THE MORNING DAWNED, Tahj woke up stiff and sore. Bashea was still asleep when he left the room. In fact, she was the last one to rise, and when she joined the others at the breakfast table, she definitely wasn't herself. She hardly spoke to anyone, and when Tahj tried to engage her in the conversation, she wouldn't even look at him. After a while, it seemed Radeem couldn't take it any longer.

"Uhh, can I speak to you outside?" Without waiting for an answer, he yanked Tahj to his feet by the back of his shirt, jaw clenched.

When they got out on the porch, Radeem released him with a shove and wasted no time in jumping him. "What the hell did you do to her?"

"What?"

It seemed that Radeem could barely control his anger. "Don't act all innocent like you don't know what's going on."

"Listen, I didn't do anything to her."

"Then why won't she look you in the eye? Huh? Huh?" He pushed Tahj in the chest with each accusation, backing him off of the porch.

"All right," Tahj said, licking his lips nervously. "Something did happen last night, but I can't tell you about it."

"Why the hell not?"

"Because it's personal."

"You've got about two seconds to tell me what's going on here or I'm going to—"

"Not that kind of personal." Tahj hesitated, trying to figure out a way to tell Radeem about what happened without telling him anything Bashea might not want him to know. "She...she was upset about...things, personal things, which happened before we came here."

Radeem looked at him skeptically. "What kind of things?"

"Look," Tahj said, becoming irate, "I told you, it was personal things, and I don't have the right to share them with you. It's up to Bashea, *in her own time*," he added threateningly, "to tell you. I don't want you pressuring her."

"All right, all right," Radeem said, backing away from Tahj with his arms held up in surrender. "You're quite the panther when you get mad."

"You have no idea."

Bashea stepped out onto the porch. "Can I... talk to you, Tahj?"

Radeem punched Tahj in the shoulder and headed inside, nodding at Bashea who gave him a weak smile. Tahj rubbed out the pain in his shoulder as Bashea approached, still not looking him squarely in the eye.

"I just wanted to say sorry about last night. I shouldn't have said... I think maybe the wine made me—"

"You don't have to say sorry."

She looked up with a relieved smile.

"I would like to know what you were doing out there, though."

Bashea sagged against the porch rail, and Tahj came to stand next to her, bending his head to catch her eye. She stammered, "I... I just thought maybe I should leave. I don't know, the wine... It seemed like a good idea at the time."

Tahj glanced down, playing in the dirt with his foot. "Was it because Radeem was with those girls?"

She laughed. "No. I mean, that was rude, but I wouldn't have left because of that."

"You weren't jealous?" he asked in surprise.

"Of Radeem?" She laughed. "Radeem? No. No! No. Radeem is like...my big brothers. I want to hit him as much as I want to hug him. No, I'm definitely not jealous of Radeem."

"Oh," Tahj replied, unable to keep the note of happiness out of his voice. There was a long pause while this soaked in. He considered her with a smile. "So, am I going to have to worry about you leaving the next time I fall asleep?"

"No. If there comes a time when I decide to leave, I'll let you know first. That's only fair."

"Good. Because I need to get some sleep tonight."

They turned to go back in. "And Tahj..."

"Yes?"

"Thanks for being so sweet last night." She bent in to give him a kiss on the cheek, and his heart took a double beat. "Radeem," she said to herself, and chuckled as she turned around to leave.

When they entered together and Bashea was laughing, Radeem visibly relaxed. The rest of breakfast was spent pleasantly. Radeem entertained everyone with stories about Tahj when he was a boy, and Tahj evened the score with a few of his own stories about Radeem. Bashea joined in the laughter and, at one point, Tahj looked over to find Radeem standing behind her chair, holding onto the back comfortably as Faraz began a tale about his three daughters as children. Radeem bent down and kissed Bashea on the head, and she reached up to squeeze his hand while still listening to their host. Earlier that morning, it would have made his stomach ache to see it, but now he just grinned with contentment. She had no interest in Radeem, so the field was clear.

But the more he thought about it, the more he wondered. If she thought of Radeem as a brother, was it possible she thought of him the same way? Bashea glanced over and caught his eye, smiling at him.

If there was a road map to help me read her heart, I would pay my last Abba for it.

CHAPTER TEN

Tahj was going to miss having Bashea riding behind him on his horse, but Faraz insisted they take some of their money back and get a "suitable" horse for her. On the way into town they talked about what they needed. Faraz and his daughters sent them off with more food than they could possibly eat for the final part of their journey, so it was decided all they needed was the horse, two tents, and perhaps some clothes. They would travel the desert by night and stay out of the blistering sun during the day in their tents.

The city of Shiraz was smaller than Avistad, but it was still a bustling marketplace filled with fishmongers, horse-traders, and people hawking a multitude of wares. A high stone wall surrounded the city, keeping in the noise of the bartering and the clip-clopping sound the many horses' hoofs made on the cobblestone. But they could not contain the myriad of smells which wafted over the walls, the pleasant scents of perfumed oils combining strangely with the briny smell of fish and the odor of sweat given off by the crowd.

Tahj enjoyed watching the way Bashea's eyes lit up whenever she spotted an unusual object for sale, or perhaps not so unusual, but still something she hadn't seen in her relatively sheltered life. She exclaimed over the many colorful carpets and blankets strung between stalls or displayed on the rungs of ladders left leaning against the sturdy walls of the shops.

The city had an interesting effect on Radeem, too. He seemed to come alive as he chatted with shopkeepers and flirted with shopkeepers' wives. The city once held a certain glow for Tahj, having not strayed much from the confines of the castle. But since taking on his father's work, he'd had his fill of cities. But he did like living the excitement anew through Bashea's eyes.

They spent some time exploring, but by late afternoon, the tents were purchased and Radeem was haggling over a horse.

"She's beautiful!" Bashea cried out happily when the proprietor led the horse out.

Radeem frowned at her, but then turned to the shop owner. "You call that a horse?" Radeem snorted. "More like half a horse." It was true; the mare was a good three hands shorter than either Balamore or the other horse Radeem had stolen. "So I'll give you half what we talked about."

The proprietor began to coax, cajole, and finally argue loudly with Radeem. Tahj shook his head. Radeem was in his element. Excitement lit his face as he argued his case, and Tahj could tell this had very little to do with money and everything to do with coming out on top.

Tahj pretended to study some bolts of material on the sidewalk, but he was really watching Bashea as she stroked the mare's velvety muzzle. He could tell by the way she was speaking softly to the horse and the way her eyes lit up when the dappled mare nuzzled her that Bashea was already in love.

The proprietor walked away to help another customer, and Radeem stomped over to Bashea's side. "You're not helping any, you know."

"What?" she said innocently. "Come on, now, Radeem, look her in the eyes and tell me she's not a beautiful horse."

Radeem complied, and his face softened as he stroked the horse's speckled white coat. "Well, sure, she's beautiful, but is she fast? We need something fast to get you safely home, and a horse with short, stubby legs isn't the ticket."

Tahj noted how Bashea reacted slightly when Radeem mentioned taking her home, but then she continued to coo at the horse. "You don't have stubby legs, do you, Star?"

"Good gracious!" Radeem said, exasperated. "You've already named her?"

"And, besides," Bashea continued persuasively, "you can't tell how fast a horse is by the length of its legs. It's all about heart, and Star, here, has heart to spare. Don't you, Star?" She put hands on either side of the mare's head and leaned her forehead on the horse's nose, near the oddly shaped black spot that had earned the horse its name.

Radeem spied his adversary inside the door helping some customer fill a flour sack. "He didn't need to wait on that customer right then," he grumbled. "He only wanted to give you more time to become enamored of his dumb horse. You fell right into his trap."

Bashea ignored him, checking the horse's legs and withers as a smart purchaser would while Radeem schemed. But then, as Tahj watched, she lifted her head and stilled, as if listening. Her face drained of color. She turned to look behind her, and when her head swiveled back Tahj could tell something was definitely wrong. She shrunk against the side of the mare, taking a deep breath, her eyes darting back and forth, though he was sure they were registering nothing. After a beat, she turned toward Radeem, but he had moved off and was again going back and forth with the owner, both men red-faced by now.

Tahj tore his eyes from Bashea and searched the crowd behind her. Within seconds he spotted the large, baldheaded man harassing some other shop owner. Gesturing widely, the big man melted back into the crowd and continued up the street, his eyes scanning the faces around him as he passed. Bashea called Tahj's name out sharply and he nodded, having recognized the beast of a man he had first seen in his bedroom a few days before. Bashea came up behind Radeem, Tahj trailing her.

"Pay the man whatever he wants," she said abruptly.

"What?" Radeem mumbled, barely glancing at her.

Tahj snatched the moneybag from Radeem's belt and plopped it on the counter in front of the startled owner. "Do you have a back door?"

THE TRIO QUICKLY CLOMPED down a dark, shady, covered walkway between buildings to a back courtyard, Tahj with his hand on the small of Bashea's back, Radeem following, looking over his shoulder nervously. They stepped out of the shadow into a bright courtyard on the far side of the shop, and the owner came around the opposite side, holding the reins to Bashea's new horse while one of his helpers led their other two horses, loaded with the provisions strapped on back.

Radeem shook the proprietor's hand while Tahj helped Bashea up into her saddle. Then the two men mounted their horses simultaneously and turned their steeds' heads toward an opening in the surrounding buildings directly across the courtyard. They spurred their horses into a canter. The setting sun's rays lit up a stone archway, and as they steered their horses through it they heard shouts behind them. They had been spied.

Their horses' hooves clamored against the cobblestone as they flew, sometimes scattering people in their path, other times finding themselves virtually alone in back alleyways. Tahj kept twisting in his saddle to check if they were still being followed. He would sometimes see their pursuers, and then leave them behind again by making an unexpected turn or dodging into the throng of shoppers.

He was so distracted with what was following them he didn't think to look ahead when he, Radeem, and Bashea turned into an alleyway that sloped upwards. Sun poured over the top of the hill where the alley met the upper street, and when Tahj turned his head for a minute to look forward, he was blinded by the rays, which seemed to be level with his line of vision. But as his eyes came into focus, he saw two small groups of men chatting with each other in a relaxed position on either side of the alley.

Time seemed suspended for a moment, hanging in the dusty air. The man closest to them turned casually at the sound of horses behind him, still laughing over something his companions had said, while holding a steaming drink in his hand. That was when Tahj realized the man, and in fact the others as well, had on a familiar uniform—a uniform Tahj himself carried in the pack behind him—the uniform of an Avistad soldier. Tahj reined in his horse so abruptly Bashea almost collided with him.

"It's them!" the young captain shouted, throwing his drink down on the cobblestone with a crash. The others turned as if on a string and then sprang to life, running around the corner of the building, presumably to get their horses.

Tahj turned his mount's head and was about to spur him in the opposite direction when Radeem came into view at the end of the alleyway shouting, "They're right behind me! Get going!"

Tahj made an immediate decision, pulling on the reins once again to lead his horse toward the top of the alley. The soldiers would probably be mounted by now, but he hoped to have chosen the lesser of two evils.

As Bashea rode behind she felt a twitch in her shoulder; a reminder of where the arrow had dug into her flesh. She knew it was likely that, in facing the soldiers up ahead, she would soon be feeling the same. The thought didn't cheer her, but she knew she would rather die with a chance of escaping than fall into the hands of Lord Boltar's men again. She spurred her horse to faster speeds, regretting now she hadn't listened to Radeem about a bigger horse. She glanced over at Tahj, whose face was beautifully, if grimly, set, and wished things could be different. At the same time, it became clear to her what she must do. Tahj was the prince, after all; should anybody survive this, it was most important that it be him.

"Hyah! Hyah!" she cried, using both arms to snap the reins and encourage Star even faster. She got a glimpse of the surprised look on Tahj's face as she pulled alongside and then out-distanced him, breaking out into the open sunlight of the street a full four horse-lengths ahead of him.

The soldiers were also surprised. They knelt or stood on opposite sides of the alleyway with arrows nocked, bows arched and ready. When she and Star burst out into the clear, strings were pulled back. Bashea waited for the twang of half a dozen bows being plucked and the searing pain to follow, but the soldiers were caught so off-guard at seeing her come flying out, and not the prince, they hesitated, glancing at each other uncertainly.

With a shout, they turned to mount their horses just as the prince emerged. A few fumbled to get their bows back up and ready, but, realizing it was too late, they turned again to their horses just as Radeem and Balamore shot past them. No longer confused, the soldiers mounted their horses, furious they'd failed to capture the threesome when they so clearly had the jump on them. They were further stymied when they turned their horses to go, and their group clashed at the mouth of the alley with the soldiers who were behind Radeem.

Tahj realized, although they successfully squeaked past the soldiers, the group would still be hot on their tails. They bent over their horses' necks, trying to present the smallest target for the archers' arrows. Tahj urged his horse up to Bashea's.

"What do you think you were doing back there?" he screamed over the wind rushing by and the driving clamor of the horses' hooves, glowering at Bashea.

"It worked, didn't it?" she threw back.

Tahj couldn't argue with that, so he just growled and turned to face forward again just as an arrow shot between the two horses.

Think, Tahj, think, a voice clamored in his head. *How are we going to get out of this one?* He envisioned Bashea's pale face as she slipped from the side of the horse after she was shot with an arrow. He was determined to make sure that didn't happen again.

He tried to get his bearings. Scores of people were still milling about, trying to finish up business before the shops closed, or chatting with neighbors on the street, unaware as yet of the chase bearing down upon them. A big bell was ringing somewhere, slowly, but with a deep, reverberating tone. Up ahead, he saw a half dozen men struggling to close the big city gates, their back to the action, oblivious to the scene unfolding behind them. They were closing up the city for the night.

That's our chance. "Hurry!" Tahj yelled back over his shoulder to Bashea and Radeem. Coaxing all the speed out of his mount he could, the prince drove for the crack of daylight the city dwellers seemed intent on shutting out on the other side of the gate.

"Hyah! Hyah!" Catching on, Radeem and Bashea pressed their horses further, watching their escape route becoming narrower and narrower.

Once through the opening, Tahj turned in his saddle to see the dust flying in thick clouds from Bashea and Radeem's horses' hooves. They sliced between the edges of the shutting doors, absorbed into the sunshine bathing the city walls, one after the other. The men shutting the gates jumped back, startled, and then shook their fists, cursing as they continued their job of locking the city up safely for the night. Once the seam of the doors was sealed, Tahj could hear shouting behind the gate.

"Open the gates! Open the gates, man!"

The mass confusion which ensued was more than adequate to provide a head start for the escapees, who thundered off into the sunset at lightning speed.

CHAPTER ELEVEN

Tahj and his cohorts thudded endlessly into the night, having lost their pursuers hours ago behind a myriad of dunes, but taking no chances all the same. The rising winds had become both friend and enemy to them, as it erased their tracks, but, at the same time, spit grains of sand into their faces like glass pellets. They wrapped as much of their exposed skin in scarves as possible, but still, the sand managed to get past this barrier and even the natural protection of their lashes to sting their eyes.

Moonlight glinted off of the desert floor as they hurried on, trying to maintain a northerly direction despite the lack of any landmarks, using stars as their only guideposts. The immenseness of the open wasteland before them was overwhelming, with a seemingly eternal supply of hills to struggle up, only to then slide haphazardly down the other side. The farther they drove on, the harder the wind began to whip at them, and, finally, they were forced to take shelter.

Tahj was grateful the wind and the speed had made it impossible for them to speak to each other over the past several hours, because he was almost certain he would have said something regrettable to Bashea if his mouth could open. With each mile they put behind them he fumed, his rage growing like a landslide that begins with just a few pebbles and swells to mass destruction.

Even now, as he dismounted and struggled to get the pack off of his horse's back, a burning anger seethed inside him. As Balamore made his mad dash over the scorching sand, Tahj replayed the vision of Bashea's back in front of him as she sped out into the bright sunlight at the top of the alley. He remembered the way his heart had clutched, expecting to see a dozen arrows pierce her like a pincushion. Sure, it had paid off, there was no denying it. But how could she have done something so foolish?

They worked side-by-side in silence, except for a few muttered directions, to erect the tents, struggling to hold on to the thick canvas the wind was trying so desperately to snatch from them. Ironically, just as they finished, the winds dropped to a far more reasonable level. Radeem wasted no time in getting under a lightweight sheet, and he began almost immediately to snore. Tahj decided to seek out Bashea. It was high time he confronted her to let her know how misguided she was. But, as he approached her from behind, his ire sizzled and melted into the sand with each step.

Bashea stood at a distance, her back to the tents, looking small and vulnerable in the vastness of the dunes, which now had a silver, specter-like glow around the edges as the sun began to rise in the distance. Her arms were crossed in front of her, and the breeze blew her sheer clothing so it flapped mildly around her. She had removed her scarves, and her gleaming black hair shone despite the dim lighting.

The prince stopped dead in his tracks five yards from her side. "Bashea?" he called quietly, not wishing to frighten her. She seemed so lost in thought.

"Yes," she replied, her voice distant.

He moved involuntarily forward until he stood next to her. "How do you fair?"

She turned to look at him with curiosity, and he could see she was troubled. Instead of answering his question, she turned and looked again at the desert. "It's striking, isn't it?"

Breathtaking, he thought, still studying her. Tahj cleared his throat and then shifted his gaze to stare again at the horizon. "It is quite spectacular at times."

"That's what I like about the desert," she replied softly. "It can be mind-numbingly boring at times, and at other times, like this, it has a kind of mystic beauty." She looked away as if embarrassed, but then turned back. "I couldn't sleep," she said in way of explanation. "I thought I'd just stay out here for a while and... think..." She bent and sat down in the sand.

"Mind if I stay, too?" She glanced up quickly. "I won't disturb you. It's just...jackals might be around." He scanned the area then looked back down into her eyes.

What could she say? He was the prince, after all. She nodded, and Tahj slid down into the sand next to her. They sat in silence for several seconds, Bashea thumbing over one of the gold medallions on her skirt, flipping it end over end between her fingers and watching it, though her mind was somewhere else.

Tahj watched the woman beside him, uncharacteristically quiet in the pale morning light, the wind licking at her hair as if it, too, was impatient with her silence.

"Tomorrow...we'll be home?" she asked carefully, breaking the stillness.

Tahj nodded. "By daybreak we should reach there."

"Mmm," she murmured, making no comment but spinning the coin in her fingers faster.

"You are worried about something."

Bashea stopped moving her hands, licking her lips, which were probably over-dry from the wind. "I'm just not sure...."

She left off without finishing her statement, but Tahj knew she was anxious about her reception when she returned home. He wished he could think of words that would reassure her. Was it really possible she would be scorned for what had been done to her against her will? He stretched his legs out in the sand, the movement luxurious after their long ride. He was beginning to feel just how tired he was. "Tell me about your family."

To his relief, she smiled. "Well...there are my older two brothers, Jahmeel and Bagrat. They are amazing, so bold and brave." He watched her eyes, wide and bright as she spoke of them. It was obvious to him she idolized her brothers. "They can tease you to tears in the morning, and then be nearly brought to tears themselves a few hours later when they see you get hurt by someone else." She laughed softly, shaking her head. Tahj stretched out on his side, his elbow in the sand, supporting his head as he listened to the musical sound of her voice. "They are like my guard dogs, though, jumping every poor, unsuspecting soul they believe has bad intentions for me—or any intentions at all, for that matter."

She paused, pursing her lips. "Then there is Gaspard, our little storyteller. He will say things—" She chuckled, gesturing vaguely. "—things no one else would ever think to say. His mind just operates in its own separate sphere." She paused, thinking. "Gaspard is smart, in his own way, but Parvaiz is also very intelligent. He will read whatever he can get his hands on. He always talks about going off to the city, but I think he loves us all too much to leave. I hope so, anyway...though I want him to be happy..." She puzzled over that for a minute, then continued.

"My sisters, Bano and Bibi, are twins, but they are as different as the sun and the moon. Both beautiful and strong-willed." Tahj smiled, noting to himself that the third sister was much the same. "But Bano, her name means princess," she added as an aside, "and believe me, she is one. She is wrapped up in herself most of the time, always concerned over what clothes to wear and how her hair looks." Bashea sighed, but Tahj could tell she was fond of her sister.

"Bibi, on the other hand, could care less about her hair and clothing. And to live in the same tent with those two, constantly going at it, day and night, as I did when we were little..." Bashea looked up at him, her face coloring slightly, perhaps realizing how animated she had become. "And Cyrus is the last of us. He's a real jewel. You'd love him, everybody does. But I've been blathering."

"No. I like hearing you talk." He reached out and grabbed her arm before she could turn away. Her loose sleeves had been blown back by the breeze, exposing skin that was soft, despite the curve of muscle underneath which came from hard work. "You sound like quite the group."

"We are. We might take a little getting used to," she said hesitantly. "We can be loud." He was happy to hear her including herself in the group again.

"I think I can handle it," he replied with a smile. She gazed at him, as if trying to read what was in his eyes, and then slowly slid down in the sand herself, mirroring his position. The move was so unintentionally sensual, he found himself licking his own lips, holding back a sudden urge to taste her. His body became hard with desire as he watched her, and his throat tightened inexplicably.

"Tell me about what it was like growing up for you, Tahj," she asked him, her silky voice sliding within him.

"Uhh...not loud. My brother, Kadeesh, was six years older than I. He wasn't around much." He breezed over the subject. "Radeem, on the other hand—" He jerked his head in the direction of the tent, where the snoring was becoming even louder. "—has always been around. Up until the last several years, when he's been a captain in the army."

"I can't imagine how strange it would be without any siblings around. You must have missed Radeem, then, when he left."

"Yes, but I was gone much of the time, too," he answered, brushing a section of hair out of her eyes, "on my father's business." His eyes strayed to her lips, and he realized then just how close they were. He had only to stretch out his head to claim those warm, full lips with his own, to cup her neck, and...

Abruptly she jerked away.

"I g-guess I am tired, after all," she stammered, rising quickly and brushing off her skirt.

Tahj scrambled to his feet as well. "Bashea..." But before he could elaborate, she was taking steps away from him.

"Thanks, Tahj, for keeping me company. Sleep well." And with that she turned and hurried away, leaving him gawking in her wake.

Tahj kicked at the sand unhappily, staring for a few seconds at the flaps of her tent, which had swallowed her up, before heading to bed himself, frustrated. Like two magnets, the closer they got together, the harder an invisible force pushed them apart.

IT HAD TO BE MIDMORNING when Tahj woke up. Strange that the sun was beating down, making waves rise above the sand when he was taking his night's rest. He wondered what woke him, whether it was just this oddly blaring light, rather than the comfort of dark which made him open his eyes, or something else. He glanced across the tent at Radeem, who had laid his shirt across his face in an effort to block out some of the light. The shirt moved up and down with his breathing, the guttural noises issuing from his open mouth as loud and obnoxious as usual.

Tahj turned over on his side, pulling his pillow over his head to block out the snores, but even through this barrier he heard Bashea scream. In an instant he was up, grabbing his sword from a peg on the tent's central post. He shook Radeem, but his breathing only changed pace; he did not open his eyes. Too impatient to wait, Tahj rushed out without him.

As he approached it, Bashea's tent wall moved and he heard her voice, muffled by something, and frightened. He crept to the door and listened, but was confused because he could hear no other voices, though there was the sound of struggling and Bashea's moans. Carefully, his heart in his throat, he eased back the flap of the door, peering inside. He could see Bashea's figure on the bed, thrashing and calling out, but as his eyes scanned the room around her, he saw it was empty.

Curious, he took a step forward, just as Bashea let out a particularly loud cry. He rushed to her side, afraid her wound pained her or some sort of infection had set in, making her feverish. He could see a bead of sweat on her brow, but when he felt her cheeks, they were cool. No fever, then. She cried out again, piteously, and he reached down to wake her just as she lashed out, catching him on the jaw and knocking him backwards, onto his rear, in the dirt.

Bashea flew up, her eyes wild, clutching her sheet to her chest. "Wh-wha-what are you doing here?" she stammered, practically upsetting her cot in her effort to move away from him.

"Calm down!" Tahj shook his head to clear it, the blow having left him unfocussed.

"Calm down?" she parroted, her voice rising. Her eyes still darted around the tent as if to assure herself her nightmarish visions were gone.

"You were just having a bad dream," he added, his voice showing the irritation born from the pain of a throbbing chin coupled with the blow to his ego. The idea he'd been knocked to the ground by this slip of a girl was embarrassing.

"A bad dream?" She rose from the bed, pulling the sheets with her for some reason, though they did nothing to hide her. Tahj noted a cut on her neck he hadn't seen before and deep bruising on an upper arm the sleeveless nightgown she wore didn't hide. "You make it sound like I'm some foolish girl, afraid of the dark, running to her *baba* for help!"

"Be at peace. I was just saying—"

"Be at peace?"

Bashea spun toward him, her eyes flashing, and he took an involuntary step backwards. "There is no peace for me now, Tahj!" She pushed her hair back with a shaking hand. "Not now. Not after what they did to me." Tahj had made the mistake of donning his uniform pants when he went to bed, and now Bashea stared at them, and, perhaps linked with the black images swirling around in her head, still fresh from her sleep, they made her snap. She rushed at Tahj, forgetting the sheet and dropping it to the ground as she attacked him, flailing and pounding him with her fists. "You did this to me!" she shrieked. "This is *your* fault!"

"Ay! Ay!" he countered, caught off-guard by the flurry of fists and the accusation. "It wasn't me!" He caught her wrists and held her.

"Wasn't it? You weren't there, granted, but it was your men." Bashea struggled against him hysterically, seeking to free her wrists, but he held her tight.

"My father's men!" he spat back, giving her a little shake. "Some of them have been around since I was in diapers."

"But they were your responsibility, were they not?" she argued, trembling with rage, her voice breaking with a sob. She dropped her head, crying. "You should have stopped them." There was a dead silence, and then she lifted her head defiantly, gritting her teeth. "You should have *stopped them*!"

The accusation hung in the air, shocking them both. He let her go and she backed away, turning her face from him and bringing hands up to rub her arms.

"You're right," he said bitterly.

Bashea's thoughts scattered like a covey of partridge frightened from the underbrush. She felt entirely too unsteady; the blood was swishing through her brain like a raging storm, battering her senses. She pressed her hands to her temples. Of course Tahj was not responsible for this. Of course he wasn't. Had he been there, he would have done whatever he could to stop the men from hurting her, she knew that now. Wasn't it Tahj and Radeem who had stepped forward to help her escape from Boltar just days before?

But she couldn't seem to keep herself from striking out; the pain, the fear, was too powerful still. She was fighting against the images in her mind, jabbing blindly as the adrenaline surged through her body, confusing her with its intensity. She had to get a grip on her rapid-fire emotions. Knowing how unreasonable she was being, Bashea tried to bring down her breathing and formulate an apology at the same time, the words becoming jumbled in her mind.

When she finally turned back, Tahj was gone.

ONCE SHE HAD TIME TO calm down, Bashea felt horrible for the things she'd said to Tahj. He could hardly be blamed for every heinous action the hundreds of men in his command performed of their own free will. She knew she had to apologize, but she needed to stop shaking first.

When she came to his tent a couple of hours later, she expected him to have fallen back asleep. They had, after all, only gotten a few hours in before her nightmares woke them both. While she waited for Tahj to rise, Bashea paced thoughtfully in the sand a few yards from the camp. It was late afternoon and the heat was still intense, but she couldn't stand to be trapped in her tent any longer. After Tahj left, she had lowered herself slowly, reaching back to feel the edge of the bed to guide her. She sat still like that for hours, the fabric of her nightgown bunched in her fists, the emotions seething inside her despite all her efforts to gain control. What had happened to her? Was she losing her mind?

In the past she had always been so in control. When her mother died, she was the oldest female in the family and so stepped up to fill the roles of cook, maid, teacher, nurse—whatever was needed. And she was good at it, took pride in it, organizing and addressing the needs of seven grieving children and her father. It had come to be a kind of running joke finally, her tiny iron fists, always able to keep it together, no matter what the situation.

Up until that night. The night she was snatched from her home and made to feel helpless and small. Where she once was so confident, so in control, now her emotions were all over the place. Of course, she had always been known as a hothead; losing control of her temper was not new. The fear, now that was new. She understood it was reasonable to have been affected by what happened to her, but yet the thought that it had changed her irritated Bashea. The idea grated on her so badly it was like the grains of sand that pelted them all day. And she knew that there was something else causing her emotions to go berserk, something to do with the prince. Was she keyed up because he was royalty? Many people would be nervous around royalty; but not her. No, he caused emotions to surface for another reason; a reason she couldn't quite put her finger on.

Radeem ducked through the flap of the tent and stopped when he saw her, a growl frozen on his face. Bashea hurried forward.

"Is Prince Tahj up?'

"Up?" Radeem queried, taking the blanket he was carrying and depositing it roughly at his feet in the sand. "I'm not sure he ever went to sleep."

Bashea stared at the tent dumbly for a few seconds and then made a move to slip past Radeem and into the tent. Radeem grabbed her arm.

"I wouldn't go in there if I were you."

"Why?"

"He's in a foul mood," the captain warned.

Bashea vacillated only a second. "I'll take my chances."

When she ducked into the tent, she could see it was almost ready to pack up. The cots had been flattened, the bedding folded, and Tahj was working at a knotted rope tied to the center stake.

"Ay! You don't waste time when you are ready to leave."

Tahj's hands stilled, but he didn't turn around. "I suppose not," he answered vaguely.

"Tahj," Bashea started hesitantly, "I want to apologize for what happened earlier in my tent."

"There's no need," he said sharply.

Bashea blinked. "What do you mean there's no need?"

Tahj tugged on his rope, and the sides of the tents drew inward. Bashea was forced to jump forward to keep from being swept up in them.

"There's no need," Tahj repeated, his jaw stony. He yanked the post out of the ground.

Radeem stood and bent over, wrestling a blanket between his knees as he tried to bind it in a roll with a rawhide cord. He glanced up when the tent began to collapse. Bashea backed out from underneath the canvas as it slid over her head, electrifying and disordering her hair, the weight of the tent nearly knocking her off-balance. She watched as the tent marched away, Tahj still underneath lifting the pole.

"Stubborn man," she murmured.

Radeem eyeballed Bashea, amused by the way her hair was sticking out in all directions, but when she cast a dark look his way, he wiped the grin from his face and cleared his throat. "What's his problem?" he asked companionably, nodding in Tahj's direction.

"Ask him!" Bashea snapped, turning on her heel and striding off to her tent.

Radeem chuckled, watching her neat figure as she marched away. "I know what his problem is, all right," he murmured, shaking his head. He turned to speak to the horse behind him, who seemed to be the only pleasant company he had today, as he hefted the pack onto his mount's back. "They're a match made in heaven, those two." The horse snorted his agreement.

In record time, Tahj had their camp broken down and everyone atop their respective horses. He and Bashea hardly spoke at all, and when they did, it was in short interjections, adding no unnecessary words to their speech.

Tahj kept going back to the discussion in his tent. She'd apologized. Tahj closed his eyes as he thought about it. How could *she* be apologizing after all she had been through?

Radeem was so openly amused by their tiff, they both became annoyed with him, and this actually forged a reconciliation of sorts as they exchanged a few words about him during a water break.

"What's with that jackass? He moves as though he has all the time in the world," Tahj muttered to himself as he watered his horse.

Bashea looked up from where she had been stroking Star and peered through the sun at Radeem, one hand shading her eyes. "He doesn't seem to know one end of a horse from the other," she added as Radeem clumsily swung his leg over his steed. Tahj chuckled under his breath. His chest lost a little of its tightness, and Bashea's face relaxed into a smile.

They road through the night, unhurriedly, but making steady progress, until they came to the top of the last sand dune and a plain opened before them, wandering up to the foothills of the mountains. With a cry, Bashea spurred her horse forward.

Not understanding what had upset her, Tahj's eyes hurriedly scoured the landscape. Ahead, he could just make out the few remaining stones of a toppled well, and, as he drew nearer, he could see the wide ring where a central fire had been and smaller rings scattered about, presumably where tents had rested.

Bashea swung off Star before the horse even came to a full stop, her eyes raking the ground. "They're gone," she murmured.

"What?"

"They've moved on. They've left me." Bashea meandered among the ashes mournfully. Here and there, small pieces of debris lay scattered on the ground: the remains of a broken pot, a ladle, a small, cloth ball, much like the one Tahj and Radeem had used as children. "They're gone," she said again, as if in shock. "I can't believe they would just leave."

Bashea came to a shattered gourd near the well. She picked it up and gingerly traced the sharp, jagged lines of the crack without speaking. Radeem and Tahj exchanged a glance and then began to wander about themselves, surveying what was left. Tahj bent and ran his hand over the ground where some sparse patches of grass tried to grow in the loose dirt. After a time, Radeem bent next to him.

"They've been here," Tahj murmured, running his hand over intersecting hoof prints. He didn't have to explain to Radeem he was speaking of Boltar's men—they both knew. Tahj looked up to where Bashea sat clutching the gourd to her chest, gazing blindly back across the desert as the sun began its climb into the sky.

"But I think they got away. There's no sign of blood," the captain noted. But Tahj hardly heard him as he straightened and went to Bashea.

Tahj placed a hand gently on her shoulder, and, although she had shown no signs of hearing him approach, she didn't jump. As Bashea turned slowly and peered up at him with tears in her eyes, his hand slid down her shoulder, coming to rest on her forearm. He left it there, bringing the other hand up automatically to lightly touch the opposite arm. "They left me." She shook her head slightly, as if astonished or confused. "I knew—"

"Bashea!" They were both startled by the shout and turned as one to face Radeem.

He was squatting down in the dirt on the opposite side of the camp, where huge boulders marked the bottom of the mountain.

"Come." He waved them over, studying something at his feet.

"Does this mean anything to you?" Radeem asked Bashea when they drew near, extending his hand out over the ground.

By staring very hard, Tahj could just make out the vague image of lines that appeared to be drawn in the dirt. One line zigzagged evenly three times, and below it a second line curved gracefully to the left and then back to the right.

Bashea studied the little picture, and then fell to her knees, closing her eyes. Tears squeezed out between her lashes as Radeem and Tahj watched her face anxiously. After a moment, she nodded several times quickly.

"Yes. Yes. It's a message from Gaspard." She opened her eyes and smiled at them. "They've gone to higher ground. This—" She pointed to the scrawling. "—means Sabalan's Crown. It is a name we made up as children for one of our encampments," she explained. Her face glowed. "They wanted me to follow." Her relief was palpable.

Tahj and Radeem beamed at Bashea and helped her rise to her feet. But as she stood, a frown slowly replaced her sunny smile. "But we would only go to Sabalan's Crown if..." Her eyes suddenly flew over the ground. Tahj and Radeem exchanged a worried glance. "They've been here!" She peered at them, and they couldn't hide from her scrutiny. "And you knew!" She turned her back on them and began to march off toward her horse.

"Bashea, wait!" Tahj called after her, but she didn't turn.

Radeem stuck a hand out to the side in front of Tahj to keep him from running after her. With a look, he told Tahj he would try to handle it. Radeem trotted ahead, catching up with Bashea and walking by her side. Tahj stayed a few paces behind. "You're right. I think Boltar's men were here." Bashea strode furiously on as if she couldn't hear him. Radeem jumped in her path and grabbed Bashea's shoulders to stop her progress. "But I don't think there was any kind of skirmish."

"How do you know?" she answered skeptically. Even in profile, Tahj could tell that her face was creased with worry.

"There's no... blood."

Bashea seemed to mull this over. "You think they got away?"

Radeem nodded.

Bashea sighed and then slid her arms around his waist. His eyebrows arched in surprise. "We have to find them."

Radeem drew her in, looking a bit tentative and unsure of himself. "We will." He laid his cheek down on her head. "I promise you, we will."

CHAPTER TWELVE

The horses plodded carefully up the slope, picking their way over stones and loose dirt, through patchy areas of pine and cedar trees. Somewhere nearby, a stream gurgled down the mountainside, tumbling like children on a grassy hill, the sound as hopeful as Bashea's heartbeat as they continued upwards. She heard the unique, chirping call of a golden eagle and knew the bark meant it was returning to its nest with food. Looking up, she caught it sailing between trees, as graceful as it was deadly, known to prey on animals even as big as an antelope or fox. Bashea watched as it banked, now silent, admiring the way it could soar so effortlessly on the wind.

As they rose, the occasional clip clopping of hoof on rock their tempo, her chest squeezed in anticipation. Was Radeem right? Had her family gotten away safely to the upper camp, or had others followed them and done them harm? If something happened to them, she knew it would be her fault, retribution for her escape. That thought chilled Bashea even as the smell of pine and cedar made her heart dance with pleasant memories.

As they rose, the landscape became more familiar, each rock and tree an old friend. "I don't think it's much farther," she said, trying to mask the excitement in her voice. "We used to come here whenever we heard of roaming bands of raiders," she explained, trying to calm her nerves by speaking of everyday things. "Though the pasture lands, for the most part, aren't as good as below, it did provide a vantage point from which to see anyone coming."

As they came over the next rise, the area unexpectedly flattened out into a huge meadow. At the far end of the plain, a number of tents seemed to spring from the ground, and smoke could be seen rising from the center of them. Bashea drew her horse up. Approaching them from across the field was a lone figure, who stopped when he saw them. Star pranced restlessly back and forth, snorting, seeming to wonder why her mistress had reined her in and was now sitting, staring at the stranger. Bashea slowly dismounted and took a few faltering steps forward.

Tahj strained to see from behind her. The stranger stepped up as well, and Tahj could now see his jaw drop open and his eyes grow wide. "Bashea?" he called uncertainly. He ran forward, and Bashea released Star's reins and rushed into his arms. "Bashea! Bashea!" The young man swung her off her feet joyfully and then shouted over his shoulder. "It's Bashea!"

Star, spooked by the cries, tried to escape downhill, but Radeem snatched at her reins as she brushed past. "Oh, no you don't," he muttered.

Cries filled the air as people spilled out of the tents and hurried forward, surrounding the two as they continued to embrace. Bashea exclaimed over and over again, drawing people to her and kissing them, forgetting altogether the pair behind her. Tahj saw a large man in a striped caftan beginning to make his way through the crowd. Bashea lifted her eyes.

"Father!" she shouted.

Tahj's gaze flew to the newcomer's face. It had the leathery texture of a man who spent his time out of doors, making Bashea's father look older than he had expected, his salt-and-pepper beard more salt than pepper. The older man's eyes took on a slightly wild aspect when they saw his daughter, and he stumbled the last several steps to her in shock and disbelief.

"*Azizam*," he croaked, the familiar term of endearment becoming stuck in his throat. He swallowed his petite daughter up in a massive hug, clutching at her as if he would never let her go again. "Bashea, you've come home to me."

"Yes, Baba!" she cried, appearing similarly moved. "I'm home."

As the two held each other tightly, the crowd emitted a low, murmuring sigh and Tahj saw people exchange glances and join hands, many wiping their eyes. He and Radeem dismounted, and as Tahj continued to look on, he noted two taller young men shuffling through the crowd toward them.

"Bagrat! Jahmeel!" Bashea squealed releasing her father and moving to throw an arm around each of them. The two laughed heartily, hugging her, and then the one she called Bagrat, slightly taller than Jahmeel, swept Bashea off her feet and into his arms.

"We knew we could never get rid of you for good," he teased, but he covered her face and hair with kisses. Bashea squirmed and giggled until Bagrat saw Radeem and Tahj standing a few feet away. His face became deadly serious and he abruptly, and a little clumsily, dropped Bashea on her feet.

"Who are these men?" he asked gruffly. All eyes turned in their direction as Bagrat and Jahmeel simultaneously took a threatening step forward. In a panic, Bashea threw her arms up, one on each of her brothers' chests, and tried to plant her feet as they slowly advanced.

"No! No, Bagrat! Jahmeel! These are my friends!"

"What kind of friends give you bruises like these?" Jahmeel growled, somewhat roughly pushing the hair away from Bashea's face, his eyes displaying both concern for her and anger for the two men he thought had harmed her. Bashea's face colored, and she glanced around at all the surrounding faces with a sense of embarrassment. Tahj looked nervously between the two mountainous men, who were all business.

Bashea's feet slid in the loose dirt, and she did little more than slow her brothers. "No, it wasn't them!" she choked out. But Jahmeel and Bagrat ignored her, coming closer and closer, as they pushed her back, to Tahj and Radeem. Tahj set his jaw. No matter what, he would not return these men's blows. They were right to be angry.

But Bashea's frantic, "*No!*", her scream shrill and desperate, finally gained her brothers' attention. They glanced down into her face, and what they saw there changed their expressions. They went from angry to two chastised schoolboys in a heartbeat. "These are not the men," she hissed, not looking her brothers in the eyes. She seemed suddenly tired. Jahmeel hesitated and then put an arm across her shoulders, though still raising his chin defiantly and staring coldly at the intruders.

The tension dispersed, Bashea broke free from them. "This is Radeem." She smiled, taking Radeem's hand and pulling him forward into the gathered circle of onlookers. "And this—" She grabbed Tahj's arm and drew him in as well. "—is Prince Tahj of Avistad." This sent a wave of murmurs through the crowd, and they now peered at the pair with curiosity. "These men helped me to escape and brought me back to you."

Bashea's father's eyes fell on them, wet and wide with wonder. He stepped forward and grasped one of Tahj's hands in both of his. "Thank you, from the depths of my heart." He turned to Radeem to do the same, but the two brothers continued to stare on suspiciously. The older man turned to the crowd and raised his hands. "Let us have a feast then, to celebrate my daughter's return."

A cheer went up, and then the crowd began to break up in order to begin preparations for the party. Though Bagrat and Jahmeel were no longer trying to get at Tahj and Radeem, they still stood their ground with a stubborn set to their chins, looking down their noses at them.

"I am Kamran. Welcome to our village." The older man's kind gaze turned to scan the tents behind them briefly and then returned to their faces. "Come, gentlemen, I will put you in my own tents." Kamran led them forward. As they passed Bashea's brothers, the pair continued to stare at them aggressively.

Kamran chatted with the men animatedly, but Tahj threw a glance back over his shoulder. Jahmeel and Bagrat were now talking to their sister, looking more relaxed as they led Bashea to a tent. But when Bashea raised her eyes and caught his, Tahj felt a strange pang, suddenly wondering if the bond they'd formed while escaping would dissipate now she was back in the heart of her family. Had he come all this way, fought so hard, only to realize returning her to her home wasn't what he wanted at all?

AT THE VERY LEAST, Tahj had to admit Bashea's father knew how to throw a feast; it rivaled any he had attended at the castle. The entire village gathered by the fire, and a goat kid was roasted on a spit. But even before it was served, they enjoyed a variety of toasted and lightly salted chickpeas, fava beans, and lentils, along with some of the biggest almonds Tahj ever laid eyes on. They were then brought nane sangak, the bread still warm from the hot stones it was cooked on. Rice and eggplant were served along with the main meal, which was subtly seasoned with saffron, cardamom, turmeric, and nutmeg. For dessert, several women brought forth platters heaped high with fruit, figs, cherries, plums, pomegranates, and grapes, along with shekar polo. Tahj loved the sweet rice dish more than anything else, but it reminded him of his youth when his mother used to make it for him for his birthday.

Feeling slightly melancholy, he searched the crowd for Bashea. They had not seen her all day, spending much of it resting in their own tent after their arduous journey. He spotted her here and there in the firelight throughout the course of the evening, talking with people and throwing back her head and laughing out loud. She had never seemed so beautiful and so unattainable. She did, however, look up and catch his eye at one point and smile. He smiled back, his body washed in a wave of warmth neither the food nor the fire provided. But as Bashea moved toward him, someone else stepped into her path and began speaking with her.

He looked away eventually and lost track of her until she was suddenly there at his side.

"More water, Prince Tahj?" She held a gourd over his cup, ready to pour, but he was so caught up in her beauty he couldn't speak at first. Something, either the firelight or her delight over being back at home with her family, gave her an almost luminescent glow. He nodded dumbly and watched as the water splashed into his cup, but the gourd emptied before she even filled it a fourth of the way up. "I'll get more," she murmured, her lips curving up at the corners as she peered into his eyes.

She stood, but Bagrat, who was making his way back to his spot after visiting with a friend and his family, heard the exchange and grabbed her arm. "No. I'll go."

Bashea shook him off stubbornly. "I'll get it, Bagrat," she announced clearly. "I can handle it." But Tahj could tell, despite her words and the unyielding tone they were delivered in, Bashea was frightened.

Bagrat took in the firm set of her chin and backed off, scowling and bending to wave his hand in the direction of the well. "As you wish, then," he muttered begrudgingly. The big man turned to watch Bashea make her way across the yard.

"You don't have to act like a guard dog, either," she tossed over her shoulder, seeming to feel the weight of her brother's eyes or knowing him well enough to instinctively guess what he was doing.

"Argh!" Bagrat spat in frustration, but he obliged by walking back to his spot and watching from a distance, though still obviously anxious for Bashea's safety. When he wasn't watching her, Bagrat occasionally shot Tahj dark looks.

Tahj turned his head to watch Bashea, too, as she walked shakily out of the ring of the firelight, wishing he'd said no when she asked if he wanted more water. After a time, he could take it no longer.

"Excuse me," he said to Radeem as he got up to leave, but the captain was in a loud discussion with Gaspard and another man Tahj did not recognize, and didn't even seem to hear him.

Tahj backed out of the firelight immediately, thinking it best if Bagrat didn't see him approaching Bashea. He skirted the others in a wide circle, moving as stealthily as possible.

"Bashea," he whispered loudly when he got near her.

Bashea jumped and squealed, turning in his direction and raising the gourd over her head as if to hurl it at him or send it crashing down onto his head.

"Bashea, it's me. Tahj," he said hastily. He stepped out of the dark, and she lowered her hands. He could see she was shaking.

"Oh, Tahj! You scared me." She folded her arms around herself, one hand still clutching the gourd by the neck. They both turned to see if anyone had noticed and could easily make out the hulking form of Bagrat making long strides in their direction.

"I'm sorry, Bashea. I-I didn't mean to..." He touched her arms in an effort to still her trembling.

"No, Tahj, I'm sorry."

"For what?"

"For what is about to happen," she explained as Bagrat came within hearing distance.

"Get your filthy hands off her!"

Tahj unconsciously took a step back. "What? I-I—"

"Bagrat, don't be a fool. He wasn't hurting me."

But Bagrat wasn't listening to her. He was within inches of Tahj now, but was still screaming, his fists clenched. "You think because you are a prince you can just have whatever you want?"

"No!" Tahj cried, shocked.

"Bagrat!" Bashea took hold of one his massive arms. "He had nothing to do with—"

The huge man turned on her. "You think he had nothing to do with it? He's the prince, isn't he?"

"Yes, but—"

"And they were his men?"

"No. I mean, yes, they were. But he is not to blame."

Heedless of his sister's words, Bagrat took hold of the sides of Tahj's vest and lifted him off of his feet. "*No one* touches my sister. Do you understand? I'm going to enjoy this. I've been waiting for a chance to be able to—"

"Bagrat!" Bashea was almost being lifted now, too, as she clutched at the bulging muscles of her brother's arm. "*He* did not hurt me. He helped me." She stopped, looking at Tahj as if she'd forgotten Bagrat was even there. "I was wrong. That's what I wanted to tell you this morning. I was wrong to say those things to you when you came to my tent."

"You went to her tent?" Bagrat growled, and Tahj didn't even see the punch coming. The next thing he knew, he was laying on the ground wondering if his jaw was still connected to his face.

"Bagrat!" Bashea said in a sort of shocked whisper. "He is a prince, for Arishtat's sake!" She glanced back toward the fire and saw a few curious heads had begun to turn their way. She took Bagrat by the shoulders and began to steer him back toward the feast. "You are going to go back now, and you will mind your own business. If I need your help, I'll ask for it."

He paused, and his big face crumpled like paper thrown on a fire. "But you did need my help, Bashea, and I wasn't there for you." He laid his forehead on the top of her head, holding her arms. "I wasn't there."

To Tahj's astonishment, the behemoth sounded as if he was going to cry. Bagrat felt responsible; Tahj could understand that. Feeling responsible for what happened to Bashea was what was making him edgy when she had come to apologize to him. All he could think of was, how could *she* be apologizing after all she had been through? He couldn't stand to hear her say it so he'd snapped at her, driving her away.

"It's okay," Bashea stuttered. "You couldn't have...it happened too quickly... It's not your fault," she said, her voice a mere whisper.

Jahmeel ambled toward them and Bagrat straightened, sniffing and rubbing Bashea's arms. Bashea dropped her head and drew a deep breath.

"Something amiss?" Jahmeel looked meaningfully at Tahj, who had just gotten to his feet.

"Everything is fine, Jahmeel," Bashea answered. "Bagrat was just heading back to the group." She gave her big brother a stern look and he turned from her.

"Come on, Jahmeel."

Jahmeel walked with him, but turned halfway back. "You coming, Bashea?"

"In a minute."

"Did you get in a fight with him?" Jahmeel whispered loudly to Bagrat as they stalked off. "Can I hit him, too?"

"No. Come."

Bashea turned to Tahj. "I'm sorry. You're not hurt, are you?" Her hand went to the side of Tahj's face sympathetically.

Tahj's heart started beating frantically but he forced a smile. "I'm fine. I could have taken him, you know."

Bashea grinned, not removing her hand. "He would have killed you."

Tahj chuckled. Bashea dropped her hand, and he caught it in his own for a second. "You know, I think he's scared of you."

She glanced toward the firelight, her eyes twinkling. "He should be." She shifted her eyes to Tahj and she smiled wider. They began to stroll back toward the others, but Tahj still held her hand lightly. It felt comfortable and right, and this time Bashea didn't pull away. After a few seconds Bashea stopped, turning to face him.

"I said those awful things to you because I was embarrassed."

"Embarrassed?"

She nodded, looking down. "Embarrassed of crying out in my sleep. I didn't want you to think I was weak."

"Weak?" He laughed now. "Weak? You almost knocked me unconscious. I think the blow you gave me hurt more than Bagrat's punch."

She batted his arm lightly. "It did not."

"Ouch," he joked, rubbing his arm.

"Stop," she said, laughing.

They continued to stroll leisurely, side-by-side, but they gazed into each other's eyes for several seconds without saying anything as they walked. It felt so natural. Bashea thought for a moment how wonderful it would be if Tahj were not a prince, if he were just some boy she'd grown up with. Could they have fallen in love? She knew it was becoming dangerous for her to think like this, or even be around him, because she desired it more, and knew she couldn't really have it. Still, one stolen moment like this, one moment to savor and wish things were different. Surely she deserved that, at least.

When Tahj looked ahead, she studied his profile as it was outlined by the firelight. Such a handsome face, such strong lines. And how good his hand felt as it gripped hers. He was a good man, like her father, like Bagrat, like Radeem. A good man with a good heart. She felt her own heart sigh, filled to capacity with a bittersweet longing for something clearly out of her reach.

As they drew nearer to the circle, Tahj stopped again. "You know, Bashea –" He looked at her, his eyes soft, voice husky. "I could never think of you as weak." He ran the back of his hand down her cheek. "You are one of the strongest women I've ever known."

Bashea stared into his eyes and felt her heart flutter helplessly.

Ahead of them, Jahmeel loudly cleared his throat. "You coming?" he asked pointedly, looking over his left shoulder as Bagrat looked over his right, glaring at them. Bashea and Tahj furtively broke apart.

As soon as Kamran caught sight of Bashea, he called her over. Later, Bagrat and Jahmeel kept her so busy Bashea suspected they were purposefully trying to keep her away from Tahj. When the festivities finally broke up in the wee hours of the morning, Bashea searched for Tahj, but he was nowhere to be found. Discouraged, she headed to bed. Just as she was raising the flap of her tent, she heard familiar voices.

"Good night, my friend," Tahj was saying to Radeem.

Radeem's big, bass voice responded, "Good night."

Bashea turned to find him, and just beyond Radeem, caught sight of Tahj. He stood like a mirror image to her, one hand holding the canvas of his tent back, pausing on his threshold. As the fire hadn't been completely extinguished yet, Bashea could see the slow grin that split his face, and her own lips curved up in response. They stood for a second, frozen, until a bucket of water brought the light to a hissing end and they moved into their tents.

Radeem turned to go into his own tent, but his vision was blocked by Bagrat's chest. He knew Bashea's older brother had been watching Tahj with a hawk's eye. Radeem raised his head to find the big man smiling down at him, though the smile looked odd. Jahmeel was lurking over his shoulder. Bagrat nodded in the direction of Tahj's tent.

"What is going on between him and Bashea?"

Radeem chuckled. "You noticed, too?"

Bagrat seemed alarmed to have his suspicions confirmed. He leaned into Jahmeel and whispered, "She will not end up with a prince from Avistad while still wearing the cuts and bruises rendered by his men. And a prince, such as he, with a sheepherder's daughter? The idea is absurd."

Jahmeel nodded his agreement. Bagrat shook his head. "No," he muttered a little louder. "Not with a prince of Avistad."

Radeem raised an eyebrow, both amused and offended. He thought back to earlier in the evening, to an image of Bashea bending to fill Tahj's cup, Tahj leaning forward. The body language was all there. "I'll bet you forty Abbas."

Bagrat snorted. "My coin purse is not that heavy, friend."

Neither is mine, Radeem thought. "Twenty, then."

Bagrat tugged on his beard, studying Radeem. His head inclined to Jahmeel's again. "This is not to be. I will make sure of it, *and* take the stuffed one's money."

Jahmeel chuckled.

Bagrat addressed Radeem. "Deal."

CHAPTER THIRTEEN

The next morning, Kamran summoned Bashea to the tent he was sharing with Jahmeel and Bagrat. As the sun was launching itself from the top of Mt. Sabalan up into the sky, she nervously scurried to her father's tent, unsure of what to expect. When Bashea approached, she heard voices inside. Entering, she was surprised to see Tahj sitting next to her father on a rug in the middle of the tent. The tent was as colorful inside as it was bland on the outside. Thick, colorful rugs swathed the floor, and vibrant blankets and cushions sat on mattresses and couches. A quick glance around the tent told Bashea her brothers were gone, much to her relief.

"Prince Tahj," she murmured with a smile, unable to move her eyes from his face for a moment.

"Good morning." He smiled radiantly back, his white teeth gleaming in his tan face, a teacup and saucer held in his hands.

Bashea, come, join us," Kamran stated with a vague wave of his hand. "Prince Tahj has just asked to stay on here for a while."

"He did?" Bashea exclaimed in surprise, turning back to Tahj.

He set his cup down hurriedly. "Only with the agreement I would earn my keep."

Bashea's eyes went wide, and she protested. "But Father, he is a prince—"

"It was not I who insisted on this," he responded. "It was Prince Tahj himself."

Bashea returned her eyes to Tahj, not hiding the question in them.

Tahj leaned forward to talk to her eagerly. "There is nothing back in Avistad for me now. I need some time to...put it all behind me...to grow...to decide what it is I want in life. Your father was gracious enough to offer me that time here." Tahj paused for a second, seeming to consider how to word his answer. "But I cannot stay and take advantage of his hospitality without offering something in return. So—" He slapped his hands on his thighs decisively and began to rise. "—I have some sheepherding to learn."

"But..." Bashea looked from him to her father. Things were moving too fast for her. She scrambled to her feet. "You're not going with Bagrat and Jahmeel?"

Tahj nodded.

"Of course he is," Kamran answered, looking confused as to why she would ask.

"I'll be fine," Tahj insisted.

"But..." She could see the faint bruising along his jaw line.

Tahj took her hand, angling his body so Kamran could not see him touch her. "I'll be fine."

Bashea noticed that Kamran watched the exchange with interest. She couldn't worry about that now. She turned to follow Tahj out, meaning to talk some sense into him, but Kamran called her back.

"Wait, Bashea. There was something more I wanted to speak with you about."

Bashea looked torn, but, as a dutiful daughter, she had no real choice. She came back to sit by her father, hoping to finish up with whatever business he had quickly, so she could catch up with Tahj.

"I wanted to speak with you..." He seemed uncomfortable with whatever subject he was about to broach, getting up to stride around the room. With a huff, he launched into his discussion. "Ladarius spoke with me last night. He wishes to court you."

Bashea was half distracted, thinking about Tahj and the very real possibility her brothers would soon be using him as sparring partner, but her father's statement got her attention.

"What?"

"Ladarius is a good man," Kamran began, as if anticipating an argument. "And you are far too independent, Bashea. It is what I love about you, but it's time you settled down."

"But Baba—"

"He is your age, and he's willing to overlook—" Kamran seemed to catch himself, then made a noise of aggravation. "I wish your mother were here. She would be much better at this," he muttered. "He does not hold...what happened to you...against you."

A light dawned in Bashea mind. "You mean he's willing to take me although I am not a virgin," she interpreted for him through gritted teeth.

Kamran's eyebrows arched, seeming surprised by her boldness. He sputtered, "Not many men—"

"So I should just run to him, Baba, because he is willing to accept a soiled—"

"Now, Bashea, calm down."

She stood, agitated. It was too much. To hear this from her father!

"I will not—"

"Bashea!" Kamran's voice flayed Bashea like a whip. Her father hadn't raised his voice to her in years. "This may be news to you, but you are a woman. And it is your place to be subservient to a man and obedient to your father."

"But I—"

"Not another word!" he roared. But then, no doubt seeing how stricken she was, he took a deep breath, softening somewhat. "Bashea, I know this is not ideal, but it is what is best for you. Trust me. I need for you to be settled. Having lost your mother, I know time is fleeting. And even if you refuse to see it, I am not a young man anymore."

Bashea found she couldn't speak through the chokehold of her emotions.

Kamran took her arms. She dropped her head and refused to look at him, but he put a fist under her chin to tilt her head up. It was then he saw the tears running down her face. "But you are crying!" Bashea rarely cried. Even when her mother died, she remained stalwart to provide strength to her siblings. And judging from the look on Kamran's face, it was tearing at his heart. "It will work out in the end, Azizam."

"No, Father," she said, her voice choked, shaking her head. "I have to go." She turned and fled, leaving Kamran standing there alone.

AT NOON, BASHEA JOINED a group of women when they took water to the upper meadow where her brothers and Tahj were tending the sheep. Sunlight tripped down the hillside, which was scattered with boulders, looking like feed-corn strewn by the giants. A stream bubbled merrily along on their right as they picked their way over the sloped ground, the temperature rising with each step as if it were attached to their heels.

Bashea's heart was heavy as she mulled over the conversation with her father. Was she wrong to want more than a man who was "willing to overlook" what had happened to her in the past? Maybe she was being too hardheaded; maybe her choices had become more limited now. But, try as she might, she just couldn't see herself making a home with a man she didn't love. Perhaps her father was right—perhaps she was too independent. But whatever the case, Bashea knew she would have to convince her father, somehow, she'd be better off alone.

The upper meadow was relatively small, but like some magical oasis, the verdant pasture land was perpetually made green by the waters trickling off the sides of the surrounding hills and flowing into its bowl-like harbor. Bashea breathed in the fragrant, fresh smell of grass and rich dirt, made sweeter by the fact it was so rarely she was able to enjoy it, since her lungs were usually full of dust and the grit of sand. It was almost as if she could breathe more freely here. Not only that, but it was also one of their better feeding grounds, one they tried to use sparingly to keep it lush, only going there when they were forced to retreat to the higher grounds by some outside threat. Far below, the sheep flecked the green plain like peaceful clouds hanging in a still sky. After a brief search, Bashea spotted Tahj off by himself, sitting on a large rock wedged into the crevice of the hillside, poking at the bottom of his sandals with a stick.

As Bashea rose higher and higher, deeper into the tree line, Tahj sat lost in thought as well in the meadow above. Radeem had stayed in bed, feeling ill after having a little too much to drink the night before, leaving Tahj at the mercy of the other herders. It was turning out to be a particularly hot day, the kind of day that left a constant, annoying trickle of sweat running uncomfortably down his body in some area or other. Tahj spit out some dirt, which had swirled into his mouth with the breeze, and gazed out over his surroundings. Strangely, he felt at peace here. The simple life of a sheepherder appealed to him. There was no weighty mantle of responsibility on his shoulders, no one watching for him to make a mistake, except for maybe Bagrat and Jahmeel. He let his eyes drift to where they sat in the shade of a cypress tree several yards below him, laughing loudly. Tahj knew winning them over was the key to Bashea's hand and was determined to prove himself worthy to the pair, if it killed him. He rubbed his bruised chin as he contemplated his best course of action.

When Tahj saw Bashea coming, he dropped the stick and scrambled down to meet her halfway up. Just as he reached her, she slid a little in the loose rock and he grabbed her arms.

"Careful. I wouldn't want you to twist one of your ankles," he said with a smile. He noticed immediately she looked a little down.

"Why are you sitting up there?" she queried. "You're more exposed to the sun up so high."

"Your brothers told me it was the best vantage point to see all the sheep."

"They did, did they?" She eyed her brothers. "What else did they tell you?"

Tahj shrugged. He took a long drink from the gourd she offered and wiped his face on a sleeve. "I'm doing well. Although I hate having to count each head constantly."

"What do you mean?"

"They yell up at me, and, since I'm new, they make me do the counting."

"Of the sheep?"

He nodded beginning to wonder why she was asking so many questions. "The sheep, the goats..."

"I see. And how often do you do this?"

"Well, let me think. I must have done it half a dozen times already. It wouldn't be so bad if I didn't have to climb down there and physically touch each one. I can see them from my rock and count, but they said I have to touch as I count, to be sure. Jahmeel said, especially in the heat of the day, the eyes can play tricks on you."

"Umm..."

"What? I can tell from your face something's not right."

Bashea shaded her eyes as she looked up at him. "I think they're...having fun with you. I've never seen them count sheep that way."

"Is that so?" He laughed at himself. "Well, I really stepped into that one, didn't I? Literally," he added, picking up his sandals where he'd been trying to scrape off sheep dung with the stick he'd discarded. Tahj's laugh came deep from his belly.

Bashea laughed along with him, but was then quiet.

"Are you well?" Tahj asked gently. "You're not angry with your brothers, are you?"

"Well, yes, I'm angry with them."

He laughed, "Don't be. I'll get back at them, don't worry."

She smiled.

"I'll see you back at camp later?"

She nodded, but a shadow crossed her face. "I'd better go."

Tahj watched her walk away. She was troubled by something—he'd almost bet money on it. He raised his eyes to take in her brothers again, napping now as they reclined in the shade. He smiled grimly. This was going to be good.

A FEW HOURS LATER, Tahj scrambled up from the lower meadow in a panic, shouting and waving his hand. The brothers sat up when they saw him coming.

"What is it?" Bagrat blurted out.

"The sheep! I don't know how it happened, but a half dozen is missing, at least."

The men jumped to their feet. "Are you sure?"

Tahj nodded, bending over double and catching his breath. "I counted them three times."

The brothers swore, picking up their staffs. "Okay, we'll go look for them. You stay here and watch the rest. And don't let them out of your sight."

The five stumbled and slid down the hillside in their haste to reach the bottom. Tahj straightened up with a smile. He climbed up the hillock and led the "missing" sheep out from a cave he'd herded them into to keep them hidden. He then strolled back down and stretched out lazily in the shade the brothers had left, sighing with sweet contentment. He took a nap.

CHAPTER FOURTEEN

By the time the men returned for their evening meal, Tahj had become one of them. They laughed wholeheartedly and slapped him on the back when they found out how he'd tricked them. When Bashea looked up from her dinner preparations and saw them, Tahj made his excuses and then separated from the group to talk to her.

"Good evening."

"Good evening," she replied softly, having met him halfway. Again he noted a sadness about her. "How was the rest of your day?"

"Better." Tahj grinned, explaining to her how he tricked her brothers.

"That's wonderful, Tahj." She laughed, reaching up to squeeze his arm. But then she looked beyond him and her face fell. Tahj turned slightly to see a man approaching who he'd seen bending Kamran's ear the night before at the feast. He was tall and slender, with a dark, sparse beard and a long, striped caftan made from rough fabric, though he wore showy rings on his hands and exuded the air of a man who was used to living comfortably. Most women would find him handsome, Tahj realized, though he had an instant dislike for him.

"Bashea, may I speak with you?" the man asked gruffly, eyeing Tahj with suspicion.

"Sure," she answered, pushing a strand of hair back behind her ear. "I-I'll see you later, Tahj."

Tahj watched them stroll away. He flinched when the man slid his hand around Bashea's waist. She stiffened and threw an anxious look over her shoulder. He met her eye just as a group of people stepped between them and blocked his view. He struggled to see through the gaps between them, but when they passed by, Bashea was gone. Tahj wondered if he should try to find them and make sure Bashea was safe, but he judged, while she seemed nervous, she didn't seem afraid, and decided to leave it alone.

LATER, AS TAHJ CROSSED by her tent, he saw Bashea through the flap she left open to catch the rare breeze. She lay on the bed on her stomach, legs bent with feet up in the air, swinging back and forth as she studied something before her. Tahj felt a smile stretch across his face. At the moment she looked like a little girl lost in a daydream, and the image warmed his heart. He approached stealthily, wanting to observe from a closer vantage point, and saw over her shoulder she held a piece of parchment in one hand and twirled a piece of hair around her finger with the other, staring off into space.

He didn't know what gave him away, but she turned suddenly, and seeing him, started, sitting up and pressing the page to her chest. "Oh! I didn't hear you."

"Yes. You seemed rather...preoccupied," he responded, a teasing edge to his voice. He reached over and tried to pull the page back to take a look, sensing she was hiding something from him. "What is this?"

"This?" she answered, her voice a little higher than usual. "Nothing." She spun to hurriedly put the parchment down, but Tahj snatched it just as it touched the top of the crate beside her bed. She sprang off of the bed to try to retrieve it from him, but her arms were too short.

Tahj held it above his head, fending her off as he tried to read it. "What is this? A poem?"

"Give it back," she fumed, jumping, but missing it by a fraction as Tahj turned his body so it was a barrier to her. He knew he was being obnoxious, but his curiosity was overriding his sense of manners. "I mean it, Tahj." Something in her voice had him looking up, and to his surprise, he found she was near tears. "Give it to me!"

"Bashea," he said quietly in an effort to calm her, "if you want it back that badly, I'll give it to you. I didn't mean to upset you." Tahj extended his arm, handing it to her, but he looked Bashea in the eye when she reached for it. "But if this is something you wrote, I would really like to read it."

This stopped her momentarily. The page stood suspended between them. She bit her lip. "You won't tease me, as my brothers do?"

"Of course not. I want to know you."

She hesitated. "I don't know. My brothers are uneducated, but you—"

"Please, Bashea," he implored earnestly.

He could see a battle being waged in her eyes. "You can read it, if you want." She shrugged. "They are nothing." She stalked to the other side of the tent, but fidgeted and he could feel her eyes on him as he read. Appearing uncomfortable with the silence, she added, "Just something to do to while away the time..." Her voice trailed off as his eyes traveled back and forth across the page, devouring her words.

Tahj found himself lost in the poem as images of nature swam before his eyes, and he immediately recognized her description of the high meadow, with its tinkling brook and grassy plain. The way she had captured the timelessness and hidden wisdom of objects that were an everyday part of her life amazed him. The flow of the words swept Tahj along and moved him more than he would have thought possible.

Bashea stilled as he lowered the page. She looked like a child standing before her father to be judged for some petty offense. Tahj felt a sort of shock. Now the bed was bare, he saw a leather-bound volume on the bed, parchment paper tied together with leather strings. His gaze flew around the room to take in several similarly bound books scattered about. "This is who you are?" he asked quietly.

She shrugged again. "I don't know." She gave a high-pitched laugh. "Sometimes the words just come to me, and I have to write them down to get them out of my head."

Tahj set the page carefully down on the crate and moved toward her. She lowered her head and fiddled with her hands.

"They're not very good, I know," she said in a rush. "Just something to do—" Bashea's breath left her as Tahj grabbed her chin and lifted her face. His other hand, grasping her wrist, felt her pulse quicken, reminding him of a baby bird's wings beating against the side of its cage when it is first captured.

"They are beautiful," he said distinctly, his eyes misty and intense, "as you are beautiful." His head bent to hers as he leaned in.

They both jumped when they heard Parvaiz's voice behind them. "Bashea!" he called sharply.

"Parvaiz," Tahj said, clearing his throat. Parvaiz gave him a hard stare. "I was just leaving." But on a whim Tahj brushed Bashea's hand as he passed, still looking evenly at Parvaiz, who barred the doorway. Parvaiz, though several inches shorter than Tahj, held his ground for a second, giving Tahj a meaningful look before letting him pass.

"Parvaiz," Bashea began, her voice a warning. "You don't need to say anything."

She moved across the room and took the single sheet of parchment and slid it into the volume on her bed.

"Somebody does, Bashea. What's going on with this prince? I came down to talk to you about Ladarius, and I find you with your arms wrapped around *him*?"

She wondered over when her little brother's voice had become so deep. "It's not like that."

"What is it like then, Bashea? Tell me," he demanded, exasperated.

"I don't think I like your tone," Bashea started, going on the offensive.

"Well, that's too damn bad!" Parvaiz shouted, his face going red.

For a second, Bashea was stunned. Parvaiz had never dared to talk to her this way before, but then her own ire rose. "Listen, Parvaiz, I don't know why you think you can talk to me like this. Are you such a big man now you can scream at your sister and order her around like a servant? What I do with my life is *my* concern, Parvaiz, not yours!"

Parvaiz looked like he was about to bite back, but he abruptly shut his mouth. This wasn't his style. He was always logical, and found most confrontations such as this a waste of time and energy. "I am sorry, Bashea. You are right. I shouldn't be chastising you. I'm just concerned." He looked up with the last and held her eyes.

The look of concern she saw there shook her, so Bashea turned to put her book away on a shelf and give herself time to collect her emotions, suddenly so raw. "You came to speak of Ladarius..." She forced herself to speak lightly and soften the edges of the seething inside her.

"Yes." But Parvaiz glanced over his shoulder to where Tahj stood by the fire, trying to look like he wasn't watching what was going on inside the tent. He sighed, gritting his teeth. "I'm sorry, Bashea, but I'm going to have to ask you again, what is going on with you and Prince Tahj?"

Bashea sighed, flinging herself onto the bed stomach-first. "Why is my love life suddenly of such interest to everybody?"

Parvaiz smiled. "It has always been of great interest. There just wasn't much to talk about before." He didn't move fast enough to avoid the pillow. He laughed, scooping it up off the ground and coming to sit down next to her on the edge of the bed.

When he didn't speak, Bashea rolled over. "He's a prince, Parvaiz," she said, trying to appeal to his logic, "and I am a sheepherder."

But, as logical as he was, Parvaiz was also a softie, and he obviously saw the pain his sister was in. He touched her face. "To me, you have always been a princess."

It was such an uncharacteristic thing for him to say, she felt like crying. But she knew it was true. Her younger siblings had always looked up to and idolized her, but being their "princess" wasn't always easy. "Father says I am to marry Ladarius."

"Well, excuse me for saying this—I mean no disrespect—but Baba will not have to live with that decision. You will."

Bashea put the back of her palm to her forehead. "Uuh, I have such a headache!"

Parvaiz smiled, patting her other hand where it lay near him on the bed. "Too much to think about." He rose. "I will leave, then, so you can do your thinking." But he turned at the door. "By the way, I came to tell you, Ladarius is not the man for you."

And he was gone.

Bashea sighed and turned her head with a groan. She stretched out her hand thoughtfully and touched a cord that hung from the tent, rubbing her fingers along its surface. In her mind's eye she could see Tahj's bedroom: soft, supple, lavish, curtained bed, carved, finished furniture, walls. She ran her fingers over the crate beside her bed and jerked it back when a splinter bit into her. Frustrated, she removed the jagged piece of wood with her other fingers and stuck the injured finger in her mouth to soothe it. The pounding in her head continued. She rolled over and closed her eyes.

TAHJ DIDN'T SEE BASHEA until dinner. They were all gathered around the fire again, and tonight there was dancing. The combination of being out in the sun and fresh air earlier, the warmth of the fire, and the tantalizing smell of the food mixed with the fragrance of the burning wood, all seemed to seduce him into a trance.

Tahj was readily able to distinguish Bashea from the other dancers, despite the veil covering much of her face, and the fact her sisters closely resembled her. There was just an unmistakable spark in the young girl's eyes, and, when the group circled around until Bashea was standing in front of him, she stopped circling, seeming to dance just for him. The other dancers seemed a bit confused with this change in the program, which left them in their own private dances, sometimes with people they did not wish to dance for, but they had no choice, as they couldn't go forward with Bashea at a stop.

Tahj grinned up at her, and Bashea's eyes became even brighter. Had Tahj taken his eyes from her for even a second, he might have seen Bagrat across the fire ring as he leaned over and whispered something to the man he'd seen with Bashea earlier. As it was, he didn't notice the man until he was upon Bashea. With his back to Bagrat and Jahmeel, Ladarius boldly slid his large hand around from behind and laid it on Bashea's bare stomach, pulling her strongly toward him and dancing in time to the music, repeating her earlier movements, and bending his knees and wriggling his hips.

Everything inside Tahj revolted, and he jumped angrily to his feet. He looked over at Bagrat and Jahmeel and saw they were laughing. His rage turned to something sharp and cold and he turned, leaving the fire hurriedly to return to his tent.

When Bashea felt Ladarius's hand slide around her waist across her skin, she was seized simultaneously with fear and anger. It was unheard of for a man to touch a woman so intimately in the company of others. Her eyes grew wide, and she grabbed the man's hand and wriggled out of his grasp. Turning to find Ladarius standing behind her, she fought the urge to slap him right there in front of everyone.

"How dare you!" she spat.

"Bashea, I told you today I wanted you for my wife."

The man was obviously drunk. His eyes were unfocussed and his tongue thick. "And I told you I was not interested," she hissed, storming past him.

When Bagrat saw her face as she marched toward him, the smile faded off his. He scrambled to his feet. "Bashea what...?"

"Don't talk to me, Bagrat." She tried to stomp past him to her tent, but Bagrat grabbed her arm and swung Bashea around.

"What's wrong with you?"

"What's wrong with *me*? Did you not just see what happened?"

"No, I... I mean, I thought—"

"Ladarius, put his...hand on me...on my stomach...like I was some common..." She couldn't complete the thought; a hand flew to her mouth as if to force her to swallow the horror back.

"What?" Bagrat roared, his eyes already searching the crowd for Ladarius.

"Let me go! Just let me go," Bashea cried, her tears finally taking her. She broke free and ran to her tent.

Jahmeel stood, too.

"You go find Ladarius and make sure he knows we are not happy with him," Bagrat told him. Jahmeel grunted his understanding. "I think I need to go and apologize to Prince Tahj."

TAHJ SAT ON THE EDGE of his cot, elbows on his knees, fidgeting with a signet ring on his finger, sliding it up and down in an agitated manner.

"Prince Tahj?" a voice called from outside of his tent. Tahj recognized it as belonging to Bagrat.

"What do you want?" he said darkly, continuing to stare absently at the ring.

Bagrat pulled the tent flap back and entered, glancing around the tent, anywhere, but into Tahj's eyes. "I've come to...apologize."

Tahj looked up. This was interesting. "Apologize for what?"

"For encouraging Ladarius to...to..." He gestured vaguely, moving his hands in wide circles.

"To what?" Tahj asked, confused.

"What are your intentions toward my little sister?" Bagrat blurted.

"My intentions toward..." Tahj repeated slowly.

"Your intentions toward my sister. What are your intentions toward my sister?" Bagrat repeated, irritated and seeming a bit uncomfortable with the conversation now.

"I..." Tahj drew the word out thoughtfully, stalling for time. "I have no idea."

Bagrat laughed heartily. "Well, I guess that's an honest enough answer." He came and sat down next to Tahj on his bed, within the circle of the light from his lantern, which sat on an upended crate nearby. "But what are your feelings toward her? Surely you can describe those?"

"I think she's great. I think she's wonderful. She's beautiful..." Tahj saw Bagrat's eyes narrow at that, and decided to move on to other territory. "She's stronghearted. I admire that." The more he talked, the more Tahj warmed to his subject. "She cares deeply for others. She can make me crazy, though," he said, almost without thinking. He looked up quickly.

Again Bagrat laughed, long and low, slapping Tahj's knee. "You are saying nothing that I do not already know. I have lived with her for many years." He chuckled. "She's a tough one, to be certain." He paused, contemplating. "She makes you crazy," he repeated. "I used to say the same thing about my Dara. Still do, in fact." He winked at Tahj and rose to leave. He stopped in the doorway. "You won't hurt her?"

"I'll do my best not to," Tahj answered quickly.

"Good, good," Bagrat answered, his face more relaxed than Tahj had ever seen it. "Because if you did—"

"You and Jahmeel would have to kill me."

"Exactly." He paused. "You know what? I like you," he added. "And, even though it made me as mad as a jackal, walking around for an hour and a half in the midday sun searching for lost lambs which weren't lost at all, I thought that was funny, what you did today."

Tahj grinned. "Thanks."

"Don't do it again."

"I won't."

"Good then, good night."

"Good night, Bagrat. Bashea is lucky to have a brother like you."

"Hmph." He grunted. "I doubt that is true after all she has been through." And with that he ducked under the flap of the tent and left Tahj to his own thoughts.

Tahj lay back in his bed, resting his head on folded arms, feeling better than before. So it would seem Bagrat put that fellow up to what he did. Although Tahj was certain Bagrat would not approve of his exact actions. That meant Bashea, perhaps, hadn't encouraged it.

He closed his eyes, thinking about the magical way Bashea's hips moved as she stood in front of him, her eyes aglow. He could almost hear the beat of the music again, like a charm, seducing each sensuous movement she made out of her, wrapping around each lovely curve of her body and swaying with her compellingly. He was pretty sure Bagrat wouldn't approve of the thoughts he was having now, but Bagrat wasn't there anymore.

SOMETIME LATER, TAHJ awoke in the dark. The flapping of his tent door created a loud noise, and a stiff breeze had blown his lantern out. As he lay trying to fall back to sleep, he was disturbed by the sound of the sides of the tent, whose violent vibrations were created by the wind's gusts. As nasty as a sand storm could be in the desert, a storm in the mountains could be murderous as well. He heard a crash somewhere in camp and recognized the sound of glass breaking. He decided to get up and see if anyone needed help.

As he stepped out into the night, Tahj realized the storm was a lot worse than he'd imagined from the relative protection of his bed. This was more than your common desert storm. Anything that hadn't been battened down was being tossed about and thrown against rocks and the sides of tents, or anything else hindering its progress. The rain was being held at bay at present, but Tahj imagined when it was released it would drive into the hillside like hurled spears.

Tahj leaned into the wind and fought his way forward, noting piles of broken crates leaning against his neighbor's tent and firewood yards from where the fire had been set up. Luckily the tribesmen always made certain the fire was totally out before going to bed, in the event something like this should happen. The wind was sharp and stung his face, and muscles screamed as he struggled ahead, already fatigued from the day's work.

Over the howling of the wind, he heard a couple of men shouting orders to each other as they tried to secure the sides of a larger tent near the center of camp. He heard the sound of a baby crying and saw a colorful blanket take flight ahead of him. Moving as quickly as he could against the force of the gale, Tahj was able to snatch the blanket from where it got hung up on the top of a tent stake before it took off again. He recognized one of the blankets they'd bought for Bashea in Shiraz.

Shielding his eyes against the bits of debris being hurtled about, he searched out and located her tent, pushing to reach it. One of her tent's ropes snapped about like a writhing serpent and bit into his arm as he tried to catch it to tether it down. He tossed the blanket inside the opening so he could have his hands free to battle the tent.

Even so, just as he secured it, two more popped out of the ground like toddlers playing a game, and a large section of the tent came loose, flailing so he had to jump to reach it. Tahj grabbed a hold of the canvas and fought it downward, finding himself on the inside of the tent, lying on top of it to keep it from flying away again.

Tahj rolled over on his back, panting from both exertion and the sheer power of the wind to take his breath. Weary, he rolled his head to one side, searching for something to use to hold the canvas down other than his body. Just feet from him a couple of crates stood. Were they filled with something heavy enough to hold the canvas down? Carefully, he rolled, making certain enough of his weight was distributed to keep the cloth down, and reached for the crates. The side of the tent began to thump and loft, quivering, but not pulling entirely away. He rocked the crates in his direction, jig-jawing them by walking one corner at a time toward him. They were plenty heavy.

By the power of utter determination, he was able to replace his weight with the crates' and spread them far enough apart to counteract the pull of the wind. Realizing it was just a matter of time before more stakes were jerked up, he decided to be proactive and worked his way around the tent, weighting down the edges. Like his own, the tent was large, and mostly empty. Tents this size were generally used for families, but it would seem there were some perks allowed you when you're the chief's daughter.

He was just standing back to admire his handiwork when a lantern blazed to life. He whipped around in surprise to find Bashea squinting at him through sleepy eyes, sitting up on one elbow, holding the lantern aloft in the other hand to try to illuminate the room, her midnight-black hair wild, but, he thought, incredibly sexy. She lay on a wide mattress covered in vibrantly colored, silken layers of cloth and mounded with pillows. A background as sumptuous as its occupant.

"What...are you doing?" she asked quizzically, a hint of amusement creeping into her tone.

"I... uh..." Tahj found himself at a loss for words. "The wind was blowing and... this part of your tent came loose and I, well...fixed it." As if to support his stance, the wind howled around the tent, circling it like a wild animal searching for a way in.

Bashea swung the lantern around and took in the books and boxes and rocks and other paraphernalia haphazardly placed around the periphery of the tent to hold it in place.

"I see." She sat up in her bed a little. "And how are you going to get out?" she asked teasingly, lifting an eyebrow.

Tahj looked around. "Uhh...I didn't...exactly...think about that," he said slowly, as if in a daze. After an awkward pause in which Tahj stood feeling both uncomfortable and foolish, he again found his voice. "I can move away a small section, and you can move it back after I'm out." The wind roared again, this time sounding like a momma panther whose babies were being threatened.

"As you wish," Bashea replied, scrambling hastily to her feet as if to escape the wrath of the wind outside. The bed projected into the room, but the canvas near her head was the only barrier between her and the thrashing night. The light of the lantern she returned to the top of a crate beside her bed cast an enigmatic glow about her which seemed to shimmer and grow with her movements. She was wearing a sheer, white gown with billowing, translucent sleeves, pleated from the bodice down and tied high on her waist, making her look so light and airy he almost expected her to take flight. She reached for a matching, sheer robe at the foot of the bed, which tied with a satiny ribbon trailing almost to the ground.

Tahj was transfixed as she moved toward him, but then, without warning, everything changed. With a mighty rush the wind gusted, forcing its way into the room like a jealous lover, come to catch his spouse in the act. One side of the tent gave way, several sections he had secured going together as stacks of books and crates flew simultaneously into the room. As Tahj took his eyes from her to look in their direction and assess the damage, he saw one of the support posts behind Bashea teeter. Like in a dream, his eyes returned to her, checking to see if she was in the line of fire, but even as he did, the post gave way and was swept forward.

His scream mingled with the sound of the wood crashing into Bashea, sending her sprawling. It bounced off her body like a rubber ball and flew with equal force into his shins, knocking his feet out from under him, and then everything went dark and oddly quiet beneath the folds of the collapsed canvas.

Dazed, Tahj pushed to his hands and knees, praying the lantern was truly out and not about to start a fire. He pushed through the heavy layers of the tent, calling out Bashea's name, though knowing the muffling nature of the canvas and the still-raging winds outside would surely prevent her from hearing him. He strained his own ears for any sound of her presence—a cry, a movement—but he heard none. He felt around at his feet for the post and managed to move it in front of him to use it like a spear, pushing the canvas outward and upward and struggling to rise to his feet. He raised the post, straining against the weight of the canvas, and opened up the room before him as he pushed forward, aiming for the place he thought the post had been. As the tent rose, he saw Bashea lying on the floor, unmoving.

"Oh, Bashea!" he cried out. He stopped, longing to drop the post and rush to her side, but he knew they would be smothered again, so he diligently worked to get his post in place, trying to hold it steady and sink it into the hole in the ground it had shot out of.

He heard a moan and swiveled his head to see Bashea stirring. Feeling a small amount of relief, he turned back to his task, finding it difficult to both keep the pole straight and aim it for the small opening in the ground while still fighting the wind. All of a sudden, he felt weight taken off the post as Bashea joined him, leaning her body forward to push the pole upright. With her clasping the pole up higher, Tahj lowered himself, guiding the end of the post with his hands into the hole. It clunked into place, but they found their work was not done.

About halfway from the corner they had just secured, down the right side of the tent a long, jagged rip in the canvas had the side of the tent whipping back and forth madly as rain now began to blow inside in torrents. Lightning flashed, a silver zigzag outlining the growling storm clouds in the night sky, and was followed shortly by the mighty crash of thunder. The air smelt burnt, wet, and heavy. Bashea and Tahj yelled over the storm.

"What should we do?" Bashea asked, holding one side of the tear as Tahj jumped to grab hold of the corner of the canvas on his side of the rip. Her hair and gown now stuck to her, as the rain drove at her face, stinging her eyes. She blinked away the water uselessly.

He played with the idea of binding the ends together somehow with rope, but finally discarded the idea as impractical. "We'll just have to secure each end as best as we can, as close together as possible," Tahj shouted in reply. With the next flash of lightning he noticed, with some alarm, a rivulet of blood trickling down the right side of Bashea's forehead. He paused in his struggle. "You're hurt!"

"What?" she screamed back, unable to hear above the chaos.

"Are you in pain?" Tahj gestured with his head to her forehead.

Bashea reached up and felt the cut, bringing her hand down to inspect it. "Fine. Fine," she answered dismissively.

Whether it was the angle of the wind or sheer luck, the end Bashea held seemed less affected by the wind. Sliding down, she managed to tuck the flap under her knees as she half turned to scan the room behind her. Seeing nothing within reach, she took a look in the opposite direction. Several feet away, Bashea caught sight of the crate beside her bed that had held the lantern which was now on the floor. The crate was knocked a little askew, but still roughly in the same place as it had been, able to resist the pull of the heavy canvas. She had to release her end, letting the storm again get its foot in the door, and move down the line of the tent, walking on her knees back toward the bed. When she was close enough, Bashea reached out and tugged the crate toward her, moving it little by little up the line.

Suddenly Tahj was behind her. "Here, let me get that." With a heave and a grunt, he shifted the heavy crate, which also served for storage of her belongings, and Bashea sidestepped back a few feet. With effort, Tahj hefted the crate on top of the fold of the canvas next to Bashea. He turned to look around for another heavy object, and she rose to her feet, returning to her former position and grasping the side of the ripped canvas in her hands. The storm abated slightly, the thunder and lightning a degree less intense, although the rain still came down viciously. As Bashea peered toward the corner during the next lightning strike, she saw Tahj had managed to get his part of the canvas all neatly tucked in with weights at evenly spaced intervals down the line of the tent.

"Here." Though his voice was gentle, Bashea jumped, surprised he was so close. He held a stack of books in his hands. Bashea backed out of his way, and he arranged them onto the corner of the canvas, bringing the room relatively to order. Exhausted, he fell back onto his backside with a loud sigh. "There." He turned to smile at Bashea, and she, too, sank to the ground beside him, breathing heavily, her back to their enemy, the tent. Without warning, Tahj reached out and stroked her face below her cut, the skin cool and damp. Her eyes grew wide. "Are you sure you are unharmed?"

She stared into his eyes as if stunned for a second and then reached up again, absentmindedly, to feel the cut. "Yes, it's not bad," she responded finally, pulling away from him.

Tahj watched coolly as she rose to her feet, trying to tug the wet robe around her more tightly and then crossing her arms, half-turned from him. He studied what he could see of her face, some light still coming in from the crack they could not altogether mend. She looked sad and frightened and... impenetrable. He found himself suddenly irritable in her presence, like every neuron was setting him on edge. He spun, mirroring her image by crossing his arms.

"You can trust me, you know, Bashea," he bit off, but then the anger simply drained away. He closed his eyes with a sigh. After a few seconds passed in silence, he turned back to her, his voice almost pleading. "You can trust me. I won't hurt you."

She turned around slowly, not reaching out to him again, just standing still and assessing him in silence. "I know," she responded, her voice small and shaky. She glanced away for a second, folding and unfolding her hands. She returned her eyes to his face, "I'm sorry, Tahj," she said without explanation. "I really am."

"I know," he murmured, not daring to reach out for her, though every inch of his body screamed to wrap her up in a huge embrace.

Bashea's gaze flitted everywhere as she tried to find her next words. "I guess y-you'll have to stay here," she said after a while.

"We could lift up a corner, and I could sneak out—"

She spun around. "But what if things come loose, or a pole comes down again?"

He crossed to her, noting how Bashea was watching his every move, and placed hands on her shoulders. "Relax, Bashea. I'll stay if you want me to. I'll sleep on the ground."

She nodded slightly, still looking a little bewildered, and he wondered just how hard the beam had hit her. "What time do you think it is?"

"Still several hours before dawn, I would guess."

She paused. "I'll get you some blankets." Bashea moved over to her bed, searching for dry blankets. Meanwhile, Tahj found the lantern, which was, miraculously, still lit, though it was on its side, the candle wax dripping onto the glass shade making its illumination hazy. He turned around, and Bashea stood behind him with a pair of blankets folded over her arms.

"Thank you, Tahj," she said sincerely and then she reached out and did something he hadn't expected, placing her hand on his arm.

"It was nothing," he returned with a gulp, her proximity unnerving him.

Her eyes searched his in the lamplight and she asked in a near whisper, "How did you know to come?"

He was mesmerized. At the moment all he could think was, *The gods led me,* but he recovered. "The storm woke me. I left my tent to see if anyone needed help, and I saw one of your stakes had come loose."

Bashea dropped her hand. "Oh." She seemed a little disappointed in the logical answer. "Thank you for coming. I would have never been able to manage that alone."

Tahj took the blankets she handed him, continuing to scrutinize her even as she turned away. She was a mystery, this woman. She seemed to pull him in and push him away like a cat playing with its prey, but he sensed it was totally unintentional.

Since Bashea had climbed into bed, wet clothes and all, he decided to do the same. He moved over to the doorway and spread his blankets out on the ground. He noticed Bashea had turned on her side, away from him, so, with a nearly silent sigh, he got between the covers, lying on his side facing her. The lantern still glowed in the night; neither one had thought to extinguish it.

Maybe twenty minutes had passed when Bashea abruptly flipped over. Tahj was lying on his back with his arms folded beneath his head, watching the shifting shadows on the tent's ceiling. Her movement caught his attention and he turned toward her. He could see now she was also wide awake.

She seemed to have made a decision. She lifted her covers.

"It's cold," she said simply.

Was she cold? Or did she think he was, Tahj wondered. He froze, uncertain of what she was asking. It seemed pretty clear, but he hardly dared to believe it to be true.

"I trust you, Tahj." Her face was solemn in the lantern light.

Tahj nodded his head without speaking and stood, bringing his blankets with him as he crossed the room mechanically. He paused by her bed for a minute, but she didn't speak, seemingly struck mute. He spread his blankets over her small figure with care and waited. She lifted the blankets again, and he sat down with his back to her, then leaned over and slowly stretched out beside her, not facing her, waiting to follow her lead. Expecting at any moment to feel her hands slide around him, his skin prickled, but she made no move to touch him. He let his breath out, still amazed she'd invited him into her bed, and wondered if she were expecting something from him.

Tahj debated his next course of action. Should he speak to her now about his feelings? Or would that make her feel uncomfortable? Had she simply asked him to join her because of the cold, with no other intentions behind her invitation? Or was it possible she, too, had feelings for him?

He could feel her smoldering heat, and in his mind could trace each curve of the body creating that heat as she flowed silently behind him, and these thoughts derailed all other thought for a time. He had never shared his bed with a woman, and the comfort of having another so close swamped his senses. He could smell the perfumed scent of her hair on the pillow. The rain had slowed to a pleasant pitter-patter, and he could hear the rhythmic sound of her breathing over the drips on the canvas and in the mud outside. It was all so comforting, he couldn't bring himself to even move for fear it would break him out of the cozy cocoon he shared with her. He drifted off to sleep with a smile on his face.

CHAPTER FIFTEEN

Tahj woke hours later with one terrifying thought. If Jahmeel or Bagrat found him in Bashea's tent, they would rip him to shreds with their bare hands.

He hastily climbed out of bed, but paused before leaving. Sometime during the night, Bashea had turned over in her sleep and now had her back to him. He crept around the bed to gaze on her face, framed on the pillow like artwork. He stood for a long time, frozen, while birds began to sing outside and a few early risers shuffled about. Bashea's face was kissed with a faint rose blush, lips slightly parted. Hands were folded together near her face, the soft tendrils of her hair tumbling recklessly across the sheets and down her shoulders. As if by force, Tahj fell to his knees in the dirt, his chest filled with a zinging ache.

"Good morning, friend," he heard outside, close enough to startle him.

He rose and made his way to the area of the tent that had ripped the night before. He pulled the edge back and saw he was facing a neighboring tent. Sliding his eyes to the right, he saw a heavyset woman bent over a fledgling fire. Footsteps faded away in the distance, and he judged this was as good a time as any to make his escape. He tiptoed out of the tent, his eyes on the woman at the fire as he backed away. He turned around and barreled straight into Jahmeel's chest, stealing his breath away, though it left the big man unscathed.

"Oh!" he exclaimed, clearing his throat. "Good morning."

"Is it?" Jahmeel responded pointedly.

"No," Tahj was quick to answer. "Not at all. Horrible, actually. Didn't get a wink of sleep. " Seeing Jahmeel's eyebrow raise he tried to backtrack. "Not because of...anything improper...the storm.... The storm was loud," he ended dumbly.

"Uh-huh."

"And the lightening..." He whistled. "I think I'll go back to my tent now and try to lie down."

Jahmeel stepped in his path and eyed him for a nerve-racking minute. Then, seeming to believe he had made his point, Jahmeel backed away, bowing and sweeping his hand in a sarcastic invitation to pass. Tahj moved by him, scrutinizing him warily, and scurried to his tent.

An hour later, when the sun had fully risen and begun its upward climb, Tahj left his tent, his encounter with Jahmeel leaving him so rattled he felt no more refreshed than when he had first opened his eyes in Bashea's tent. Tahj made his way over to the fire and was pleased to see Bashea there, dishing out some sort of hot mash from a pot on the fire to a group of men who were gathered, grumpily eating their breakfast, on logs around the central fire. Kamran sat, flanked by two older men nearly his age, on the largest of the logs. Jahmeel and Bagrat sat together, chewing in synchrony, and Radeem sat beside the two of them, looking like he wasn't fully awake yet, clutching a cup of some steaming liquid. The brothers looked at Tahj curiously as he approached, but he had eyes only for Bashea.

"Good morning, Bashea," he murmured, his lips involuntarily parting in a smile.

"Is it?" Bashea responded sweetly, but Tahj detected a slight edge. Tahj blinked, confused.

Bagrat and Jahmeel, who heard the exchange, sat up a little straighter, continuing to ladle the gruel into their faces, but paying closer attention to the pair in front of them. Radeem, too, lifted his head and followed the proceedings with interest.

Tahj glanced in their direction and lowered his voice, though it still carried to the threesome. "Did you sleep well?" he asked, boldly hinting at their secret, shared intimacy of the night before. Her eyes flew to his, and he could feel the heat they contained searing his skin.

"Did you?" she countered, her voice razor sharp.

Bagrat and Jahmeel's spoons clattered into their bowls simultaneously, and their eyes shifted to his. Tahj stood flabbergasted, jaw dropped open. He slid his eyes to them in desperation.

"What's going on?" Radeem whispered under his breath to the brothers. The pair shrugged. Tahj's eyes begged them for help, and they looked like they would have almost felt sorry for him if they were not so entertained by their sister's reaction to everything he said. They mouthed Tahj encouragement, telling him to not give up, to continue to prod Bashea and find out what was upsetting her. Tahj believed they were half fearing for him, half hoping for some sort of volcanic eruption.

Tahj cleared his throat, glancing at Bashea's back. She had turned away from him, flinging her spoon into the pot, which was suspended from a big, iron hook she now swung over the fire. Uncertain, Tahj looked back at his friends, who nodded and gestured in Bashea's direction. "Umm...did I...do something wrong?"

She spun back to him. "'Did I... did I...'" she repeated, the incredulity pitching her voice high. "No, Your Highness," she hissed icily. "You didn't..." Her voice cracked and she looked around, becoming aware they had an audience. Her face clearly displayed her struggle to rein in her emotions. "You didn't *do* anything wrong," she said more calmly, but when she looked back at Tahj, her eyes began to fill again. "You didn't *do* anything...at all," she finished just loud enough for Tahj to hear. She scanned the circle of men, all now staring at her, and then turned and marched off without another word. Tahj gulped, watching her leave, knowing he had done something to hurt her, but not understanding what it was.

Bagrat peered at Jahmeel and Radeem, who shrugged, and then he stood up with a sigh. He crossed to clasp a hand on Tahj's shoulder and said with forced joviality, "Did you know Bashea means 'lips of the gods?'"

Tahj didn't want anyone to see how upset he was by Bashea's reaction to him, so he faked a half laugh. "Are you sure you don't mean tongue of the devil?" All the men chuckled to themselves, each recalling a time when their spouses had been unhappy with them. But Tahj continued to watch Bashea's retreating figure until she lifted the flap on her tent and disappeared inside.

BASHEA SAT IN HER TENT stewing. She had never felt so utterly confused before. What was wrong with her? She was so angry she could hardly think straight, which wasn't helping matters. So Tahj had acted the gentleman last night. So he wasn't interested in her, so what? The last thing she'd ever wanted in life was a man. Who needed someone else to look after? Not her. She had her brothers and sisters and her dad...she didn't need a man, and she certainly didn't need Prince Tahj of Avistad.

To think, she'd actually cried over him. Actually shed tears. And then she got up and washed the tears from her face. She did not need anyone. Who did Tahj think he was, anyway, waltzing into her tent in the middle of the night and... what? Why had he come there in the first place? She was about to go over everything again, from the beginning, to try to make sense out of it, when Bibi stuck her head in the tent.

"Father wants to see you."

"See me?" Bashea asked in surprise.

Bibi nodded. "Right away."

Bashea hurried out of her tent. When she got to Kamran's, she found him pacing.

"Father, you called me?"

"Yes, yes. Bashea, have a seat." He gestured to a sitting area and pulled a chair up so close to her their knees were almost touching.

"Bashea, I'm just going to come right out and say it. I overheard your argument with Prince Tahj this morning."

Bashea blinked, her cheeks suddenly hot. "You heard..."

"And let me just say, I think it is fine if you like the Prince—"

"*Like* him?" she practically shrieked.

"Yes, but I have some advice for you—"

"Father, I do *not* like Prince Tahj."

"You don't?" For a minute, Kamran seemed genuinely confused, but then, reading his daughter's face, he seemed to understand.

"You seem to be under the illusion I need a man, Father," Bashea blustered, jumping up and pacing back and forth as she talked. "First, Ladarius, now Tahj—"

"Bashea, do you think loving this man makes you less strong?"

Was she really so easy to read? Exasperated, she collapsed into her chair again. "Loving...?"

"You are wrong. Loving someone makes you stronger, better, less selfish. Bashea...*azizam*," he said tenderly. He took a deep breath. "I was wrong to not let you see me cry when you were little. I know it terrified you when I was grieving for your mother." Bashea dropped her eyes, and Kamran lifted her chin. "But do you think I would give up one moment with her, even one moment, to have never felt that kind of pain?"

Bashea could tell it would do her no good to deny her feelings anymore; Kamran could see right into her heart.

"Oh, what should I do, Father?" she breathed.

"What? What's troubling you?"

It was enough he knew she liked Tahj; he didn't need to know all her insecurities, too. "It's just...I don't know..." But when she peered into her father's wise and kind eyes she had a change of heart and told him anyway. "I don't know how to act when he's around."

"Oh." Kamran chuckled. "Is that all?"

"Father, don't laugh at me!" Bashea barked, jumping up from her chair again.

Kamran stood and put a hand on Bashea's arm to keep her from running out. "No, no, daughter. I'm not laughing at you." He led her over to a loveseat where they could sit together. "It's just, I remember those times." Again he chuckled, reminiscing. "I wasn't sure if your mother liked me or not. After all, she was so pretty and I'm...well, I'm not exactly a looker."

"Father!" Bashea cried out, frowning at him.

Kamran raised a hand. "No, no, my girl, facts are facts. But your mother had a way of seeing right through all that, right into your heart. Did I ever tell you she had another suitor when I asked for her hand?"

Bashea shook her head. As her father spoke, she could see the years melt away from his face, and he became for her the young Kamran, helplessly in love with her mother.

"Yes. His name was Rostam." He said the name with such distaste Bashea nearly laughed. "And he was tall and fair and rich beyond your wildest dreams. But your mother knew I loved her with all my heart—still do, in fact—and she chose me." He clapped his hands on his knees with fresh satisfaction over the idea.

Bashea stood thoughtfully and went to the door of the tent, pulling it back a little and peeking outside. The new morning light warmed her face as she gazed off into the distance. "But," she said quietly, "I'm not even sure if he likes me."

"Bashea!" he scolded, coming over to stand next to her, looking down at her with a scowl. He again touched her face gently. "You are beautiful, both inside and out, and if he doesn't see that, he's a fool."

"Oh, Baba!" she interjected dismissively, her face coloring.

"I speak the truth," Kamran assured her, placing his hand over his heart. "But..." Kamran took her hand and led her over to the loveseat again. He sighed. "Bashea, I have raised you to be too independent. I leaned on you after your mother passed, and you had to grow up too fast. It is my fault." He held her hand without speaking for several seconds.

"Father, what are you saying?"

"Prince Tahj is a man used to getting his way. He orders soldiers and servants. He asks, and things are given to him."

Bashea thought this was not the Tahj she knew, but she listened anyway.

"You need to be more submissive," Kamran stated bluntly.

"Submissive?"

"Yes, submissive. You must bow to his will in all things if you wish to make him yours."

Bashea hung her head. She knew it was true. She spoke her mind without thought about whether she was contradicting Tahj or not. She lashed out at him in anger, letting her hurt feelings get the best of her. But could she learn to tame her tongue? Somehow, she doubted it. But she still had to try. If only it wasn't too late.

CHAPTER SIXTEEN

Tahj sat on the edge of his cot, thinking about everything he'd said and done with Bashea the night before. He had done this a lot lately, sitting and thinking about Bashea. What could have caused her to become so angry with him?

A few minutes later, when Bashea whipped open the front flap and strode into his tent, he looked up in surprise. It was unheard of for an unmarried woman to enter a man's tent, unless summoned there by him. Tahj was expecting another tongue lashing, but instead she hesitated.

"May I come in?" she asked awkwardly.

Tahj just stared. Wasn't she already in?

Tentatively she slid over to where he sat, never taking her eyes off him. To his surprise, when she got within a foot of him she knelt on the dirt floor. Tahj licked his lips, trying to think over the intolerable pounding of his heart. Before he could come up with an opening sentence, Bashea placed both hands on his thighs and began to rub them. Startled, Tahj flew to his feet, almost knocking her over.

"Wh-what are you doing?" he squeaked.

Bashea was taken aback. "M-making myself submit to you."

Tahj took a step back, pushing his bed with him. "Why?"

Bashea's face flashed red. She rose to her feet and began pacing.

"You know, Prince Tahj," she spat, "usually when a woman makes herself submissive to a master, he doesn't ask her why she is doing it."

"B-but you're not just any woman, Bashea," he stammered.

Bashea's brow furrowed. "What is that supposed to mean?" Before he could answer, she interjected, "Isn't that what you want?"

"No!" Tahj shouted emphatically.

Bashea's face fell. "I see," she murmured. "I'll just go, then."

She turned to flee, but Tahj grabbed her arm. "Bashea, no. Please, wait!" She stopped, but kept her face turned from him. His frustration got the better of him. "You are the most difficult woman I have ever known!" he lamented involuntarily. "I just don't understand you."

She whirled around, and Tahj could see there were tears in her eyes even as they flickered over his face. Unconsciously his hands slid down to hold hers loosely. Bashea found her voice. "That is strange, because sometimes I feel as if you are the only one who can."

Prince Tahj's eyes searched hers. "I want to," he murmured earnestly. "Please, can you just sit down and talk with me for a while?" he pleaded.

Bashea nodded with a sigh, dropping her gaze self-consciously as he led her over to his bed, where they sat down next to each other. An awkward silence settled over the tent while Tahj contemplated what he wanted to say.

"Can you tell me why you are so angry with me?"

Bashea bit her lip. "Do you not find me beautiful?" she finally blurted out.

"Of course I find you beautiful! What man wouldn't?" Tahj responded, flabbergasted by her question.

She seemed confused by this. "Then...you are simply not attracted to me then?"

"What?"

"You are not attracted to me," she repeated, mustering some resolve. "That is fine. I can understand—"

He jumped to his feet. "As if you didn't know I was insanely attracted to you, that my heart skips a beat whenever you are near—" Tahj's mouth froze. Had he really just said that?

Bashea stood as well, her eyes clouded with bewilderment. "Then why did you not touch me last night when you were in my bed?"

A light went on in Tahj's head. Now he understood. How could he have been so thickheaded? Bashea felt like he was rejecting her. He reached out and touched her hair, letting it slip through his fingers, a gesture filled with longing. "Bashea, I respect you. And..." He hesitated. "I know what those other men did." She shook her head adamantly as if trying to ward off the thought. "But I don't want to hurt you." His face was earnest, and then his voice became husky with emotion, though he spoke distinctly. "And I don't want you to think I am like them."

Bashea gazed up at him, searching his eyes. "Will you touch me now, Tahj?" she asked quietly. "I want you to touch me."

"Bashea," he murmured, his voice full of tenderness. He took a step forward and brushed a finger over her lips. She closed her eyes, her faced etched with pain, a single tear sliding down her face. He slid his arms around her and her eyes flickered open. *Good. I want her to see how much I love her.*

He slowly lowered his lips to hers. The kiss contained the suppressed longing of every minute they had spent together from the beginning. It started off sweet, but when he pulled her in closer he felt a strange sense of possessiveness overtake him. This was the woman for him, the one he had waited for, and he simply had to have her. He changed the angle on the kiss and his fingers clutched, wove themselves into her lush hair, claiming her.

Tahj hadn't meant to let the kiss get out of hand. He knew he had to control himself with Bashea, so as not to scare her, but the fragrance of her skin, the taste of her lips, the desire he saw in her fathomless, dark eyes just before he kissed her—all these worked together to scramble his thoughts, and all he could do was dive in deeper to try to find himself again. He felt Bashea melt against his body, and it was as if he could feel the anger and hurt seep away from her, absorbed into him, somehow, and then it just dissipated. Her mouth was unbelievably sweet and soft, and when a small moan escaped her it rang in him, fueling his want more.

Tahj felt an animal tear from a cage inside him, incensed and yearning to take, and to take, and to still take more, until it was satisfied, but even as he did he heard a small voice calling the beast back. Reason told him this wasn't the time or the place to give in to his desires. *Wait,* it told him, and with each heartbeat it got louder, *wait!* until it shouted down the animal which growled in him and, with effort, he drew back, still holding her arms.

"Wait!" he found himself shouting into her face.

"What?" she asked, looking confused.

"We can't!" Tahj released her arms and turned in a tight circle, pacing away from her with hands on his hips. He stopped a few feet away and then made the mistake of raising his eyes to hers. She was breathing rapidly, face flushed, lips full and moist. She looked so beautifully off-balance. And the animal leapt.

"Dammit!" He took two swift steps forward and grabbed her, tilting her head up to again ravage her mouth. This time Bashea gave as well as she took, her tongue dancing with his and causing a bright shaft of desire to spear to his loins. He felt her quiver and pulled her closer. She allowed her hands to slide up his back as her chest pressed against him.

She arched and he nibbled on her neck, reveling in the alluring fragrance of her hair and the taste of her milk-honeyed skin. "Tahj," she murmured feverishly. The sound of her voice caressing his name aroused him to new heights, and he thought he would never tire of this woman; the need for her would never run dry.

And then, with a sigh, he pulled away and laid his forehead on her shoulder. All that could be heard was their panting and the simultaneous pounding of their hearts. More composed, Tahj raised his head to look at her briefly before they slid into an embrace.

Clearly overwhelmed with emotions, Bashea laid her head on his chest, and Tahj rested his cheek on her hair, closing his eyes and treasuring her closeness at last.

After several seconds Bashea's voice came, muffled, from his chest. "I'm sorry I was being mean earlier."

He smiled. "I understand."

She pulled back and looked him in the eyes. "Why is that?"

He laughed, kissing her on the forehead. "I just do." He sighed, unwilling to let her go but knowing he must. "Now, you'd better get out of here before your brothers find out you're in here and hunt me down."

She smiled up at him teasingly. "What, are you afraid of them?"

"Are you kidding? They could pulverize me." He trapped her wrists behind her back and pulled her in again, hard. She giggled. "And I think they know I am in love with you. Bagrat's been giving me the evil eye since I showed up here." He released her hands but didn't step away.

In an uncharacteristic move, Bashea reached up and stroked his face tenderly. "I don't want to go."

"And I don't want you to go." He let his lips brush hers again and then sighed. "But you are an unmarried woman."

She closed her eyes. "I know. I know," she murmured, her voice a mere whisper. Appearing to draw on some inner strength, she pulled away a little, but still held his hands. "I'll see you later?"

"Yes," he responded confidently. "You'll see me later."

Bashea backed away, a wistful smile on her face, letting his hands drop. Without another word she turned and was gone.

THE REST OF THE DAY was agonizing. For see her he did. He saw her when she brought water to the fields, but they were not alone. He saw her at the noontide meal, but they were kept separate by the fact that her brothers seemed to be ever-present. And just as they were striding toward each other in camp with relieved smiles on their faces, glad to have finally found each other alone, Kamran strode out of his tent in between them and their faces fell. How infuriating to have finally spoken of their feelings for each other only to never get a chance to be together again.

Dinner was no better. Radeem had decided to leave in the morning and return to his home, and he demanded all of Tahj's attention as he planned his cross-dessert journey to Vadeed, anxious now to return to his wife and family.

"So, if I stick to the foothills here," Radeem repeated, gesturing with a stick to the crude map they'd scratched into the ground, "I should be able to avoid the most paralyzing heat and reach Vadeed in... about four days, correct?" The pair sat on a log by the fire.

"Hmmm?" Tahj answered absently, searching again for Bashea in the dimming light.

Radeem poked him in the foot with the end of his stick.

"Aow!"

"What's the matter with you? I've had to repeat myself, like, four times. I might as well have left already for all the attention you're paying me."

"I'm sorry, my friend." Tahj turned to face him squarely. "Now, what was it you were saying?"

"Ugh!" Radeem cried in frustration, jumping to his feet. He jabbed his stick at his makeshift map, dragging the end through the dirt to obliterate it. "What's the use? I got it figured out without you."

"I'm sorry," Tahj said sincerely, also rising. "I'm just...distracted." Bashea came into view behind his friend, and again Tahj's eyes strayed to her. "... a bit."

"I can see that," Radeem retorted peevishly. "Just what is it that's got your mind so occupied, anyway?" When Tahj didn't answer right away, Radeem followed his line of vision. "Oh! It's Bashea, isn't it?" Noting the startled look on his friend's face, he continued. "So, what was with that little tiff you guys had earlier? She seemed really angry."

"Nothing, nothing...who...Bashea?" he added innocently. "We just...we always fight."

"Yes. I noticed. You've got feelings for each other, don't you?"

"What? No!" Tahj responded adamantly, but noting the frown on Radeem's face he decided to come clean. "Perhaps we do..."

"I knew it! I knew it," Radeem boasted.

Tahj pushed him out of the firelight, slapping a hand over his mouth. "Be quiet, you idiot," he hissed. "Do you want Bagrat and Jahmeel to hear you?" He glanced over to where the brothers were adding wood to the fire.

"What? What's the big deal?" Radeem responded in a whisper when Tahj finally removed his hand. "Don't they approve of Bashea having a relationship with a crowned prince?"

"I'm not a crowned prince," Tahj reminded him. He glanced in the pair's direction and thought about Bagrat's visit to his tent earlier. He almost seemed to be granting Tahj permission to pursue Bashea, but... One look at the duo's frowning faces had him changing his mind. "And, no. They do not approve. I don't think they would approve of anyone courting Bashea."

"Courting?" Radeem said in surprise, loud enough to earn him a smack in the arm. "Courting," he whispered loudly. "It's courting now, is it?"

"Be quiet!" Tahj shouted, drawing more attention to their discussion than Radeem had. He grabbed his captain by the sides of his shirt and dragged him farther out of the firelight. "If you don't stop now, I swear I'll kill you in your sleep," he hissed, dropping his voice belatedly.

"What's going on?" Bagrat asked as he ambled over from the other side of the fire. Tahj lowered his head, but Radeem spoke up.

"You owe me twenty Abbas."

"What?" Bagrat's head swiveled from Radeem to Tahj. "Have you been after my sister?" he growled.

"No! No!" Tahj answered hurriedly. But then he turned his back to the big man and took a few steps away from him. After a beat he shook his head and whirled around. "All right, yes!" He stepped forward defiantly. "Yes. I'm 'after' your sister, as you so tactfully put it."

To his surprise, Bagrat smiled and began to chuckle, clapping him on the shoulder. "The god's blessings then, my brother."

"Th-thank you," Tahj responded in surprise.

"You'll need it," Bagrat added, shaking Tahj's hand with his free one, his eyebrows raised and his eyes twinkling. "Jahmeel! Come here! The young prince wishes to court our sister, Bashea."

"No joking?" Bagrat's brother answered sarcastically, showing no surprise at all. "It is about time."

"You knew?" Tahj asked in shock.

Several men grunted and snorted in response as they sat around the fire, not even glancing up from their dinners. Bagrat and Jahmeel guffawed over Tahj's reaction, bending over to slap each other on the back. With a scowl, Tahj turned and tramped away to the sound of Jahmeel trying to get his wheezing laugh under control and Bagrat counting out coins into Radeem's open palm.

THE DAYS PASSED IN a torturous haze for Tahj and Bashea. Time together had to be stolen at odd moments, but, in spite of their overall frustration, they treasured those moments together. With a look, they'd know just when to sneak away from the others and meet up above the upper meadow, or in the woods. They would talk quietly about their pasts, about growing up in a palace, practically alone, and growing up in a tent with people breathing down your back night and day.

Never before had Bashea felt that smothering closeness so drastically. She wished only to spend her time with Tahj, to be in his arms forever, but they were constantly battling just to be alone. While Bagrat and Jahmeel approved of the relationship, there were certain proprieties to be considered. To be found, even kissing, while unwed, would be scandalous indeed.

But it wasn't just this that weighed on her. Lately she had become increasingly aware what they shared together was just a fantasy. As Tahj moved from discussing their pasts to discussing a future together, she'd become more and more uncomfortable with their present. She loved Tahj with her whole heart, but she could not imagine him a sheepherder all his life. Though he said he was content, Bashea still had a nagging feeling she would be robbing him of something if she were to consent to become married to him.

It was just this she was thinking of, while collecting kindling in the woods, when she heard Tahj's strained whisper.

"Bashea!"

Unbidden, her heart leapt. "Here, Tahj!" She dropped her kindling when she saw a sweep of his robes between the trees and ran to him. He caught her in his arms, and immediately their lips met, creating a blinding heat, which was a constant when they touched.

"Umm..." he moaned when they parted briefly. He buried his face in her hair. "I never thought I'd be able to get my hands on you."

"I know." She sighed, heady with his scent and the warmth of his hands on her sides.

"Lie down with me," Tahj said, tossing sticks aside to make a nest for them among the cypress needles on the floor of the forest.

The fragrance of the needles was said to soothe anger and frustration, but it only reminded Bashea of the time they'd spent together, curled up beneath the trees, and made her want Tahj more. When she was stretched out beside him, Tahj sat up on one elbow, turned toward her, and trailed his hand slowly down her side, enticing them both.

"Bashea," he whispered, lowering his mouth to hers. "I love you!" He kissed her neck, and she murmured something unintelligible in response. He shifted so his body was on top of hers, pressing her into the soft earth. "I want to be with you." His breath was warm, his words edged with an intense need as he whispered, his lips brushing her ear. "I *need* to be with you."

"I know!" she cried, even as her body bowed in response to his.

His mouth covered hers, drowning any further words as his kisses became more frantic. They had only minutes together, and it was just enough time to drive them mad.

"Let me ask your father for your hand, *please*, Bashea. Do it for me. You know I love you."

Through the fog of her own passion, Bashea heard him, and, as the words sank in, she shoved him to the side and sat up so abruptly her head spun. "No! Tahj! You know how I feel about this. Do we have to go through this all again?"

Tahj sat up, too, pulling his knees up so he was sitting flatfooted. "Uuh!" he growled. "You are being so unreasonable!" He turned toward her. "Why can't you see *this* is what I need? This! Here... with you. I don't need anything else."

"You say that now, Tahj," she retorted, scrambling to her feet. "But someday you will regret it."

Angered, he came to his feet as well. "So you know my heart now. You think you can choose what is right for me?"

"Yes!" she spat back. "Yes. Because my head is not clouded by...by..." She waved her hands, frustrated the words were not coming to her. She knew that, as a man, Tahj was blinded by lust. He wished to have her body, but it was too high a price for him to pay.

"My head is not clouded, Bashea," he threw back. "I can see clearly what I want." He reached for her again, desperate to make her understand, but it was the wrong move. He didn't know he was only reaffirming her own conclusion that what he desired most was to have her in bed.

"No!" she shrieked, moving away from him. She turned and braced herself against a tree trunk with one outstretched hand, shaking her head. They had argued the point over and over again. She had hoped he would come to understand, but now she saw that he would never change his mind. He would stay here with her until he grew to resent everything he had missed out on, and then he would hate her. A prince didn't marry a sheepherder. And suddenly she knew what she must do. Her whole body had gone cold and quivery. Her hands trembled against the bark as she drew in a shaky breath, steadying herself. She turned back and her face was set "This cannot go on."

"Wh-what are you saying?"

She wrapped one arm around her stomach, where it felt as if a huge hole had ripped open, a coldness rushing inside to stagger her. "You have to leave. You have to go back to your people."

"What are you saying?" he repeated more forcefully. "I have no people. My place is here, with you and your family."

"No. You are wrong, Tahj. You don't belong here."

"You don't mean that."

She retreated. "But I do."

He straightened, his jaw clenched. "Bashea, don't do this!"

I already have! her head screamed. *Can't you see the hole?* Drawing upon her last ounce of inner strength, she made her voice even. "You need to leave here before the fortnight is over, or sooner." She forced herself to turn and bend to pick up sticks.

He stared at her as she performed the everyday task. "You're throwing me out?" When she didn't answer he took a step forward. "You don't mean that."

She hesitated, squeezing her eyes shut for a few seconds before turning back to him. "If you don't leave, I'll have Bagrat and Jahmeel escort you." She knew it was a low blow.

He stared at her in shock for several seconds, and then, without another word, stormed off.

Bashea stood stone still for a full ten seconds before she began to shake uncontrollably. With a sob that tore through her throat, she collapsed to the ground, bent in half, rocking back and forth as she cried. It would kill her, but she had to do it. It was what was best for him, whether he could see it or not.

THE NEXT SEVERAL DAYS, Tahj did so much thinking his brain hurt, but it was like he was stuck in some eternal loop; every thought circled around to where it had begun. He needed to prove to Bashea they belonged together, but how?

And to top it off, Bashea looked as miserable as he felt. Her smiles, as she talked to her fellow tribesmen and women, were feeble and lifeless, her eyes shadowed. She seemed to do everything she could to avoid him, instead sticking close to Bagrat and Jahmeel.

Until the night they arose and approached Tahj, who stood, staring into the fire wordlessly. Hearing their lumbering footsteps, Tahj looked up. Bashea appeared to be watching nervously from across the ring.

When he reached Tahj, Bagrat opened without any of the usual preliminary pleasantries, asking bluntly, "Did you and Bashea have a fight?"

"What do you mean?" Jahmeel jumped in. "They're always fighting."

"Not like this, you fool!" Bagrat growled. "I mean, just look at her." All three turned to peer at Bashea, who looked away, lowering her head. "She hasn't got any fight left in her," he finished sadly. He looked accusatorily at Tahj and then stepped up so only a sheepskin's worth of space lay between them. "I told you once not to hurt her."

"I didn't! I swear!" Tahj shot back. "At least I don't think I did." He sat back down on his log despondently.

Jahmeel and Bagrat exchanged a glance. A woman carrying a tray passed them, and they stole a jug from her and sat down with a sigh, bookending Tahj on the log. Bagrat pulled the cork out of the bottle with his teeth, spat it on the ground, and handed Tahj the bottle, putting an arm around his shoulder. "What happened?" he said with empathy.

Tahj took a long swig. "I told her I wanted to ask for her hand."

"That doesn't sound bad," Jahmeel uttered, his brow furrowed. He gestured for the bottle.

Bagrat sat thoughtfully, scratched his head as if contemplating so hard made him itchy, and then reached for the bottle, concluding, "No. That sounds right." He took a pull, and then handed it back to Tahj, encouraging him with a motion to drink up.

Tahj obeyed. "That's what I thought." He frowned, staring into the fire. "She's got it into that pretty little head of hers that, because I'm a prince, or something, marrying her would be wrong."

Bagrat grunted, nodding, as if agreeing this was wise, and took back the bottle to chug a bit. "Well," he said with a sigh, "when Bashea gets something into her head—"

"She's like a cougar with a cub," Jahmeel finished, taking the bottle from his brother and raising it to his lips again. All three glanced up at Bashea, who was talking closely to Bibi and watching them. They nodded, making sounds of assent.

The trio continued to drink glumly. "I wonder what she's saying," Tahj said, his voice wistful.

Bagrat nudged Jahmeel, who fell off the end of the log into the dirt. "Go over there and find out what they're saying. But, ssh." He put a finger to his lips and hissed loudly, swaying a bit. "Don't let them know."

Jahmeel's head bobbed in a sloppy nod, and he began to stagger toward his sisters, listing here and there and teetering a little too near the flames, but then righting himself, much to his cohorts' amusement. Bagrat nodded his satisfaction when Jahmeel sat down on the log next to Bashea, practically in another woman's lap, who slapped at him and scooted over to save herself from being squished. Jahmeel, none too subtly, pretended to be busy adjusting his sandal straps, but looked up to give Bagrat and Tahj a loose smile and a wink to tell them he was on the job.

"Idiot!" Bagrat said into the bottle, waving at him with a giggle and returning to his former conversation with Tahj as they discussed various ways to win Bashea over to their side, for it was their side now—Bagrat and Jahmeel were firmly on board. "Perhaps if I say something..." Bagrat suggested.

Tahj's felt a glimmer of hope.

"Nah." Bagrat waved his hand. "She'd only dig her heels in deeper."

"We don't want that," Tahj concluded logically.

"No, my friend." Bagrat handed Tahj the bottle and he drained it, shaking it upside down, confused to find it empty, and then holding it up to try to look inside for any spare drop. Bagrat blinked his eyes, focused in on another bottle that was passing by on a tray, and reached out to clumsily grab at it, getting it on the third try.

Tahj looked up and discovered that the woman bearing the tray was Bibi. She pushed the bottle into her brother's hand with a look of disgust and then appeared to be hunting for something on the ground, picking up discarded cups and litter as she went.

"I just don't know why she doesn't believe I could be happy here with her. Do I seem unhappy to you?" Tahj asked indignantly.

"No!" Bagrat answered, adamant. "You're the happiest damn man in all the world!"

"I agree," Tahj commented, leaning heavily on the bigger man's shoulder.

Bagrat looked up to check on Jahmeel, who seemed to have fallen asleep, and then glanced over at Bibi. He looked across the fire again. Bashea seemed to avoid eye contact. With a quick, if not accurate, grab, Bagrat caught Bibi's wrist as she bent to pick up a cup. "Ay!" he cried loudly, as if something had just dawned on him. "Bashea sent you over here to spy on us."

"You're crazy," Bibi answered petulantly, slapping at his hand.

"I am not...well, maybe I am, but I'm not wrong about this. You're s-spying on us. That's-s a dirty trick!" he slurred.

Bibi freed herself but had to reach out quickly to push Bagrat back upright before he fell off of the log altogether. "Oh, and you didn't send Jahmeel over there to do the same?"

"I didn't!" Bagrat insisted, sounding offended by the idea. "Did I, Prince Tahj?"

"Hmm...oh, no. Never!" Tahj responded belatedly. "He's too good a man to do that." Tahj swung a hand over his friend's shoulder, nearly connecting with Bibi's face.

"Ugh!" Bibi said with disdain, letting go of Bagrat so the two of them fell forward into the dirt. "You're a pair! I'd expect as much from you Bagrat, but you, Prince Tahj?" She tutted and trudged off.

Tahj pushed himself up from the ground. "I need to talk to her."

"Who? Bibi?"

"No! Bashea." He dusted himself off and strode purposefully forward.

"Oh!" Bagrat responded, finally seeming to understand.

Bashea caught sight of Tahj and scurried away, giving one last hurried look over her shoulder before ducking inside her tent. Tahj stood at the edge of the firelight with his hands on his hips, stymied. Bagrat clapped him on the shoulder, kicking Jahmeel awake at the same time.

"I've got to talk to her," Tahj repeated.

Bagrat spun Tahj around. "I'm going to give you some advice, my friend. And, drunk as I am, I think it's pretty good advice." He chuckled, but then straightened, trying to appear serious. "Sober up before you talk to her."

WHEN TAHJ ENTERED BASHEA's tent unannounced, she spun at the sound of the tent flapping open. He felt the familiar squeeze in his chest with the accompanying race of his pulse; a feeling she never failed to give him. It was apparent she had been expecting no one and was just getting ready to climb into bed. He gazed on her form, always enchanting in the lantern light, in its gauzy, white choli top and a long, billowing white skirt that reached the ground, leaving her midriff bare. Her hair, which was still elaborately done up from dinner, had an equally filmy, white ribbon wound through it, set off by her dark tresses, reminding him of the creek at night, silvered by the moon.

"Tahj." She took a few stumbling steps backwards and grabbed at the post at the end of her bed, as if steeling herself. "You're drunk."

He shook his head vigorously, droplets of water flying from him. "No. I laid down in the creek." He smiled stupidly. "Believe me, mountain water will sober you up in a heartbeat."

She ignored him. "So you're drunk and wet."

"Bashea..." he pleaded. He was moved by the tears he saw in her eyes and by the way her chin had quivered when she first breathed his name. He took a step forward, and she threw a hand up in front of her to stop his progress. "I've nothing left to say, Tahj. You need to leave." She was trying to appear strong, but her arm shook. She turned away from him.

"But damn it, Bashea, I have more I want to say to you, and you're going to listen." He took two swift strides, grabbing her arms and turning her to face him.

"Don't, Tahj, please." Her voice trembled and became weaker. "You have to leave. Can't you see?"

Why was she doing this to them? He reached for anything, and the lie came to him. And being a desperate man, he used it. "I've come to say goodbye, then. Surely you won't deny me that." If it was goodbye she wanted, then goodbye he would give her. But in his heart, he was hoping that once she saw how much he loved her, if, maybe, his actions could persuade better than the words he'd given her, she would finally understand that they were meant to be together. She blinked away her tears, appearing stunned he was giving in. "You won't deny me that, will you, Bashea?" He shook her slightly, his emotions raw. He could not leave her; it would break his heart.

"No...no," she whispered.

"Good." He bent to take her lips, clumsily at first, as he tasted the lie, but then he pushed it back and vowed only to show her the love he felt for her. He pulled away to watch her face, etched with the pleasure he aroused and the pain of being eager for even more of him.

Once he tasted her, he could only want more. Tahj pushed her back against the bed, recklessly fumbling with her hair and pulling it all down around her bare shoulders, black against bronze. "Yes, that is how it should be," he murmured, more to himself than to her. He reached up and gently tugged on the ribbon still loosely laced through her thick hair and then set it on the crate by her bed. His hands touched the skin along her sides, as soft as a buttercup's petals, and ventured to her back where he found the bottom tie of her top.

He knew it was wrong to be here, to be doing this with an unmarried woman, but if the woman wouldn't marry you, what were you to do? He watched her eyes grow wide with surprise and then soft with acceptance. She reached up herself and untied the top, pulling it off over her head.

He wondered if he should say something. He wondered if he *could* say something. But how could words capture the way he was feeling? Not just the passion tingling in his veins, threatening to set him on fire, but the way his heart was filled with her, how moved he was she would lay herself bare for him, physically and emotionally, share herself with an intimacy which could allow for no turning back, no deception. He wanted to thank her for this, but the words just didn't seem right. His lips, unable to form words, sought her heart in other ways; they cruised over her jaw, nibbled as she clung to him, then rose to meet hers.

Bashea knew at once his intentions, even as she knew her own. She let the kiss swirl slowly down inside her, making her weak. She felt his arms pull her in more tightly, possessive, and her heart leapt. But then he changed angles on the kiss, and the heat whipped into her like hell-fire, slicing and burning down to her core. She trembled with the strength of the emotions he was eliciting and with her desire for him to take her farther.

This is what she'd wanted all along, she knew now; she wanted simply to belong to him. She wanted him to hold her and make her feel safe and valued. But she knew it could not be. So she simply allowed herself to be swept along by the kiss and decided it was okay, this was better, she would allow him his one night of passion. She knew that others would think what she was doing was wrong, but if she was going to let him go forever, she needed to have this. She reached up to rake her hands through his dark hair, intent on remembering the way it felt as it slid through her fingers, the smell of his skin, the taste of his breath, the feel of his long, hard body pressed against hers. She knew she would never have another in this lifetime, for her heart truly belonged to Tahj and Tahj alone.

This was to be their one time together, and she would not be ashamed of it or regret it. Rather, she would treasure it, let each touch leave a permanent imprint on her heart. If she had to let him go, she would at least have this. His fingertips cruised across her stomach to the base of her breasts and lingered there, letting her fill his hands with her curves. He brushed his thumbs across her nipples, and she let out a purr of pleasure.

His face showed surprise when her hands found his shirt at the waist and yanked impatiently. Within seconds, his shirt lay on the floor, along with their other clothing. As if tied with a string, their hands rose from their sides and met, fingers entwined like fairytale ivy.

They stood about a foot apart, and Tahj let his eyes wander.

"You are so beautiful. So beautiful."

He stroked the side of her face softly. She turned and pulled the covers down on her bed, sliding beneath the layers of silk and holding it open as she had one other time, inviting him to share her bed. This time he seemed to know what to do, what she wanted, and he gave to her of that full heart, melding their bodies together, slowly, sensually, letting his lips traverse her body, forcing soft, moaning urgency from her lips.

Bashea arched and let him take her higher. She had never imagined it could be like this. She forced herself not to think of this as the last time, but as the only time, the best time, the moments she would cling to forever in the still of the dark. Despite this, she found the way he touched her, looked at her, whispered her name, and made vows of his love without words so beautiful that tears squeezed from her eyes, and she fought back sobs of joy, and gratitude, and ecstasy.

When they finally lay in each other's arms, complete, Tahj stroked her hair, and Bashea feathered a kiss along his throat. In the dark he smiled, and dozed off. She knew he believed they were now one. In the dark, she lay awake, trying to quiet her breathing. Bashea choked back the sharp edges of her weeping even as she basked in the warmth of his closeness, not wanting to wake him or ruin a single minute of their last hours.

She watched the sunrise paint across the inside surface of the tent, the glowing rays a picture on canvas. Finally, with one large sigh, she drifted off to sleep.

BIBI THREW THE TENT flap wide. Bright daylight illuminated Bashea and Tahj as they lay in each other's arms. Bashea's hair was splayed across Tahj's chest, his face turned toward her, his lips still touching the top of her head, their fingers threaded together on the pillow near his head. They began to stir. Bashea lifted her head, her eyes blinking. She saw Bibi hesitate in the doorway, then step inside, letting the flap close.

With a loud intake of breath, Bashea flew up, clutching the covers to her breast. Tahj also opened his eyes.

"It's Father," Bibi whispered urgently. "You had better come quickly." Bibi glanced at Tahj and then lowered her eyes. "I will wait outside."

Without a word, Bashea got up and began to dress.

Tahj, too, rose and began to search for his clothing, cursing himself for not rising before dawn, like he always did, and risking Bashea's reputation. But, in reflecting, he had seen no condemnation in Bibi's eyes, no anger...perhaps, even, sympathy. Hearing the flutter of the tent flap Tahj looked up, and found he was alone.

BASHEA AND BIBI WALKED together without speaking at first. They nodded politely as people passed by, but once they were alone, Bashea couldn't take the silence anymore.

"Please. Let me explain."

"There's no need to explain," Bibi insisted.

"Yes. Yes, there is."

Bibi glanced over at her sister for the first time. "I do not judge you."

"Well, you should. You should be shocked."

Bibi tilted her head. "I was shocked. But to tell you the truth, I felt a strange surge of love for you both."

Bashea simply stared. "What?"

"I am happy for you, Bashea. And proud of you, in a way, for being brave enough to love again after all you have been through."

Bashea was flustered. "I don't know how to respond to that."

"You know, you never speak about that night, but on a clear evening I can hear your screams, when you dream—"

"Let's not talk about that," Bashea interrupted. "What is wrong with Father?"

They had reached Kamran's tent, and Bibi pulled back the flap so Bashea could enter. "See for yourself."

TAHJ FLEW IN THE DOOR behind Bashea, out of breath, his shirt left untied. He glanced around at all the faces that had turned his way, and then his eyes fell on Bashea. She had fallen to her knees beside her father's bed, which was laid directly on the carpeting that covered most of the tent. He could not see her face, as she was hunched over her father's bed, but he could see her clutching Kamran's nearest hand desperately.

"Father! What's wrong?"

"It's nothing. Nothing, my girl," her father responded dismissively, though the edges were tight around his smile. "Just this old heart of mine." He tried to chuckle, but it brought on a bout of coughing. Bano, who knelt on Kamran's other side, raised a ladle of water, but the old man batted it irritably out of the way. "Tahj. Tahj," he called, his voice strained.

Again Tahj looked at the faces gathered, as if asking permission, and when Bagrat nodded, he squatted down by Bashea. The second his gaze touched Kamran's face Tahj knew something was terribly wrong. He was alarmed by the pallor of the older man's skin. "Yes, Father."

"Tahj...you love my Bashea?"

The question startled the prince, especially after having just rolled out of the bed they'd made love in.

"Father, this is unimportant..." Bashea began in an effort to deflect the question.

Tahj caught Bagrat and Jahmeel's eyes. "Yes, I love her with my whole heart," Tahj answered firmly. Bashea's head bowed.

Kamran grasped Tahj arm with his free hand. "And you will take good care of her," he reinforced, though his speech was now halting.

"Father..."

"Bashea!" Kamran barked, surprising everyone. Bashea dropped her head to her chest and began to cry onto her father's hand, which she still clasped tightly. Kamran softened his tone, his voice gravelly. "I am tired, Azizam, so tired. Forgive me." Bashea looked up at him then and nodded, the tears falling freely down her face.

Kamran's eyes shifted slowly to Tahj. "Take good care of her. Make her your wife. She is a good woman."

"Oh, Baba!" Bashea cried.

Kamran continued as if uninterrupted. "She is a bit headstrong," he added with an attempt at a smile, "but her heart...her heart is good as gold."

"I know this, Father," Tahj said gently, laying a hand on Bashea's arm.

Kamran suddenly clutched at the cloth of his tunic over his chest, bunching it in his fist and making a struggling gurgle in his throat. The brothers and sisters exchanged panicked glances. But after a few seconds, the pain seemed to have passed. The head of the family lay panting, trying to regain his strength. He gestured for Tahj to come closer, and the prince leaned in. "You must promise me now. Promise me you will take Bashea as your own and care for her all the days of your life."

Bashea shook her head, her tears flying everywhere.

"I will," Tahj responded solemnly.

"She is my dearest one," Kamran whispered, closing his eyes. He raised his voice one last time over Bano and Bibi's sniffling. "Now, everyone out. An old man gets tired. Out!"

The brothers looked at each other and then sheepishly shuffled out. Bashea nodded to Bano and Bibi, and they followed. Tenderly, Bashea brushed Kamran's hair back from his forehead. "Do you need anything more, Baba?"

He didn't bother to open his eyes. "No, my child."

Tahj helped Bashea as she staggered to her feet and left the tent. No one had gone much beyond the entrance to the tent, and they were gathered in a semi-circle, comforting each other. All eyes fell on the couple as they stepped out into the sunlight.

Bagrat immediately stepped forward and grasped both of Bashea's hands in his own big ones. "It's bad, isn't it?"

Bashea gazed off in the distance, tears brimming in her eyes. She took a breath, seeming to gather herself, and looked at her brother for several seconds. She nodded her head.

Bagrat spun away from her and walked off a few steps. Everyone watched him. He turned back with a sigh, wiping a hand across his tired face. "It's obvious that having all of us there is too much for him," he said, taking charge for the first time in his life. "We will take turns caring for him. I'm first." When a few mouths opened to object he thundered, much like Kamran had minutes earlier, "I'm the oldest. I'm first." He ducked inside the tent, and the rest stood lifelessly.

Bashea turned to the sister beside her and took Bano's chin in her hand gently. "You look tired."

"I had nightmares last night. Maybe a premonition."

She nodded at Bibi. "You two, get some sleep." Seeming to anticipate their protest she added, "We'll come get you if anything changes."

"We'll stay close," Jahmeel's wife stated, moving with Jahmeel toward the fire circle. The rest dispersed, already being approached by others who wished to comfort or find out more about what had happened.

BASHEA TOOK A COUPLE of slow steps around the side of Kamran's tent, harrying a loose thread on her garment. Tahj followed, his arm still around her shoulder. When she stopped, he came around in front and took her hands loosely in his. Bashea looked up, gazing into his eyes, her eyes darting from one to the other.

"You are not held to that vow."

"What do you mean?" Tahj responded, his voice sounding shaken.

She looked away, blinking back tears. "Vows such as that...the obligation..."

"It is a vow I took freely. A vow I had already taken the night before."

"Tahj!" Bashea cried in desperation. "You don't understand what you're saying—"

He cut her off angrily. "Was I the only one who took that vow last night, Bashea?"

She swallowed. She felt like her own heart was squeezing in her chest, much as she was sure her father's was. "No, Tahj." Her voice was raspy and fragile. "I took a vow with you, too." She brought a hand up to touch his face tenderly. "I will never love another man. I pledged myself to you and you only. But that still doesn't change the fact that you are a Prince of Avistad and I am a sheepherder's daughter."

"So what? We're just supposed to love each other and go our separate ways?"

She tore at her shawl. "You'll find someone new," she murmured, looking down.

Tahj took her arm roughly, obviously too angry to care if he was hurting her or not. "There is no one else for me, Bashea. Why can't you understand?"

She didn't raise her head to look at him.

He released her and paced off, coming back to stand in front of her. "And what if the roles were reversed? You were the princess and I the shepherd. Would you love me less?"

"No."

"If you had taken me to bed as a princess, would the love we made be any less real?"

Bashea thought about it. "I would not make a vow where one could not be made."

"What's that supposed to mean?"

Bashea lifted her head, and her eyes flashed with pain and anger. "I would not take you as my husband knowing you would be unhappy at my palace."

He took her arms again, bending to hold her eyes. "Is that what this is about? You're afraid of life at the palace? But I told you I wish to stay here with you—"

Bashea exploded, shaking her arms free. "Can't you get it? Are you just too thickheaded to understand?" Her voice became a dangerous hiss. "This," she gestured between them, "cannot happen."

"'This—" He, too, gestured wildly. "—*did* happen!" he shouted back, apparently not caring who was hearing their conversation now.

She lowered her head and was silent for several seconds. "It was a mistake," she said distinctly. "I was weak. And I wanted to have you." She looked him straight in the eye. "But it was a mistake. I have to attend to my father."

Tahj looked like he'd been kicked by a camel, but she couldn't let that stop her. Taking one glance over her shoulder as she walked away, Bashea saw him standing in the same place, staring at the ground. He couldn't even react when she walked away.

BAGRAT ENTERED TAHJ's tent to find him in the same position he had the last time, sitting on his cot, playing with his ring. Only the scene was vaguely different.

"You're packed?"

Tahj stood. "I'm leaving."

"What? Why? You promised my father—"

"And I intend to keep that promise," Tahj asserted, stepping up. "But your sister is a stubborn woman."

A twinkle found its way back into Bagrat's eyes. "I never tried to hide that fact from you."

Tahj turned and trod back to his bed, walking in a slow, wide circle as he talked. "And I've also been thinking about another promise I made." He stopped briefly to look Bagrat in the eye. "A promise I made to my mother, as I held her, dying, in my arms." He took up his circuitous route again. "I promised her I would return to avenge my father's death and reclaim the throne."

Bagrat nodded, suddenly serious. He stepped forward. "I will come with you, my brother."

Tahj clasped the big man's hand and put his other hand on his shoulder. "I appreciate the sentiment, Bagrat, I do. But your place is here now, while your father is sick."

Bagrat nodded, but seemed sad. "I will miss you."

Tahj was touched more than he would let on. "And I you, friend."

"What about Bashea?" he asked, suddenly alarmed. "She will be beside herself."

Tahj looked down for a second, wiping at something in the dirt with his foot. When he looked up, he was grimacing. "Actually, she ordered me to leave."

"She...*ordered*...you?"

"Yes. It's a long story, and I can't say I even understand it much, but I think I know a way to fix it."

Tahj left without saying goodbye. He was sorry for it, but he didn't feel like his resolve would hold if he were face-to-face with the woman he loved.

BASHEA'S HEARTBREAK over Tahj's leaving was soon coupled with the heartbreak of her father's death. Looking back on that time, she often wondered how she would have pulled through it if it hadn't been for her little secret.

The night was cold, and Bashea couldn't sleep. She wrapped a shawl around herself and headed out of her tent. The sting of the wind had her pushing her shawl up around her wild hair as she walked, feeling sad and lonely. Her father had been buried months ago, but she still found herself turning during a story around the campfire with a laugh to ask for his comment, and finding the laugh dying on her lips.

And the hole in her life, which could only be filled with Tahj, became wider with each passing day, her longing a physical craving which left her edgy and irritable by day, sorrowful and sleepless by night. She trudged across the encampment, her head bent to the wind.

Shortly after her father's death, they broke camp and came down from the mountainside to their lower camp, the colder weather in the mountains forcing the move.

Bashea had been glad to go—there were too many memories. But then she found, like their tents, the memories moved with them.

The cold air bore into Bashea and bit at her skin. She shook her head, wondering why, like most normal people, she wasn't snuggled in her bed right now. Arriving at the edge of the encampment and the well that marked it, she reached out for the cold stone as a sudden blast of wind almost knocked her off-balance. Using her hand for support, she skated around to the far side of the well and leaned against it, facing the desert. With a sigh, she felt the ring that squeezed her heart loosened a fraction. How strange she would now seek comfort in the very spot where she had been abducted and dragged away from her family.

But here, at least, she felt closer to Tahj. Bashea knew it was stupid—a hundred paces closer, at best—but somehow she felt connected to Tahj here. For he was out there, somewhere, and so she was drawn to this spot night after night. She didn't even realize she had been crying when she felt her cheeks were wet. She pulled her shawl down to her shoulders and let the wind whip through her hair, closing her eyes and imagining him there.

Bagrat had let slip, mere days after Tahj's departure, the prince's intentions of retaking the castle, and how it all had something to do with proving his love for her. Since that time Bashea had been wracked with guilt and worry. What if Tahj were to lose his life in an attempt to win her over? Could she bear that? And how would she know? It wasn't like they had daily visitors from Avistad who could update them on conditions there. Those visitors who did stumble into their camp were grilled by Bashea. Had they heard of any uprisings? Met a man of Tahj's general description? Did they know any-thing that would settle her heart?

"Oh, Tahj!" she said out loud, rubbing a hand over her stomach without thinking. "What if I was wrong to have sent you away?"

That was the one thought that haunted her without ceasing.

TAHJ PACED OUTSIDE his tent like a caged jackal. Sleep had evaded him again. He was just no good at waiting. It seemed like such a damned waste of time. He had spent five long months recruit-ing soldiers and was now back in Radeem's hometown of Vadeed, where he'd started, on his way out to another town in search of those sympathetic to his cause. He was forced to be cautious, not know-ing where Boltar's strongholds were, but was pleased to have found a number of leaders who swore to back him. The fact Boltar was squeezing extremely high tributes out of these cities made it easier. Not to mention he was...personality-challenged.

But it wasn't Boltar he was thinking about now. The fact was, he was missing Bashea horribly. It didn't help that any number of leaders offered him slave women whose beauty rivaled the gods, since none of them, in his mind, came close to what Bashea offered. By Asman, he'd even found one in his room tonight. Completely naked, in his bed, and now all he could think about was the day he found Bashea trussed up on the floor, beaten and full of fight. He laughed now, to think of it. That should have been his first clue she was impossi-ble, and impossible to live without. Besides, he felt sorry for the slave women. They had as little choice in this as Boltar and his men had given Bashea on the night she was abducted.

With a sigh he ceased pacing, putting his hands on his hips and looking up at the stars. He was already weary of this battle, and he hadn't even drawn a sword once, except the time they made the mis-take of propositioning one of Boltar's closest friends. Being away for so long had its disadvantages, like being unfamiliar with the field of play.

He wanted so badly to be back in Tamook with Bashea. He never wanted this life of royalty, never enjoyed the responsibility, the weight of it, was not, in fact, cut out for it. The only reason he did it now was to keep a promise, and to prove to Bashea they belonged together. He prayed it would work.

He closed his eyes and tried to let his thoughts of Bashea soothe instead of ruffle him. He imagined her laughing over something he'd said, remembered her jumping and trying to get her poetry back from him, thought of the alluring fragrance of her skin and the way it felt beneath his fingertips...but tonight the comfort wouldn't come. He stormed back into his tent, then stood still, wondering what to do now.

Glancing about restlessly, he went to his cot and pulled out a leather-bound book. He had taken it from Bashea's tent before leaving. He untied the bindings that held the cover on and opened the pages, leafing through them until he found one of his favorites, which compared a desert storm to the whirlwind of Bashea's emotions after her mother's death. She must have been pretty young when she wrote this, he mused. What had she said...ten, eleven? He shook his head in amazement. The way she captured her feelings and put them on paper in such a way that they became so palpable...it was as if she were living and breathing in the same room with him. And finally, this, he found, soothed him.

"GO AWAY!"

"Not a chance, Your Highness," Radeem growled, pulling on the arm that was extended beyond the bed. "Now get your royal buttocks out of bed." Tahj groaned but made no effort to move. Radeem scowled, looking at the papers scattered across the floor, seemingly from a volume just beyond the prince's fingertips. "What is this any-way?" he mumbled, curious.

Tahj opened his eyes and then quickly turned his head to see Radeem bending down to pick one of Bashea's poems up off of the floor. He sprung from his cot, lunging at his friend. "Give me that!" He slapped a page from the captain's hand and snagged it in midair before it reached the ground. "Oh, no," he lamented, gathering the papers like the tribe's lost sheep.

"Why are you so upset?" Radeem queried, annoyed. "What is this, strategies?"

"No." Tahj stuffed the papers back into their leather cover and quickly tied it off.

Radeem stood staring at him with his arms folded across his chest.

"It's personal."

Radeem rolled his eyes. "Whatever you say, Your Highness."

Tahj hit socked him in the arm. "Stop saying that."

"You'd better get used to it. It's what you want, isn't it?"

"It's not what I want, and you know it," Tahj answered, looking at him meaningfully. "You relish swaggering around and ordering people to do this and that. Not me. Maybe we were switched at birth."

"Not a chance. You look too much like Kadeesh."

"Do you think so?" Tahj asked, glancing in the mirror behind Radeem.

"Every feature," Radeem assured him. The captain rubbed his arm. "Oww! That really hurt. Save that for the battle."

"The battle, the battle... I don't think there is ever going to be a battle."

Radeem laid a hand on the prince's arm. "It will be here fast enough, my friend, and then you'll wish it had never come."

Tahj sighed. "I know. I'm sorry, Radeem. I just didn't get much sleep."

Radeem bent and retrieved one final page from under Tahj's cot. He waved it under his nose, breathing in, just as Tahj had done, to catch a whiff of the familiar perfume. "Missing Bashea?" He raised his eyebrows, and the corners of his lips turned up.

Tahj glowered at him, snatching the poem from his hand; it was her "Desert Storm." "Easy for you to jest, curled up next to your wife every night."

"Not every night, friend. There have been plenty of nights on the road with you."

"I know. And I thank you for it. I do." Tahj changed the subject, knowing his captain would be excited about whatever they were going to tackle today. "What's on the slate this morning?"

Radeem pulled up a chair and straddled it, talking while Tahj got dressed. "I have to tell you, this one makes me nervous."

"Go on." Tahj buckled his pants, listening raptly.

"King Qubad of Havna. He and your father never saw eye to eye on much. He's kind of an ass. And I've heard told he's had some recent emissaries visit from Avistad."

"You think Boltar got to him?"

Radeem stroked his chin thoughtfully. "I think there's a chance."

"Then we don't go to him," Tahj responded, pulling a shirt down over his head.

"But to win him over to our side would be quite an accomplishment. He commands a great army."

"Is there any other way?"

"I don't think so."

"Then we win him over," Tahj answered with a smile, gesturing for his sword.

Radeem tossed it and he strapped it on. They were off by noon.

TAHJ GLANCED AROUND the throne room trying not to give away his nervousness. He recognized the king at once and remembered a rather unpleasant experience he had when he was a young boy, in which he accidentally knocked off the king's hairpiece during a ball. King Qubad himself was an imposing figure, let alone the two men stationed on either side of him who dwarfed everyone else in the room. A huge purple banner hung from the ceiling behind the throne, emblazoned with a fierce golden dragon and fringed in gold. The man's throne was massive, his robes rich, and his mood dour.

With others, Tahj had been able to draw on their previous loyalty to his father, but here he had to watch his step. "King Qubad, I am grateful for the opportunity you have given me to speak with you today."

"Yes, boy. Get on with it," the king interrupted.

Tahj bristled at the term "boy," remembering the way others of Boltar's clan mocked him before the uprising. He consciously swallowed his pride and continued. He felt Radeem shift beside him and knew his captain was scanning the room, computing the odds, but Tahj would do what he could to avoid a fight. Tahj bowed slightly, but held the king's eyes. It was important to remain polite without appearing weak, and he knew how to play the game. "Let me be frank then, Sire. I need your assistance."

Qubad raised his eyebrows. "And why should I help you? Your father was a tyrant and your mother—"

"Stop there!" Tahj ordered, his voice as steely as the sword at his side.

"You will not order me in my own court!" the king roared.

Tahj felt Radeem's hand cover his own as he unconsciously fingered the hilt of his sword. He knew it was Radeem's way of signaling him they were too outnumbered. "I will not hear you speak poorly of my family. If this is all the discussion we can have, then perhaps I should leave. But I warn you," he hastily added, "what I have to say will be to your benefit."

Tahj glanced at Radeem and then around the room to take in the odds himself. He had an entourage of about sixteen, including Radeem, and there were at least three dozen guards in the room alone, not to mention the other half-dozen or so in the hall outside. He let his gaze fall coolly on the king again, who seemed to be considering his worth.

After a long, uncomfortable pause, the King cleared his throat. "You have spoken up to me, which speaks well of your bravery. You did not fly off of the handle when you were angered, which speaks to your self-discipline. You do not appear cocky, like your father, nor are you an arrogant, evil cur like Boltar." He nodded his head. "Go on."

Tahj relaxed; he knew he had his man now. "Lord Boltar—"

"He calls himself King Boltar now."

"Whatever he calls himself, the fact remains he is extracting two times the tribute from you that my father did."

"You are well-prepared."

"Should you support me, I will cut that number in half."

"If you win."

"If I win."

Qubad studied him again. "How many men do you need?"

"How many do you have?" Tahj asked with a grin.

Qubad chuckled and reached down to take Tahj's hand. "You have my support. Bring us some wine to seal the deal."

BASHEA'S HAND FLUTTERED to her stomach. Why was she so anxious? Of course, she knew why she was nervous. In a short while, her family could be throwing her out in the desert all alone when they discovered what she had done, but she hoped and prayed they wouldn't.

It was hard to judge which way it would go, especially now her father was gone. Although she wasn't even sure what his reaction would have been to such news. But, with Bagrat in charge...she just wasn't sure how temperamental he would be when he learned the truth.

"We'll be okay," she murmured, and stepped up to open the flap to Bagrat's tent, where the family meeting had been called.

Laughter quieted as she entered, and everyone turned to look at her expectantly, but without tension. She fought an urge to turn around and run. Everyone sat on cushions in a semicircle, facing the door, where she stood. She chose not to take a seat. It would be easier this way.

"Bashea," Bagrat prompted, "you wanted to tell us something."

"Yes. Yes, I did."

She looked at each of their loving, encouraging faces and found her throat had dried up. Her stomach did a wild flip, and she put a hand over it and took a deep breath.

"What I have to say will come as a surprise to you." She looked around, hoping, somehow, someone would guess her secret, but they all just looked on curiously. How was she to say this? Best to get it over with quickly. "I'm...expecting a child. Tahj's child." She winced as she said it, and every muscle tightened as if expecting a blow.

All heads swiveled to Bagrat, whose mouth lay open. Slowly, the big man rose to his full height, and stepping over some pillows he scooped his sister up in his arms. "Congratulations!" Overwhelmed, Bashea could do nothing but cry. "Are you okay? Do you need anything?" he asked, concerned.

"No," Bashea blubbered. Bagrat's wife, Dara, handed her a cloth to wipe her eyes, and everyone gathered around offering their congratulations. Bano and Bibi seemed especially pleased. "I was afraid you'd throw me out," Bashea offered, laughing through her tears.

"Of course, not," Dara answered for the group. "We know what you've been through, and how hard it was for you and Tahj to...work things out, when it was clear you were in love with each other. We don't judge you, Bashea, and we'll make sure no one else does, either."

She knew they could not keep people from talking, but just knowing they were behind her made Bashea feel like she could handle whatever else was to come. "You all are the best," Bashea proclaimed tearfully, stretching her arms out to pull in as many as possible. There was much laughter and sniffling within the circle, and much laughter about sniffling in the circle, and teasing, but finally Bagrat spoke again.

"Bashea, I just want you to know, even though Tahj isn't here right now, you are not alone."

Bashea thought it was the sweetest thing she'd ever heard and started crying again.

"Oh, look now," Dara scolded, "you've got her going again. She's going to dehydrate that poor baby of hers." Everyone laughed, and Bagrat called for a private celebratory feast to be shared in his tent.

As twilight passed into night, Bashea looked around the circle of faces lit by a small fire, animated as they conversed with each other, and felt the ring around her heart grow tight again, but this time because her heart was swelling with love. Later, she made her excuses and snuck out to the well.

It was a mild night, and the sky was full of stars, as if the gods had scooped up handfuls of sand and thrown them up against the black, radiant and glowing as far as the eye could see.

Bagrat's gruff voice startled her. "You miss him, don't you?" He put an arm around her shoulder.

Instead of answering, she laid her head down on his chest. They stood quietly. From a few feet away a cricket began to chirp, and beyond him they could still here the murmur of late-nighters around the central fire.

"Do you think he's okay?" Bashea questioned, breaking the peaceful silence.

"Who? Tahj?" Bagrat asked, cricking his neck to look down at her. "Oh, yes. He's fine. He's a tough one, for a prince." They were quiet for a moment longer, and then Bagrat started chuckling. "Remember when he hid those sheep on us? Heh, heh. That was a good trick."

Bashea smiled and hugged herself tighter to his side. "Thank you, Bagrat. You are a good brother."

"Ahh, now," her brother countered, getting choked up, "don't go sayin' that. You know you'll only regret it in the morning." He sniggered and pulled her closer, protecting her from the night air.

TAHJ TOOK IT AS A GOOD sign when Boltar did not kill his emissaries. He agreed to meet with Tahj to discuss his claim, but only if the prince was willing to come to him.

"You've got to be crazy. There's no way I'm letting you go in there."

Tahj strapped on his hard, leather chest plate. "If it will spare Avistad blood, then it is worth the chance."

"What good will it do any of us if you are dead?"

Tahj smiled, picking up his sword. "But you will avenge my death, dear brother."

"Tahj, do you think this is a game?" Radeem cried, exasperated.

"No, my friend," he replied soberly, laying a hand on his captain's shoulder. "I know very well the risk I'm taking."

A head ducked into the tent, soon followed by the body of a handsome fifteen-year-old.

"Sarfraz," Radeem asked with a scowl, "what are you doing here?"

The young man bowed politely to his father without answering his question. He then proceeded to kneel before Tahj, taking his hand.

"Oh, Mighty Prince Tahj, I have come to serve you. I wish to fight beside my father."

"I thought I told you—" Radeem blustered, but Tahj waved a hand to silence him.

"Rise," Tahj said to the boy regally. He stood thinking for a beat or two. "Sarfraz, you have proven yourself brave and true in your request, and I have need of such a man...but not at the front. It is for something very important, however. Can you be trusted with such a task?"

"But I wish to fight with my father," Sarfraz responded, perilously close to a complaint.

"A real soldier goes where his leader needs him without question," Tahj stated sternly.

Sarfraz bowed his head for a second. "What do you need?"

"I will need someone to deliver a letter for me to Tamook. It is several days' ride across the desert. I will send you with two others in case of attack or emergency. Will you do this for me?"

"Yes, Sire," he answered at once, kneeling to take Tahj's hand again.

Tahj grimaced at the title. When he looked up, Radeem was smiling widely, but as Sarfraz rose, he replaced the look with a frown.

"I don't like the idea," he growled, but when Sarfraz looked to Tahj, Radeem winked at the prince.

"He is fifteen. It is the boy's choice." Tahj looked down at Sarfraz. "I will prepare the letter. Saddle your horse."

BASHEA WAS BENT OVER a pot in the fire when the three riders came charging into camp at a full gallop. She shielded her eyes with one hand in order to see them better through the late-afternoon sun, and stuck her other hand, involuntarily, into the small of her back, frequently sore now from the additional stress of her rounded belly. Bagrat and the rest of her family were constantly warning her not to overdo this close to her time, but she needed work to ease her mind.

The horsemen stopped some feet from her and dismounted. The tall one in the middle stepped forward. He looked somehow familiar. "This is Tamook?" he asked, and she could see now he was just a boy.

Bagrat stood up and strode over to meet him. "It is."

The young man reached into a leather pouch tethered to his side, lifting the flap and bringing out a neatly folded piece of parchment. "I am looking for Lady Bashea."

Bagrat's eyebrows lifted at that, and he turned with a smirk. "*Lady* Bashea?"

Bashea straightened and strolled regally over to the messenger, swatting Bagrat as she passed him. "I am Bashea," she said kindly.

The young man's eyes opened wide, staring at her. "Th-this is for you," he stammered, handing her the paper.

"You look familiar to me. Have we met before?"

"No, I am sure we haven't," he answered dreamily.

Bashea smiled and elbowed Bagrat, who she could feel behind her now, knowing he was about to laugh at the boy, who seemed taken with her. She glanced at the paper, tapping it against her palm, her curiosity over the boy superseding her interest in the letter's contents at this point. "You are from...?"

Sarfraz shook himself. "I have come from Vadeed."

Bashea was immediately keyed up. "This is from Radeem?"

"No. Prince Tahj."

Bashea would have swooned, were it not for Bagrat's thick arm.

"Let me get you some coins, lad," Bagrat said quickly as he steadied his sister.

"No need. I am just following orders," he answered smartly.

Dara put her arm around him and led him off. "A meal, then. Surely you are hungry..."

Bashea heard all this as if in a daze, a low, background buzz to the humming in her ears. She stared at the paper now as if it were a finely cut diamond.

"Bashea," Bagrat said gently. "Are you well?"

"He's alive! Ooh!" Her hand went to her stomach.

"What? What is it?" Bagrat asked in alarm, looking over his shoulder for Dara.

"It is nothing. The baby only kicked me hard."

"Let's get you out of the sun." Bagrat led Bashea into her tent. "Water?"

"Please."

When Bagrat returned with some, minutes later, Bashea was still sitting on the edge of her bed, staring at the letter, wonderstruck.

"Aren't you going to read it?" he probed gently.

"Read it?" she responded, as if a million worlds away. "Yes. I will read it."

"I'll leave you alone then," Bagrat murmured with a smile, though it wasn't even clear if she heard him.

Several minutes after Bagrat left her, Bashea looked up to find him gone. She rubbed her belly comfortingly. "It is from your father," she told her constant companion, and she felt a sort of shimmery glow descend on her. "Your father." Tears left her eyes now. She'd never known if her baby would have a father; now it seemed like there was a chance.

Slowly, as if it were the most ancient, holy epistle, she opened the folds and spread it on her lap.

My dearest Bashea—

I cannot think to start this letter without saying first how much I love and miss you. These many months have been an agony for me, and

I could not go on if not for knowing it was all to win you over to my side, to prove to you my only happiness lies with you, to make you my wife, the mother of my children.

A small sob escaped Bashea. "He has no idea, Baby." Her hands shaking now, she continued reading.

Except for this constant ache in my heart which comes from your absence, I'm doing fine. Radeem and I have been gathering quite an army. I am touched by the amount of support I've gotten, even from unexpected corners. Yesterday, three of Kadeesh's old friends showed up in Vadeed to swear their allegiance to me. Men who were boys I looked up to as a child, kneeling at my feet. It is very humbling.

But throughout it all I think of you, and count on the promise we made to each other...though, truth be told, I often wonder if some man hasn't come and swept you off your feet yet, and all this will be for naught.

But I hold on to the hope we will be together again soon. When I miss you most, I hope you will forgive me for this, but I stole a volume of your poetry. I read it and it makes me feel close to you. So, I thought I'd try my hand at it, please forgive my inexperience—

When the sun's rays are stretching across the Western sky—
And the night animals begin to wake,
It is then I think of you, far from my side,
And my heart begins to ache.
My lids cannot close without
The ghost of you floating before my eyes
And I'm tortured for want of you,
You're the breath within my sighs.
For when the circle is done
And again the sun begins to rise
The pink edges melt with the blue
And become the swelling skies.
Then I rise to face another day,

A false smile upon my face
Duty drags me along
Though I see you with each reluctant pace.
The space between us is both great and small
The chasm insurmountable when you are not near
But, at times, bridged by my thoughts of you
I find that you are here.
Bashea, the time is nearing
When I'll stand or when I'll fall
But it's not the battle which scares me
As I march through castle hall.
It is the thought of me returning to you
When all is said and done
To find what my heart's longed for
With each rising of the sun
Is not what I imagined,
Or what is designed to be
Yet, I pray, somehow, you'll
Accept my love and, finally, marry me.

Here the poem ended, but Tahj had added more.

Ahh, the joke's on me, Bashea, for you made it look so easy, but I cannot make the words bend to fit my thoughts or show you the way I feel. I long for you to show me the way, even now.

Should I not return to you, and our upper meadow, know I loved you, and with the last beating of my heart, it beat for you.

—Tahj

"Oh, Tahj!" Bashea wept, imagining him in each stanza of the poem. She rose, but then a pain gripped her so hard she doubled over, letting the letter flutter to the ground. "No! Not now, Little One," she ordered. She gritted her teeth and stood up, leaving the tent determinedly.

She rushed to the fire and found the boy where he was sitting spooning food into his mouth as if he hadn't eaten for days. Just like his father. She quickly crouched in front of him, her hands on his knees. "Prince Tahj—he was well when you saw him?"

The boy's eyes were wide with surprise, but he answered. "Yes, quite well."

A smile warmed her face like a sunrise. She patted his knees. "Good! Good." She rose, but then grabbed her stomach, bending over. "Ohh!"

Immediately Bagrat was at her side, gripping her arm to support her. "Bashea, what is it?"

Dara hurried to her other side. "Is it the baby?"

"Yes, I think it is!" She panted, her eyes frantic.

"Get her to our tent," Dara ordered.

"But not now, Dara. Not yet."

"I think the baby has different thoughts on the subject, Bashea."

"No!" she screamed, the next contraction taking her by surprise.

"The tent, Bagrat!" Dara raced ahead to prepare the way.

Hours later, Bashea was crying out in pain. "I need Tahj! I need Tahj!" She sobbed.

Dara laid her forehead on Bashea's, repeating reassuringly over and over, "I know, dear one, I know."

And in the twilight hours, Bashea gave birth to a baby girl.

TAHJ MARCHED ALONG, almost feeling claustrophobic in the circle of soldiers. Surrounding him was his entourage of handpicked men, sixteen of the bravest and strongest, including a handful of Kadeesh's friends and, of course, Radeem. Surrounding them were men who had once been loyal to his father but now vowed allegiance to Lord Boltar—for he would always be Lord Boltar to Tahj. They were escorting Tahj and his men to the throne room for an audience.

It felt strange to be within the castle walls. Where once his family crest hung on the wall, there was a tremendous shield with a wickedly taloned, black eagle on a background of red. Overhead, where multi-colored flags used to wave, were now row upon row of black and red flags. He watched them flutter a warning and snap with the breeze like so many dragons' tongues. Where once he heard the chirp of the small birds who darted in and out of the sunny archways, now the only sound to accompany the steady and somewhat ominous march-ing of men's feet was the sad cooing of a lone mourning dove, which could be heard, but not seen.

Radeem nudged him as they reached the throne room, whose large, cypress doors had always remained open in invitation in his father's time, but now were closed and cold. The men stood ner-vously waiting while sentries on either side drug open the doors, the iron locking pulls dragging against the tile with a grating, metallic sound. As they passed through the doorway, Tahj again thought of the mouth of a dragon, and for the hundredth time wondered if he had made the right decision to meet on Boltar's grounds. *But these are my grounds, my home, and he has intruded long enough.*

As Tahj came into view of his father's throne, he almost stopped short. Although he had, of course, known Boltar would be sitting there, it still came as a shock to his system. When he looked at the steps, now bearing a red-and-black-fringed carpet, he saw the corpses that had been lying there when he fled for his life. Although he'd tried to prepare himself for this, he just hadn't been capable of it. Pushed forward by the others, he came to the center of the room and stood before the throne of the man who'd murdered his mother and father, and probably his beloved brother, too.

Boltar sat on the throne with a golden staff in his hand, two guards flanking him with golden spears. Where glass lanterns had been on the columns of the stairs, there now burned crude torches, a rather odd addition, Tahj thought, but he supposed it made Boltar appear more menacing to some. Tahj knew he was only a coward who hid behind the might of the masses and felt no fear, only loathing. Boltar's snake-like eyes glinted in the light cast by the torches.

"King Boltar of Avistad," someone announced loudly. The whole of the crowd bowed their heads in respect. Tahj commanded his head to bow, but the best it could do was a slight nod. Now came the problem of how to address the fraudulent king with respect without vomiting. But Boltar saved him the trouble by speaking first.

"Ahh, young Tahj. How good to see you."

The sound of the man's voice made the hair on Tahj's arms stand up, and he was well aware his proper title had been dropped.

Radeem glanced at Tahj. He could see the veins in the prince's face and neck pulsing, but he was surprisingly under control.

"Yes, Boltar, I am glad to be back in *my* home."

Score one for Tahj, Radeem thought, and he had to cough to hide the smirk he couldn't keep from his face. Radeem scanned the area expertly and was surprised to find no more soldiers were posted in the room besides the four standing at attention on the balcony behind more of the garish, self-glorifying red and black banners. The captain felt confident, however, some were now amassed behind the large doors they entered. But he would see to that when the fighting started. *If* the fighting started, he reminded himself. He smiled. The odds were much more favorable than he'd anticipated.

"What can I do for you, Tahj?" Boltar asked in a bored tone. He snapped a finger at a servant who hurried off to fetch something.

You can vacate the throne, you officious ass! Radeem thought.

"I have come to make a proposal to spare many Avistad lives, which would, of course, be both your and my topmost concern."

Boltar leaned forward, "Oh, are there Avistad lives at stake?"

Tahj ignored his remark. "I am willing to offer you one hundred thousand Abbas to step down as...leader of Avistad, so I may resume the throne given me by birth."

"Don't you mean given *Kadeesh* by birth?" Boltar emphasized Tahj's dead brother's name in the hopes of infuriating him and forcing him to act, which he almost did.

Tahj clenched the hilt of his sword, and then consciously relaxed his grip, his eyes never leaving Boltar's face. That was why he noticed the briefest flick of the man's eyes upward. As he continued to talk, Tahj also glanced in that direction, and caught the smallest shadow of a figure behind the banners gracing the upper railings.

"Yes, you are right." Tahj stuck his hands behind his back and began to walk around in an oratory fashion. "It should have been inherited by my brother, Kadeesh, but he met an untimely end, didn't he?" He chanced a glimpse at the south end of the balcony as he turned back to Boltar, and realized they had been led into a trap. Archers were stationed above, and he and his men had now become easy targets for their bows. While Boltar formulated an answer, Tahj's gaze darted about, searching for a solution.

"Yes," Boltar said slowly, "what an unfortunate end." The servant arrived with a jar of wine and Boltar accepted a cup. "Perhaps he was in need of a swordsmanship lesson."

Before Boltar could even bring the glass to his lips, Tahj lunged, drawing his sword in one swift motion and whacking at a torch above the servant's head. The torch, cut in two, dropped onto his tray, upsetting the jar of wine and knocking it all over Boltar's lap even as the alcohol caught fire. It was just the distraction Tahj needed.

"They're above us! Take cover!" Tahj shouted.

How could I have been so stupid? Radeem thought, even as he buried his sword in a man's chest after ducking and barely missing having to part with his own head. As he fought off those around him, Radeem located Tahj halfway up the steps. The prince was exchanging thrusts with one of Boltar's personal guard, sword against spear. Radeem took another man down and tried to move through the throng toward Tahj. From his position slightly above the fray, Tahj's back was totally vulnerable, but Radeem knew he was after Boltar.

I SHOULD HAVE KILLED him when I had the chance. If my men weren't so inept, he never would have escaped Avistad in the first place. Boltar's anger raged. *But then the boy waltzes in here, just waltzes right in. So like Tahj, so trusting, the little fool. The boy's father, who I had little trouble disposing of, was smarter than that, as was his treasured brother, Kadeesh. And now, to have turned the tables on me when I was just about to squash him for good.*

Boltar was not unaware there were many who had been hoping for the prince to return someday. The overlord had sent out parties far and wide, offering huge sums of money to the person who would find and kill the prince, but without success. *And now the boy sees through my own trap?*

Boltar was seething on the inside even as he blistered on the outside from the burns the flaming alcohol had left. *Well, no worry,* he thought as he brushed at the charred edges of the robes he wore, knocking off bits and pieces of the ashes, striding quickly down the back hall to his bedroom, *my men may have to work a bit harder, but I'm sure they picked off a great number of Tahj's group before they were able to scramble for cover, and will dispatch with the rest of them quickly.*

And as for the boy prince—well, Tahj was sure to be killed in the first few minutes of battle. He was an excellent swordsman, probably even better than Kadeesh was, but he didn't have the businesslike attitude of a true fighter, like his brother once had. Tahj just didn't have the killer instinct. Boltar knew for a fact, each blow Tahj dealt created a wave of remorse in the prince. Any emotion at all was an opening for death in a battle.

"Lord Boltar!"

Boltar turned slowly and recognized the man on top of the steps at the end of the hall right away. Hurmoz, a friend of Kadeesh's. The boy had an arrow stuck in his right bicep and blood dripping down his leg from some other wound. He had a lighter complexion than most, and though probably in his thirties by now, still looked all of eighteen. His face was wide and expressive, his hair curly.

He stumbled down a few steps. "I have come to fight for Prince Tahj's throne and to revenge a good man, Kadeesh!"

Pain was etched on the young man's face, and he looked pale. He held his leg stiffly when he advanced, but there was a grim determination about him. Boltar wanted to kill him, but he just didn't have the time. He swirled around, his back to the younger man. "Go home," he said dismissively. "I've no time to kill you today."

Boltar climbed the two or three stairs to his bedroom and opened the door. He heard the *stomp, drraag* of Hurmoz as he made his way down the hall and rolled his eyes. *Very well.* He stood just behind the door, drawing a short dagger from the inside of his cloak, counting with a bored expression until the young man entered, listening as the *stomp, drraag* got closer, his hand on the doorknob.

But Hurmoz, who knew how wily Boltar was, turned out to have a plan of his own. As he passed through the doorway, Hurmoz yanked hard on the outside doorknob, swinging around the edge of the door, ready to slay Boltar on the doorstep.

But since Boltar grasped the handle on the other side, the unexpected move threw Hurmoz off-balance, saving the older man's life. The soldier's blow only nicked him as he fell forward, and he still managed to find an unnatural sheath for his dagger in Hurmoz's chest. The young man dropped his dagger with a clang and fell hard on his knees with a tortured cry, his hands trying feebly to disengage his enemy's hand from the dagger piercing him. Boltar lifted with all his might on the handle of his weapon, wreaking further damage to his opponent's insides, from which a sickening noise issued, then Boltar released his grip, letting Kadeesh's friend fall face-forward onto the tiles.

Boltar straightened up to his full height, slightly winded, and examined his side. His tunic was torn, a long but shallow scratch oozing a little blood onto the edges of the fabric. "Every one of you is out to ruin my wardrobe today," he muttered disdainfully, stepping on, rather than over, the body at his feet.

Hurmoz groaned loudly, his breathing labored as the dagger probably punctured his lung, and the impact of the hilt, as deeply as the blade had gone in, would have crushed some ribs. But the groan turned to a scream of pain when Boltar grabbed his arm, dragging him across the floor to the bed, the pressure on his rib cage so intense it would feel like being ripped apart. Hurmoz screamed in agony.

Blood poured from his wounds upon the tile, and smeared in a trail to the spot where Boltar finally released him, his body falling with a loud noise to the ground. Ignoring the man's pain, Boltar reached around the side of an ornately carved bedside table and found the minuscule hook there, flipping open a secret door. He pulled the front of the table open and reached in, taking out sackloads of coins.

FOLLOWING TAHJ'S ORDER to take cover was a little easier said than done, as the balcony encircled the throne room on all four sides, so even the huge columns in the room could only provide cover on one side. Not only were they surrounded from above, they also had soldiers hemming them in from all directions as well. But at least Tahj's warning saved them from a full-out slaughter.

Tahj fought desperately on the very steps where many of his father's counselors had been butchered, several of whom, he recalled now, were weaponless. Well, he had a weapon, and he would put it to good use. His opponent jabbed with his spear, and Tahj jumped high in the air, tucking his knees up under him and landing lightly on his feet as if playing some dangerous game of jump rope. The soldier then rushed at him with a roar, holding his spear across his chest. He hoped to push Tahj backwards and impale him on the sword of a soldier who was rushing him on the other side, who the prince didn't seem to be aware of yet.

Tahj took a mighty, two-handed swing at the spear handle and cracked it in two, but his momentum took him crashing to the steps, which turned out to be a good thing, as the man behind him was just bearing down on him with his sword. As Tahj looked on with surprise, the guard he had been fighting was run through by his own man's sword. Both soldiers looked at each other with wide eyes as the guard collapsed to his knees, inches from Tahj, his mouth open in a scream.

Above the sounds of clashing metal, death screams, and victory howls, Tahj heard Radeem yelling his name in warning. The prince looked up and saw the second guard, spear raised high above his head, charging down the stairs above him. He rolled to the left just as the spear came down, ringing on the steps, the pole shattering and launching the man who bore it head over heels until he came to his final resting place at Radeem's feet, the captain's sword penetrating his chest.

Meanwhile, the soldier who had killed his own man had managed to pull his sword back out of him and was cutting a path to Tahj on the stairs. Tahj had regained his footing and was sparring with another soldier. He saw the second soldier approaching out of the corner of his eye, but was too preoccupied with his own fight to do anything about him. His sword was tied up in a test of strength with another man, each pressing forward, their muscles straining. Just before the second soldier reached him, Tahj managed to finish off the first by throwing his elbow hard into his face. Without hesitating, he brought his sword around while the first man crumpled to the ground, slicing through the second man before he even had a chance to react.

Momentarily unchallenged, Tahj took a second to glance around the room. To his horror, he saw one of Kadeesh's old friends slumped in a seated position against a column, blood smeared behind him, more splattered on his face, his eyes wide open and lifeless. It was easy to see they were outnumbered. Several of his men were taking on two opponents at a time, and as he watched, several more fell. He heard shouts and a loud banging at the door, whose very timbers shook. Suddenly Radeem was at his side.

"If they break through that door, it's all over." Radeem lunged suddenly and went to the aid of a friend.

Tahj took a deep breath and found his next target.

It seemed as if the fighting had gone on forever. The prince's muscles began to shake with each new strike. Several times it looked as if he were about to meet the wrong end of a sword, and one of his men would bail him out. In turn, he fended off numerous attackers for others, saving their lives, but the battle was still pitched against them.

He heard the sound of the door finally splitting in two. Alarmed, he turned his head to behold a strange sight. In pushed Bagrat, Jahmeel, and their youngest brother, Cyrus, along with several dozen tribesmen, still in their dusty work clothes, but now with stolen swords—swords won off of the men they'd fought to gain entrance to the throne room. Bagrat caught Tahj's eye and grinned, then dove into the fray like it was a party.

Tahj finished off his man, trying to fight his way over to Bagrat. Soon it was clear the tide had turned in their favor. Tahj worried about the newcomers. They were field hands, not swordsmen, but what they lacked in skill, they seemed to make up for in enthusiasm. Not realizing he had gotten so near, he was surprised to find himself fighting back to back with Bagrat, who said in a jovial voice, "Good to see you, Tahj."

"*Fantastic* to see you, brother!" Tahj returned with a grin.

"Why don't I handle things here and you go off and take care of that ugly King Boltar? You've got to hurry up and get back to Bashea and your daughter."

Tahj froze, until a blade whistled past his head. He came alive, arcing his sword and meeting his opponent's next maneuver easily. "My daughter?"

BOLTAR LOOPED EACH coin sack through his belt and tried to secure them as best he could. He was so intent on his project, he didn't hear Tahj enter behind him.

"I'll have to ask you to leave."

Boltar whirled to face the grim-faced prince. His eyes flicked to his sword, left by the door, and back to Tahj's.

Tahj lowered his sword. "Retrieve your weapon," he ordered.

Boltar smiled. Tahj was nothing if not predictable. *Instead of finishing off his enemy, he offers him a sword. Fool!*

"I won't kill an unarmed man," Tahj stated.

Boltar's eyes went hard and he recovered his weapon. "You should not have come back, Tahj." In a flash, Boltar reached up and lowered the wooden bar, which locked the door with a thud.

The two began to circle each other. Hurmoz sputtered, coughing, and Tahj took his eyes off Boltar for a second to check on him. A second was all Boltar needed to strike. At the last moment, Tahj brought up his weapon and was at least able to keep the shot from being deadly, but Boltar stabbed him in the right shoulder. With a cry of agony, Tahj fell to one knee, his sword clanging to the floor. Without his sword hand, he was useless.

Radeem began to shout outside the door, and they could hear him ramming himself against it in an effort to get in.

"Did you really think you would come here and defeat me?" Boltar taunted. With all his strength, he kicked his boot into Tahj's wound, knocking him back several feet. Tahj let out a cry of pain.

Hearing Tahj's scream, Radeem began to throw his body even harder into the door, cursing.

"Oh, do be quiet, will you?" Boltar taunted. "Let me finish off the prince in peace, and then I'll let you in and you can have your turn."

Radeem cursed loudly and let Boltar know, in very colorful terms, just what his turn would entail.

Boltar stood over Tahj, his sword point to the prince's throat. Tahj's hand groped desperately along the tiles for his sword. "How appropriate you should die here where I drained the life from your dear old mother and father," Boltar jeered. He removed the sword from Tahj's throat so he could bend down to taunt him at closer range. "Where's your Baba now, Tahj?"

Tahj's fingertips felt the cold metal of his sword. With a weak but well aimed swing, Tahj struck where he could see the blood on Boltar's side. With a cry, the self-crowned king fell to one side, his eyes wide with surprise over Tahj having managed to take Hurmoz's cut deeper. Tahj staggered to his feet. In a rage, Boltar made the mistake of coming at Tahj wildly, allowing Tahj to sneak under the blow and kick his hand, sending his sword flying. It hit the wall just as the loud sound of wood splitting had them turning toward the door. The door shook but didn't give.

When Tahj turned back, Boltar was bent over the prone body of Hurmoz, pulling his head up by the hair with one hand, the other holding a dagger to the man's gurgling throat. Tahj saw the young man's wide eyes and grimace of pain, and suddenly he was seeing

Kadeesh's face again in his dying friend. Tahj fought back the tears rising in his eyes and tried to refocus.

"You won't watch this man die, will you, Tahj?" Boltar smirked, happy to have used the prince's own weakness and compassion against him. "Drop your sword!"

Tahj looked at Hurmoz again and knew he was gazing on a dying man. His face was gray, his breath rasping so loudly Tahj could hardly think. Boltar jerked the poor man's head back even farther. "*Drop the sword*!"

Resigned, Tahj let go of his sword. Even before the metallic reverberations had ended, Hurmoz made a loud, choking noise and the light went from his eyes.

Suddenly three things happened at once. Tahj dived for his sword at the same time as Boltar relinquished his hold on Hurmoz's body and it slid, lifeless, to the tile. With an ear-splitting noise, the door gave in, and Radeem flew into the room. Radeem stood, taking in the scene for a second as Tahj clambered to his feet.

Boltar had reached a tapestry and drew it back, opening a door behind it. Tahj and Radeem reached it just as it closed behind him and they heard the clank of a bar being set in place. With a frustrated and exhausted sigh, Tahj slid to the ground, his back to the wall. Radeem, still panting, followed his lead, sitting shoulder-to-shoulder with the prince.

They heard a sound, and both looked up quickly to see Bagrat's large form blocking the doorway. His tunic was torn and blood-spattered, but the big man seemed fine. With a grin he announced, "The castle is ours!"

BOLTAR SPURRED HIS horse to greater speeds as he tore across the desert. The steed's black, glossy mane matched its coat and whipped back as his feet churned the ground. The thrill of victory he'd felt when he escaped from Tahj and Radeem was short-lived. When he turned to see if he was being pursued, Boltar caught sight of what he was leaving behind. The castle loomed gloriously in the setting sun, the city below tucked in like children gathered around their mother's skirts. He turned his back on it.

It had been his. And then some whelp came along and just stole it right out from under him. How could this have happened? He'd worked so hard. But one thing was certain—he would have his revenge. He was not to be stripped of power again. He would make sure of that. He would gather an army and return, and, when all was said and done, he would drink Tahj's blood in a goblet.

But first, first he would make him suffer. He would kill...well, he had already killed all of Tahj's family. Who then? That stuffed, excuse-of -a-captain, Radeem. Yes. And the girl he escaped with...his men had reported seeing them together in Shiraz. She meant something to the prince; she must. And he knew just where he might find her.

Boltar's thoughts were interrupted by the sound of hoof-beats behind him, and he quickly turned in his saddle. He was able to distinguish the pack behind him as his own men, riding to catch up with him. At least a couple dozen. Enough to take Tamook by storm.

"LET ME TAKE OUR LITTLE Keiara. You both need your sleep."

It was true, Bashea was nodding off, but handing over her precious daughter was going to be like ripping off a limb. She looked away, blinking away the tears welling in her eyes. This was asinine. Keiara would be right across the room. After she made the baby comfortable, Dara came back to Bashea's side.

"Do you need anything, Bashea?" she asked kindly.

Bashea took her hand. "No. You've been wonderful."

"You're crying!" she said with mild surprise.

"I know. I'm sorry. It's just...she's beautiful, isn't she?"

Dara pulled the blanket up to her patient's shoulders. "She is," she agreed immediately. "She will have Tahj wrapped around her finger the minute his eyes fall on her." She meant it to comfort, but she saw a shadow of pain cross Bashea's face. She stopped fussing with the blankets, leaning in. "You miss him, don't you?"

Bashea sighed. "Like he was the sun."

"Hmmm." Dara paused. "You rest now. I'm going to go get you some more water." She rose, and when she turned back at the door saw that Bashea was already asleep.

Dara practically ran into Bibi at the door.

"How is she?"

"Resting," Dara said pointedly. "They both are. Bashea had a rough time of it, but she's a fighter, through-and-through." She sighed. "I only wish Tahj were here for her. I almost told her, *almost*, that Bagrat had gone to bring back her love. But I didn't want to get her hopes up in case...in case..."

Bibi nodded. "That was wise. If you'd told her, she would have only worried about both of them."

Dara made a clucking noise and stirred herself, moving with her pitcher in the direction of the well. "They will come home safely. There can be no other way." Bibi fell into step beside her.

"Keiara is a pretty baby, is she not?"

"Beautiful!" Dara confirmed. "Those big, expressive eyes of Bashea's. And all that hair!" She laughed, raising her eyes to the desert. She came to an abrupt halt.

Bibi looked in the same direction, shading her eyes with one hand. She saw a cloud of dust on the horizon. Dara squeezed her arm.

"Horsemen! Traveling fast." Her smile was as bright as the setting sun. "Go get Parvaiz and Gaspard."

BASHEA STIRRED IN HER sleep. She had been dreaming of Tahj, high up on a throne, smiling down on her. But when she climbed the steps to him, the stairs just kept getting longer and she couldn't reach him. She was carrying Keiara, wrapped in blankets. Bashea gazed down into their child's sleeping face, but when she looked up at Tahj, he was frowning at her. "Here she is!" he cried, his voice an open accusation.

Bashea opened her eyes. Someone was standing in the doorway, holding the flap for someone else to enter. It was a man. There were loud noises outside, shouts...and fighting. Bashea sat up on her elbows, clutching her blankets to her chest. When Boltar ducked inside the tent her face froze in disbelief.

"Ahh. We meet again," he said, his voice smooth, clearly reveling in the girl's terror. "What's this?" he queried angrily, having spotted Keiara's bed.

"No!" Bashea wailed, sitting up too rapidly. The world began to spin and she gasped, the pain was so great.

Boltar picked up the child, who woke, but didn't cry. "A daughter," he said, clearly delighted with his find. "Is it his?" he asked coldly.

Bashea's mind reeled. He was touching her baby, her Keiara. What was she going to do? Grimacing, she struggled to her feet, fighting the wave of pain threatening to overtake her. Boltar handed the baby to his henchman, who had let the tent close behind him.

"*Is it his, I asked?*"

Bashea stood, her mouth hanging open for a second. Then she screamed. "Help me! Somebody help me!"

Boltar crossed to her in two great steps, wrapping one arm around her and covering her mouth with his other hand, squeezing her mercilessly. "You will tell me, woman!" he threatened. When she didn't answer, he brought his face within inches of hers. "I don't need an answer. I can tell you whored around with him just as you did with me." Bashea raged against him and fought to free her hand.

"Ahh, yes. You were a fighter. What a turn-on that was." He licked his lips, sneering at her, but then seemed to make an attempt to rein himself in. "This will end where it began, then." He released Bashea, but the scream never left her lips as he backhanded her so wickedly she spun, and flew across her bed, face down. She didn't move a muscle. It was strangely quiet for a second, and then they baby started to cry.

"Give me the child!" Boltar ordered, marching across the tent, an evil smile on his face.

The soldier who had found Bashea stood stunned. But after being witness to what had happened, he had no intention of crossing Boltar. He held the baby out, and the enraged man snatched her from him, holding the baby like a bag of sugar while she cried.

TAHJ AND BAGRAT WERE headed back to Tamook with the rest of their crew, those who had survived, which, happily, were most. Tahj left Radeem in charge, with intentions of coming back and crowning him king, but right now he just wanted to get home to Bashea. Home. That sounded good.

Bagrat was beside him, in the lead, and was animatedly describing some of the action he'd gotten into during the fight.

"And then I took his head," he chuckled, "and forced it into my knee and almost got caught by the other one's blade, and that would have been the end of Bagrat, I'll tell you, as it was aimed at my neck, but I...."

Cyrus galloped up to their side. "What's that?" He nodded forward, and their heads swiveled as one to take in what he was gaping at.

"Oh, by heaven. We left them alone." Bagrat spurred his horse into a gallop, racing forward.

Tahj was still squinting in the direction Cyrus had indicated, and could now make out a dust cloud and smoke.

"Bashea," he whispered, his throat hoarse. He kicked his stallion and flew after Bagrat as fast as he could.

They were still a way off when they heard shouting, the sound of swords meeting, and children crying. Having the head start, Bagrat reached the battle first. He saw a soldier dragging Dara forward and dove off of his horse on top of him, wrapping his arm around the man's neck.

Tahj didn't stop to get involved in the skirmish, heading straight to Bashea's tent instead. He swung off of his horse before it even stopped, and it continued on, riderless.

Calling out her name, Tahj dashed into the tent, only to find it empty. A sense of panic flooded him. He went back out and searched the crowd. He saw Parvaiz breaking a crate over a soldier's head in defense of a fellow tribesmen. He saw more of those who had come with him from Avistad jumping off their horses and getting into the fray. Then he saw Bagrat hugging Dara. He crossed and took a hold of Dara's arm.

"Bashea, where is she?"

"Oh, Tahj! They're both inside." She motioned to the tent behind her, and Tahj ducked through the flap. His stomach turned hard when he saw Bashea lying sideways across her bed, half on it, half off.

"No!"

Dara and Bagrat entered behind him and Dara screamed. Bagrat held her.

Tahj prayed the worst hadn't happened. He crossed and turned Bashea over gently, a hand flopping loosely beside her. The right side of her face was red and looked swollen, and her lip was bloodied. Tears came to Tahj's eyes, and his heart clutched with fear. He took one of her hands, and with his other hand smoothed the hair back from her face and tried to speak, though his throat was tight. "Bashea...my love..."

Her lips moved, pronouncing his name.

"Bashea!" His head fell to her chest.

Bashea opened her eyes and stroked his hair. "Tahj?" she said in amazement.

"Yes, I'm here." He kissed her hand, swamped with relief.

Bashea struggled to sit up. "Keiara!" Then suddenly her memory came rushing back. "Oh! He took her. Oh, Tahj! He took our baby!"

"Who?"

"Boltar! He was here." She struggled to her feet.

"Bashea, you're in no shape to—"

"He has our baby!" she repeated frantically. Her brow creased, and then she gasped. "I know where he took her!" Her eyes were wide with the discovery. "He took her to the well, Tahj."

Tahj disengaged his arm, giving hers a reassuring pat. "I'll get her back, Bashea. I promise." Even as he said it, he prayed it wasn't a lie. He turned and swiftly left.

When Tahj stepped back out into the light of day, he saw a riderless horse running by. He reached out to grab the reins, and then mounted it.

"I'm going with you."

He looked down, and Bashea was by his side, reaching up to him. Bagrat came out, rubbing his ribs and looking angry.

"No, Bashea. Stay here with Bagrat."

She stuck out her chin, her eyes firing. "I'm going with you," she demanded, her words spoken with icy clarity.

Tahj knew precious moments were ticking away. He also knew with Bashea at the well he would have two people there he'd have to protect. Having little choice, he offered Bashea his arm and pulled her up. "Hyah!" The horse tore through the dusty spaces between tents, weaving through tent tethers and combatants alike. It was as if their ride knew where she was going.

When they had skirted all the fighting and came around the last tent, they saw Boltar's robes, black and red, blown back by the breeze as he marched across the fire circle, their child in his arms. When he heard their horse, Boltar ran the last several lengths to the well. He took the baby, and, holding her by the neck with one hand, extended her over the well. Keiara flailed her tiny fists and kicked her legs, crying the bleating cry of a newborn whose lungs aren't big enough for a full cry. The blanket fell from her, fluttered briefly, and was swallowed up by the black of the well.

Tahj jumped from the horse. "Stop!" His eyes connected with his daughter's, wet and wild from crying, and his heart was seized. He had never beheld anything more beautiful in his life.

"And why would I want to do that?"

Tahj found he was speechless. At the time when he needed his words the most, they failed him. Bashea slid off of the other side of the horse and took a few teetering steps forward, holding one hand out in front of her.

"Please," she begged, her voice ringing with emotion. "I will do anything, *anything* you want."

Boltar paused, studying her for several seconds. As their eyes locked, Tahj looked from one to the other. Bashea was desperate, quivering; Boltar was...tempted.

"But you already have, my dear, remember?" His voice was a sinister whisper. He started to turn back toward the baby, but Bashea screamed, throwing herself on the ground.

"*Please, don't hurt her!*"

Bashea hoped it would provide the distraction Bagrat needed.

Bagrat had ridden his horse through a little copse of trees that extended into the desert to the right of the well and then approached, crawling, for the last part, on his stomach, so as not to be seen by

Boltar. Bashea saw Bagrat as he slinked across the sand, a great love filling her heart. Bagrat, her big brother, he would save her baby.

Bashea was sure her heart had stopped beating. She watched helplessly from afar as Bagrat made his move, screaming just as Bagrat started to rise, and Boltar was about to spin in his direction. For those few seconds, it was as if the world stopped turning...and then Bagrat had her; Boltar turned back to Bashea, and Bagrat snatched the baby from the overlord. Bagrat's hands, strong from the field and sure, pried Boltar's from Keiara's tiny neck and he scooped her up, bringing the baby to his chest triumphantly.

Tahj rushed forward, his sword drawn, and Bagrat ran toward Bashea, to get his niece to safety. Boltar pulled a dagger from somewhere inside his sleeves and swung with all his might, driving it into Bagrat's back. The big man let out a heartrending cry of both confusion and pain and fell to his knees, his eyes wide with astonishment.

Bashea's mouth fell open, the tears that had threatened before spilling onto her cheeks. Not Bagrat! "No," she cried softly, her voice shaking.

Bagrat pitched forward, but caught himself, one hand in the sand, one wrapped protectively around Keiara, who had stopped crying. Bashea pushed up on one arm, mirroring his position. Bagrat, breathing heavily, stretched out his hand, holding the baby out to her. Bashea shifted, taking Keiara from him, drawing the child to her bosom. She gazed at Keiara, amazed to find her unharmed.

Bashea looked up. Maybe a foot in front of her, her big brother's hand had cradled her sweet baby. Now, her eyes followed her brother's to the ground, as she repeated quietly, "No, no, no..." She crawled to his side, shaking her head slightly as if to will it all away.

"See, Bashea," Bagrat said, his voice weak, "I saved her." He held on for a few more seconds, and then shut his eyes.

AS TAHJ RUSHED FORWARD, he saw the flash of the blade in Boltar's right hand. He screamed, but it was too late. Boltar plunged it into Bagrat's unprotected back. The only thing he could think was, *I should have moved faster! It should have been me. I started this.*

Wasting no time, Boltar pushed Bagrat away and drew his sword in order to meet Tahj. With all his strength, Tahj swung his sword over his head and brought it crashing down. Boltar met it, but the force of the blow drove him to his knees. With a yell, Tahj kicked him in the midsection and Boltar flew back, smashing into the well. Tahj heard the sound of bones breaking. He had never wanted to kill a man before, but he wanted to see Boltar die, wanted to hear him take his last breath, wanted to watch the life drain from his eyes.

Bracing himself with the well at his back, Boltar was able to rise unsteadily to his feet, but his breathing was raspy. He took a weak swing at Tahj, who parried it easily, his face cold. Boltar showed no fear, although it was clear now the fight was over. His face only showed his endless contempt for Tahj. He stumbled, feeling along the stone of the well to right himself.

"I am the king!" Boltar raged. "You will never be king."

"I have no desire to be king," Tahj said simply.

This seemed to confuse Boltar for a second, but then he again thrust his sword at Tahj. This time Tahj only batted it away, sending it flying through the air. Boltar eyed him, then rose to his full height, letting go of the side of the well. The only sounds that could be heard were Bashea's low, mournful cries and Boltar's harsh breathing. Tahj tossed his sword into the sand near Boltar's and raised his hands in invitation.

Boltar gathered himself and charged, his eyes sparking. Tahj reached out and grabbed the man's head, thinking about the good people he had killed—Kadeesh, his mother, his father, Hurmoz, and now, possibly Bagrat—and brought his knee up into the man's face. Boltar stood, bent over and wobbling. Tahj kicked him, using his whole body, throwing his hands backwards as he did, and Boltar's body flew through the air and crashed against the well. He landed in a seated position, his head cocked to one side, blood dripping from one corner of his mouth, his eyes open but lifeless.

Tahj turned away in disgust.

EPILOGUE

Bashea bounced the baby on her shoulder, hoping to get him to stop fussing. He was teething, she'd put money on it, as he babbled, drooled, and complained in equal measure. She was standing talking to Bibi and Dara, having just finished breakfast, when Keiara tugged at her skirt.

"What is it, baby?"

The little girl turned and pointed to the west, her black curls bobbing. "Baba!"

Bashea raised her eyes and saw Tahj approaching, walking his horse through camp alongside his brothers-in-law. The group had been in to Avistad to counsel the good King Radeem and had been gone nearly a week.

Spotting them, Tahj quickly handed the cloth camel he had brought for his daughter to someone behind him and squatted, holding his arms open wide. With a squeal, Keiara took off running in his direction. Without even looking, Bashea dreamily handed off her son, Shahzad, to her sister, and followed in her daughter's wake.

Bashea noted that, unbeknownst to Tahj, the someone he had given the camel to squatted down behind him and off to the side a little, holding out the camel and pretending to make it walk through midair. Enamored by the camel, Keiara sped past Tahj and into the waiting arms of her Uncle Bagrat, who stood with the girl in his arms and tickled her with the camel, laughing at Tahj's expression.

"Well," Tahj snorted with his hands on his hips, "a man leaves for nearly a week and this is all the love he gets?"

Bashea walked up behind him and slid her arms around his waist, whispering suggestively in his ear, loud enough for Bagrat to hear, "I've got some love for you...."

Tahj smiled at Bagrat. "I'll take it!" He turned and gave Bashea a loud, smacking kiss on the lips as she swayed and giggled in his arms. Then the kiss turned more serious as Bashea took the sides of her husband's face into her hands, and then more passionate. Suddenly, Tahj bent and swept Bashea off her feet. Bashea squealed in surprise, hugging herself closer to him. "Take care of the kids for a while, Bagrat," Tahj called boisterously over his shoulder.

"Oh, ho!" Bagrat chuckled. "What do we think of that, Miss Keiara?" He nuzzled his niece's neck and she giggled, squirming and scrunching up her noise happily.

Bashea looked back over Tahj's shoulder as he marched off with her toward their tent. Her heart warmed to see her daughter in Bagrat's arms. It wasn't long ago they were worrying about whether or not Bagrat was going to make it through the night. She thought of that time with an inward shudder, and she felt a pang of love for him. He looked up and caught her eye, and it seemed as if he was thinking the same thing, his look fleetingly serious. Maybe Bagrat's being gone with Tahj had stirred up those old emotions and worries about him. She smiled, and then blew him a kiss. He winked at her, and then raised Keiara over his head, where her camel came to make a nest in his hair, its legs swinging in front of his eyes, blocking his view.

"Be careful with her," Bashea warned as Tahj ducked with his burden into the tent.

Once inside the tent, Tahj put his wife down gently on her feet. "I *really* missed you!" he said, grabbing Bashea by the hips and walking her back to the bed as he kissed her.

"I missed you, too!" The kiss she gave him was meant to entice him further, and entice it did.

He started peeling off his clothes. "I've been thinking about this for days."

She was thrilled. "Mmm...me, too."

He began to kiss her again, running his hands over her skin feverishly, his movements becoming rough and reckless. He laid her back across the bed, joining her as he tore at her clothes in an effort to assist her in getting them off. He felt the cloth give and the sound of fabric ripping. Instantly he pulled back, "I'm sorry."

She heard the guilt in his voice, and it infuriated her. "Why, Tahj?" she snapped, sitting up suddenly.

Confused, he sat up, too. "Because. I vowed to always respect you, Bashea."

She got up, crossing arms over her chest and walking away from him. "It's been four years, Tahj, nearly five, and in all this time you've always been so...controlled. Horribly, awfully, controlled." She turned, and, seeing the look of hurt in his eyes, she came back quickly, taking his face in her hands as she stood between his legs. "Not that it hasn't been wonderful. And being together like this...has been beyond my wildest imagination. But, I feel you pull back, hold back sometimes instead of...I don't know, being too wildly in love with me that you can't hold back. You can't refrain. You've just got to have me."

"Bashea, I feel that way all the time. But I just can't go...ripping your clothes off."

"I know."

"Then what is it that you want?"

She took in a deep breath, and then blurted out, "I want you to take me, take me hard and fast without thinking about respecting me. Just stop thinking at all! Go with your feelings—"

He grabbed her roughly by the hips and swung her around onto the bed. "Be still, woman!" he demanded, and then he did as he was bidden. Taking her as he had always longed to, with abandon, with wanton recklessness, without any other consideration other than satisfying himself, and in so doing he drove them both wild, to a place they'd never been before, a new, electrifying, and exhilarating place.

And when at last they took that sweet, final plunge, they lay together in the golden afterglow, both thinking about their relationship without speaking. They were happy. They had their children, who gave them great delight. They had their family, Bagrat, Jahmeel, and all the rest, Radeem and their friends in Avistad, and even Faraz and his daughters, who had come to visit a time or two. And they had their home in Tamook. Boltar had tried to take it all from them, but they had prevailed together, better, stronger for having done it with each other. They appreciated each other more, and everything they had, because they had been forced to fight for it.

Their relationship had been tempestuous from the start, a whirlwind of strong emotions, much like the storms that gathered over the desert, shifting huge sand dunes, reshaping the terrain. But they had made it through the winds to the stillness, the quiet, refreshing stillness after the storms, where things began anew, and love grew stronger each day. And they thanked the gods for it.

NOTE FROM AUTHOR

Thank you for reading TAKEN BY STORM, part of my RO-MANTIC REALMS COLLECTION. I hope you enjoyed it. Now that you've read the book, won't you please consider writing a review? Reviews are one of the best ways readers discover great new books. They don't need to be fancy or long, just a sentence or two honestly describing your opinion of/experience with the book. I would sincerely appreciate it.

Want more from M.J. Schiller?

Page forward for an excerpt from

AN UNCOMMON LOVE

Book Two in the ROMANTIC REALMS COLLECTION

AN UNCOMMON LOVE
CHAPTER ONE

Adriana lifted her head, straining to see through the thorny bramble of the bush she lay behind with Garin. Her father's Royal Commander plucked a leaf from her golden hair.

"What is it, love?" Garin asked, still wearing the silly grin she put on his face. He plucked a leaf from her golden hair.

She could barely make out the sounds of jeers and cries coming from the outer courtyard of her father's palace, the Castle Ramport. "What is that? What is happening?"

"Oh. It must have something to do with the commoner who struck Derrick."

She gasped. "Somebody struck Derrick?" Even though he worked for her father, she was terrified of the hulking beast of a man.

"Aye," he answered with a chuckle. He looked over to where the crowd was entering the grounds, too. "But he is probably sorry for it now, the poor fool."

She frowned, noting there was little pity in his voice. In fact, his words sounded mocking. The princess tugged at the gold laces which held her bodice together, trying to thread them hastily through their looped cording. When she attempted to struggle to her feet, he sought to press her back down to the ground.

"Adi, honey." He pressed his lips to the skin still accessible above the low cut of her neckline, but she was no longer in the mood.

The noise of the crowd surged and she again tried to make out what was happening, but saw only snatches of color and movement through the branches surrounding her. Her heart was racing.

"What will they do to him?"

"Oh, I do not know," he said, shrugging. "Whip him or beat him or ..."

"What?" Incensed, she succeeded in scrambling to her feet.

Garin sighed, gazing at her with ill-hidden lust. He sat up, bending one knee and languidly resting on one elbow, his shirt left half-opened.

"Adi, I do not know if I can make it to our wedding night. The very scent of your skin these days sends a fire burning in my groin." He rose from the ground. Pushing aside her fingers, he helped to tie her bodice. She fumed at the delay, half-ready to fly, tied or not. He smiled at her. "It is so strange how these feelings have awoken in us. Forever you have been my best friend, the one who explored the creek with me, who fought with me, who fished with me, who got in trouble with me. Soon you will be my lover, and that thought consumes my mind throughout the day. And tortures my nights." His movements stilled and he gazed into her eyes. Swinging an arm towards the patch of ground they had just abandoned he begged, "Adi, darling, come back and lie with me." He seemed not to care about how unmanly the pleading made him.

"Garin," she scolded. "I cannot lie with you in the grass while some man is being tortured within my hearing."

He grabbed her even as she turned from him, and pulled her in roughly, his strong fingers claiming ownership of her hip bones. He pushed his groin against her and brought his mouth to the base of her ear. "You *will* give me some time later," he growled.

She turned her head towards him, her arms crossed in front of her, hands covering his. She leaned back against his lean body, her lips curving up in an effort to seduce. "Would you doubt that?" she asked, her voice stroking him needlessly.

He chuckled low in her ear, letting his hands slide up, hard, along the sides of her bodice, coming in to cup what she had hidden away from him. "You will be mine soon, Adriana, and then there will be no running away."

The sound of his voice thrilled her. The need she heard in it was intoxicating, his hands, masterful, even as they clutched at her desperately. She turned in his arms and pulled his head down, pressing her warm, open lips to his. Snapping her head back, she watched the haze of passion lift from his eyes. She raised her hand to run a finger down his face from his temple to his lips, her gaze traveling its course. He nipped at it playfully and she lifted her head to peer into his eyes. "It will be worth the wait," she promised.

"Had I any doubt, I would have taken you on the grass today despite your protests."

"Oh. You, wicked boy!" She spun towards the sound of the crowd and fought her way out of his arms. "Come, now. Hurry, Garin. I must see what is happening!"

With that, she broke from his grasp and lifted her skirts to free her feet. Running down the stone pathway that curved around the corner of the building, she followed the uproar. As she ran, parallel to the crowd following the road, she peered between branches of the oak trees planted at regular intervals along the edge of the garden. She could see a man with his arms tied in front of him, struggling against his captors as he was pushed, shoved and pulled. He wore a loose-fitting, beige-colored linen shirt. His blond hair was long on top, and flew in front of his face as he swung his head violently. He seemed to be trying, at the very least, to injure someone with his skull.

She hastened her steps, and was actually the first person to reach the courtyard, angled as it was in her direction. She broke from the tree-line and stood just beyond the edge of the wide, hexagonal, stone court. High above, a small balcony jutted out from what she knew to be her father's conference room.

She continued to hear the whistles and cheers of the crowd, though they were briefly out of sight up the roadway, and it filled her with apprehension. In the past, her father had never let her see the goings-on in cases such as this, and now she understood why. It frightened her. Her heart beat faster as a few guards poured into the courtyard, walking backwards as they took in the actions of the mob that trailed. She could see Derrick, her father's Captain of the Guard. Even from this distance the purple bruising on his chin was obvious. He held the rope tied to the captive's wrists and jerked it, a cruel move that sent the man crashing to the stone pavers.

Adriana gasped, but then covered her mouth. She stood, barely visible, at the fringe of the trees. If her father or his men saw her, they would order her away, of that she was sure. The man struggled to his feet and defiantly shook the hair out of his face. His white teeth flashed as he bared them, glaring with disdain at Derrick. His heavy work pants were torn at the knees, whether from the fall she had just witnessed, or from some other fall, she could not tell.

The prisoner's gaze lifted and caught hers. For several seconds it was as if no one else was there besides Adriana and the stranger. The air seemed to shimmer between them with the intensity of their stare. The noise of the crowd thundered in her ears, but was now accompanied by the sound of her own blood pounding through her veins. His eyes were the most startling blue, reminding her of the flash of a blue jay she sometimes caught a glimpse of in Ramport's gardens.

Adriana's cheeks grew warm. She gazed at the stranger, her mouth hanging open. He was easily the most gorgeous man she had ever laid eyes on. His shirt, which should have been tied at the neck, was torn and open, revealing his well-muscled chest, which glistened with sweat in the late afternoon sunlight. The veins on his powerful arms, captured on each side by a guard, bulged as he fought to free himself, despite being wildly out-numbered. Adriana felt an unfamiliar acceleration of her heart-beat when he, despite the flurry of activity around him, did not take his eyes from hers. His face at first seemed open, thoughtful. But then, as his gaze trailed over her gown and the thin circle of gold and jewels laced through her hair, his jaw became set. His stare turned cold, almost hostile. Adriana pursed her lips, uncomfortable with the change.

Her father stepped out on the balcony, and she at last tore her eyes from the prisoner's and looked up.

Garin appeared, grabbing her around the waist and trying to steer her away from the scene. "You should not be here."

Adriana slapped at his hands. "Leave me be, Garin," she whispered, her voice hoarse and tense. At her words, his eyes flashed, and he pulled his hands away, holding them up in a sign of surrender.

The crowd quieted as one, and all faces turned upward as the king spoke. "Why is this man brought before me?"

Adriana stared at her father. She did not recognize his voice as it rumbled forth from on high, so uncaring, so...icy. As she turned her head to hear Derrick's response, she noticed another face in the crowd. A woman was looking on with her hands clasped over her mouth, her eyes filled with tears. She was beyond beautiful, with huge, meadow-green eyes and long, wavy hair the color of deep mahogany. She had high cheek bones and a delicate nose, and she was watching the prisoner's face with rapt attention. So, he had a girlfriend, or wife, she surmised, taken aback by the wave of disappointment that swamped her heart.

"Sire, this is the commoner who assaulted me earlier today."

"Has he not been scourged?"

The attractive brunette in the audience winced.

"Aye, Sire." Derrick answered with a wicked grin.

Adriana thought her father's lips turned up as well as he nodded. "And...?"

Here, Derrick's formerly cheerful countenance clouded. "The prisoner refuses to apologize."

The king's eyebrows rose in surprise. "Perhaps a trip to the river will change his mind." His tone was ominous. The brunette gasped and a woman nearby grabbed her arm to support her as she seemed to swoon.

Adriana turned to Garin. "What does he mean?"

"Adriana, you should not be here—"

"Garin," she hissed, desperate to understand what was going on, "*what* are they talking about?"

He shrugged. "They will take him down to the river and hold his head under water until he apologizes or until he drowns."

"What?" She stared at him in disbelief, her stomach dropping like a bucket in a well.

"You wanted to know," he responded blandly.

She turned slowly to catch Derrick chuckling, and her father looking on in, what appeared to be, amusement. She saw a shadow of fear flit across the prisoner's face, but then it became like stone. He looked at the dark-haired woman apologetically, but seemed resolute. The group as a whole turned to leave.

"Wait!" Adriana shouted, her voice ringing out across the expanse. Without even realizing she was doing it, she had stepped out of the shadows and into the open courtyard.

"Adriana!" The king gave Garin a hard stare. "What are you doing here?"

"Father." She caught her breath. "You asked me what I wanted this morning for my birthday—" She thought quickly, chancing a glance at the prisoner, who was peering at her now with wide eyes, his mouth hanging open a bit.

"Ana—" The king responded affectionately, and, while dismissive, his voice sounded more like what the princess was used to, "—we can discuss this at dinner." He turned to go inside.

Angered by his condescension, she struggled to contain her voice. "Nay, Father!"

He turned and stared at her, eyebrows lifted.

She stepped forward so as not to be heard by the crowd. "Papa," she cajoled, switching gears, "I want you to free this man, *please*!"

"What?" He took another look at the commoner bound before him. "What is this man to you, Ana?"

Her cheeks blazed as if she had been sitting by the fire for hours. She purposefully did not look at the others, only peering into her father's eyes. "Nothing, Father. Nothing. I just... I do not wish to see him hurt."

"Ana, this is none of your business—" he began.

"Father, this *is* my business," Adriana stated firmly, but softened her voice, noting the anger spark in her father's eyes. "This is your business, and so it is mine." She stepped closer, almost within the shadow of the balcony. "I do not wish to anger you." Now she chanced a glance backward and saw Derrick glaring at her with conspicuous irritation. "But, if I am to celebrate my birthday this evening, I cannot do it knowing this man is suffering."

"He will not be suffering long," she heard Derrick murmur under his breath.

"Are you sure this is what you want, my Ana? I had picked out something very special for you, a piece of jewelry from your mother's collection."

"I am grateful, Father, as always, for your generosity. But I know all the work you have put into making this evening special for me, and I only wish to enjoy it as you meant for me to. I cannot do that knowing this man is to be tortured." She gestured in his direction and then paused, holding her breath.

The king seemed to consider her argument a moment. He shrugged indifferently. "Well, if that is what you want." He smiled at her, waving a hand over the gathering beneath him. "Release the prisoner."

There was a cheer from the small part of the crowd that had come in support of the accused commoner. The brunette rushed to the prisoner's side and threw her arms around him.

Adriana was about to turn to go, when the prisoner raised his head from where he had laid it on the woman's shoulder and studied her. Her breath felt tight in her chest.

The man's arms, which a guard had been working to release with a small dagger, came free and he swooped the woman up, closing his eyes for a beat, and then saying something to her with a tender smile. He set the woman on her feet and slipped an arm around her shoulder. He glanced in Adriana's direction one more time as he turned to go.

She dropped her eyes, filled with confusion. When she glanced up again, all she could see was the man's back. His shirt was ripped to shreds and bloodied from the blows he had received, but he walked away with a happy ease she found enviable.

Garin's hand clasped her shoulder. "Why did you do that?"

"I do not know," she answered honestly.

"It could not possibly be because the commoner was—" he quirked an eyebrow, "—somewhat handsome."

"Nay." Feeling her response was a bit too adamant, she hurried to add, "I just did not want to see anything happen—to anybody, boy, girl, good-looking, or not." *Besides he is not somewhat handsome, he is gorgeous!* She looked back over her shoulder just as the object of her thoughts was passing under the stone gate of the castle's outer walls and sighed wistfully. Then she turned back to Garin with a smile. "Let us go get ready for my ball."

He smiled in return and gave a little half-bow. "After you, m'lady."

To purchase AN UNCOMMON LOVE go to my-book.to/AnUncommonLove

ABOUT THE AUTHOR

M.J. Schiller is a retired lunch lady/romance-romantic suspense writer. She enjoys writing novels whose characters include rock stars, desert princes, teachers, futuristic Knights, construction workers, cops, and a wide variety of others. In her mind everybody has a romance. She is the mother of a twenty-three-year-old and three twenty-one-year-olds. That's right, triplets! So having recently taught four children to drive, she likes to escape from life on occasion by pretending to be a rock star at karaoke. However...you won't be seeing her name on any record labels soon.

ROMANTIC REALMS COLLECTION:

TAKEN BY STORM
AN UNCOMMON LOVE
LEAP INTO THE KNIGHT
LADY OF THE KNIGHT
A KNIGHT TO REMEMBER

ROCKING ROMANCE COLLECTION:

TRAPPED UNDER ICE
ABANDON ALL HOPE
BETWEEN ROCK AND A HARD PLACE
ROCK ME, GENTLY
MIDNIGHT MELODY

REAL ROMANCE COLLECTION:

UPON A MIDNIGHT CLEAR
THE HEART TEACHES BEST
DAMAGE DONE
HOMETOWN HEARTACHE
TAKE A CHANCE ON ME
BLACKOUT

DEVILISH DIVAS COLLECTION:

TO HELL IN A COACH BAG
DAMNED IF I DO
THE DEVIL YOU KNOW
SATAN, LINE ONE
PITCHFORK IN THE ROAD
SIN WORTH THE PENANCE

www.ingramcontent.com/pod-product-compliance
Lightning Source LLC
Chambersburg PA
CBHW061141170626
46809CB00003B/940